Say Goodnight to the Bad Guy

Edited by TW Brown

Cover Art and Design by Shawn Conn

Say Goodnight to the Bad Guy

Printed in the U.S.A.

ISBN - 9781936730063

Dedication

Dedicated to the realists who understand that good exists, but doesn't always triumph

Foreward

Some people may well be wondering what sort of daft twit publishes an anthology of stories where the *Bad Guy* wins, gets away, or…<gasp!> triumphs. Considering the number of stories we received…the better question might be: "What sort of person sits around and writes such things?"

This is not a selection of stories that you want to cuddle up with on a bad day; rest assured, there is some seriously nasty stuff inside. I wouldn't share this book with your future in-laws. They might wisk your soon-to-be beloved far away (and have the local authorities digging up your backyard and/or basement).

So, as you push forward into this very dark place that we've created especially for you, don't blame us at May December Publications. Take a look at the by-line. Check out the author bios in the back of the book. Tell those sickos how you feel.

Last, I feel that it is necessary that I say this is not a book for the youngsters. It is definitely rated a Hard R. It has all kinds of mature themes and age-inappropriate material. You've been warned.

Are you being followed?

TW Brown
June 2011

Contents

Chinked

By: Aaron Garrison

I

October 19th, 1981

The phone rang like any other. Buford did not say hello.

"A sample," said the grievous voice from the other end.

Buford's reply: "A day."

The line went mutually dead.

II

October 20th

The photos came on a Good Day.

Manhattan floated past the taxi's windows: brownstone row houses, enigmatic winks of harbor, a jigsaw of skyscraping architecture. Barnaby Tasle luxuriated in the uncomfortable back seat, whistling an off-key "Strawberry Fields Forever." Not that Barnaby was much the Beatles fan; his rock and roll persuasions started around Simon and Garfunkel and ended in ABBA territory. The song just seemed apt: his Tuesday was shaping into an exemplary Good Day.

Preceded by The Good Night's Sleep, the Day had started with The Good Breakfast, which had given way to The Good Bowel Movement. Shedding his monogrammed bedclothes, Barnaby had then assumed The Good Outfit, a houndstooth Armani ensemble he was especially fond of, next up in his revolving choice of apparel. And finally, he'd hailed The Good Taxi, also known as *any* taxi.

As Barnaby stop-and-go'ed through the mazy borough, his sense of weal only grew. This was a lazy-Sunday-afternoon day, an it-can-wait-till-tomorrow day, a pass-the-buck day. Nowhere was the usual dread regarding his "job" at Harrison Bank, nor any of the superfine emptiness that plagues the well-to-do; he felt queerly equipped to deal with his tedium, much as a carpenter must when gripping his hammer, or a dirt farmer his plow—not that Barnaby knew either. His history of physical labor stopped at counting greenbacks, which some might say is a burden unto itself. But there were no burdens today, fiscal or otherwise. For the first time in a while, Barnaby found himself unbothered by his contemptible status, or the sinecure bank-seat inherited from his late father, or...other things.

He blinked, the whistling suspended. The taxi continued on, indifferent.

Other things. The words were predatory, lurking in the underbrush of his thoughts. Part of him wanted to pick this scab, reveal the raw ugliness beneath, but soon the words were drifting, drifting...until there was only John Lennon duetting a Rickenbacker.

Living is easy with eyes closed ...

Barnaby glanced at his Rolex, a cute little graduation gift from The Good Dad: not even eight o'clock. Making Good Time. His whistling returned, stronger now, almost in-key. No aliment for whistling like Good Time.

Two bars from the song's unwhistlable conclusion, the cab crawled to a politic stop at the Harrison Bank of New York. The cabby twisted to Barnaby. "Twenty-one even," he spat.

Dodging the waterworks, Barnaby produced a healthy wallet, then a twenty and a ten. He fed the bills over the seats. "Keep the change."

The jowly face lightened, almost unrepulsive. "Thanks, Mister."

"Good Man," Barnaby quipped, flashing his winning smile. Then he was gone.

***

The Good Day continued as he approached the Bank. After completing the riot of bodies preceding the door, he was allowed entry by The Good Doorman—who wasn't a man at all, but a delectable brunette Barnaby'd been eyeing for the past couple weeks. Becomingly small, black denim pants, a tight red vest not unflattering to her cleavage—a real ginch. Coloring coquettishly, the brunette dimpled and greeted Barnaby by name, to which Barnaby encored the smile he'd shown the cabby, tossing in a flare of his not-quite-middle-age charm. Then, employing his resounding I'm-a-man voice—office legend claimed it could vaporize women's undergarments—he offered a friendly greeting and entered the Bank's warm foyer. Tempting as the woman was, she would have to wait.

Things continued for the Good as he slipped last into a closing elevator; rotten egg. He felt whistly again, but spared the underlings keeping him company. He watched them leave one by one. When the elevator reached the penthouse, he was alone.

After a little chat with his secretary, Charlene, Barnaby entered his opulent office. Larger than many apartments, and some homes, it offered everything but a bed and a mini bar. Behind Barnaby's gigantic desk, his oxblood chair accepted him with a gentle creak, and he at last resumed his solo of "Strawberry Fields," even singing a few snatches. He shuffled some papers, finger-walked his Rolodex, and smiled; his morning was free of commitment. Good.

He leaned in the priapic chair, *V*'ing his arms and tucking them at his neck. "Let me take you down, 'cause I'm go-wing to ..." he hum-sung, conniving excuses for summoning the doorwoman upstairs. Rocking and smirking, he toyed with the idea of a dinner out, some wine, his place; and if that went well, maybe he'd take her up north, to The Patterson—

He stopped singing, hands dropping heavily to his sides.

Other things. Tat-tat-tat...

A shiver traced his natty spine, making him shake. He grappled with the thoughts, smothered them from mind, pushed them down, down, down...and slowly they dissolved, back into the frothy of his unconscious.

Barnaby eased into the chair. He grasped for the song, but it was gone, scared off like a bird.

***

Despite losing its anthem, the Day continued well past morning. The paper bore Good News—the Yankees had won; his stocks had gone up, save for a stinker he'd grabbed on a pity-buy; Good Weather was on its way—and by afternoon he felt he couldn't lose. The Day seemed to take a turn when he spilt coffee on his Good Jacket, but, miraculously, one of the gofers had it dry-cleaned by quitting time. Barnaby gave the man a raise.

Though ultimately benign, the coffee incident did serve as an unsettling omen: The Good Day had a habit of hooking a hard right into Badsville, Barnaby knew. Therefore, he procrastinated his move on the brunette, wanting only to cool his heels back in the fastnesses of his flat (though he did relinquish another devilish look on the way out, groundwork for when he overcame his Bad Day willies). Unknown to him, he would never see her again.

The Day began its deviation just after work, when he was damnably unable to hail a cab. It was outright remarkable: many zipped past, unoccupied, but none stopped. One was even the morning cabby, recognizable by his pug-like face and mighty chins; the man avoided Barnaby as plague, motoring past with a bare back seat.

Guess I'm losing my touch, Barnaby thought, and started for the subway. Though put off, he refused to acknowledge his descent into Bad Day territory. Couldn't this be a Good Thing in disguise? God works in mysterious ways, after all; closing one door and opening another. Maybe he'd meet a nice young lady, get laid for the thousandth time.

Barnaby navigated the swarming street, empty attaché in tow, his footfalls lost in the downtown din. Random cried words. Pumping cylinders and angry horns. A gumbo of loud. The city's strange tribe flooded past, looking hurried in the way only New Yorkers can. They avoided Barnaby's eyes, and he theirs.

Pair that apathy with a full bladder and my burning hair, Barnaby cynicked, *and I'd be in the market for a toupee.*

Half a mile saw him round Liberty Street for Maiden Lane. People were everywhere, mingling like cogs in a titanic machine, the sidewalks lousy with feet. A traffic cop jigged amidst gypsy traffic. A paperboy enthused his wares. Gang-bangers crowded doorways, trying to look innocent. Even the birds appeared on a time schedule. Car exhaust assaulted Barnaby's nostrils, inducing a raspy cough despite his city upbringing. The bustle was overwhelming to one on his own, enough to strike any man small. Barnaby yearned for his flat and a high-ball.

The jungle scene forced Barnaby into his head, his legs continuing on instruments. He went through his day like a dog perusing trash—his stocks, the jacket fiasco, his evening, the brunette doorwoman. The brunette: soft ochre eyes, bedroom smile, gourdlike curves. A short girl—and maybe a tad stout; he wouldn't be surprised to find some extra padding under her little red vest—she stood lower than Barnaby's shoulder, childlike, incredibly sexy.

Just like Zoe.

Barnaby stopped mid-step, ebbing the flow of bodies. Zoe: it circled his head, threatening to at last wretch his Day into the wastelands. The name, and the iceberg it played tip to, danced dangerously close to conscious scrutiny, like a tenpin about to fall.

Other things. Tat-tat-tat...tat-tat-tat...

Barnaby broke into spontaneous sweat. A shapeless man brushed past, knocking Barnaby off-kilter, and Barnaby removed himself from traffic, veering off like a broken down car. He stopped in the doorway of an unfriendly bodega, struggling to keep the vomitous thoughts in their place. Then, just when the floodgates were trembling, his repression mechanism kicked in, working its magic. The hateful name disappeared.

Barnaby coughed unnecessarily and smoothed his jacket, then returned to the pedestrian crush. Firmly back in the Good, he resumed his journey down Maiden, all things right, God in His heaven. It was so Good that as he crossed an intersection, moving with the herd; he even heard Mr. Lennon inviting him to strawberry fields.

Before Barnaby could accept the invitation, however, something caught his eye: a Polaroid picture, tucked between the quoin bricks of an approaching building, like a printed receipt. The building appeared to offer the picture to passersby, daring them take it. No one did, though; Barnaby seemed to be the only one who noticed.

Suddenly dubious, he glanced left and right, as if the Polaroid were made of gold, but The Tribe continued, oblivious to both him and the picture. He tried to ignore it with them, but felt oddly magnetized to the thing, how a fish might as it sees a lure. He took one funky step, hesitated...then two more, accepting that tidal pull.

Wedged loosely between two weathered bricks, the thick stock flapped haphazardly in the breeze, perhaps waving hello. Thumb and forefinger in an *L*, Barnaby reached out and tweezed the plasticky paper—then pulled back as though yelled at: touching it had zapped him with Bad Day dread, a hot slap from a heavy hand.

Don't, cried a voice not his own, *forget it and go home*. Barnaby considered this...but, no. By then, curiosity had drowned his better sense, proverbial felines be damned.

He callipered the photograph, plucked it free, turned it over. Then, anticlimax: the photo displayed only a fuzzy, sallow square under a too-close flash, what appeared to be fabric or tawny skin. Barnaby sighed; the image was no more frightening than a visit with his bed sheets.

"It's nothing," he said aloud, as though the lump was benign. But then recognition waved from the back of his mind: there was a weave there, in the photo's yellowish blur. It seized him with fear, his brow crumpling—he was looking at It.

The Polaroid fell to the concrete, back-flipping in the breeze.

Impossible, he exclaimed internally, stumbling from the building. *Didn't see that, didn't happen. Strawberry fields, nah-nah-nah-nah-nah...*

He considered letting the picture flip its way into a nearby storm drain, but ornery hands soon consigned it to his pocket. He turned clumsily to passersby, mumbling half-formed questions, face beseeching. "...some kind of joke?" he muttered indignantly, directing the words to no one in particular. The Tribe passed as if he were made of cardboard.

Other things—didn't see that—just a coincidence—tat-tat-tat—

His heart stuttered and feverishly resumed, each pulse felt in the ears. Feeling criminal, he sidled into the alleyway, the swell of his back finding gritty brick. He distantly realized he'd damaged his jacket—his *Good* Jacket—but he paid no attention; vanity had suddenly grown very small and far away, as it might in war. To think someone had photographed *It*...impossible. And to have planted the picture for him to find, in the middle of Manhattan, when he should've been in a cab anyway—it was insane.

"Nonsense," he said, but his heart slowed none. Sweat caged his forehead, thick like wax. He planted a hand into the pocket with the offending Polaroid, played some pocket pool... and emerged empty.

If it's just a coincidence, why not look at it?

Barnaby snorted with offense, conjuring a thousand fictitious reasons. Before he voice them however, his attention was diverted further into the corridor: there was a second Polaroid, fluttering from the lid of a trashcan.

Barnaby lost his color. He scuttled to the trashcan, pawing the brick for support, and snatched the picture petulantly to his face, ignoring the high stench of rotten food.

It revealed a second patch of that repugnant beige weave, unmistakable.

Barnaby staggered backward as if punched, anger joining his fear. *"Where are you?"* he screamed into the alleyway, head darting about. Three agitated plunges of his hand joined the second picture with the first. It was all a farce, he knew. A crew from *Candid Camera* or *I Spy* was waiting in the wings, would soon spring from nowhere and announce the ruse amidst prerecorded laughter. Ha-ha. Joke's on you, Mister Tasle.

There was no one, though, and soon another white square caught his eye, from the alley's far wall. He raced through the trash-littered corridor, his eyes in manic study, a scowl devouring his good looks. Standing as far away as possible, he shot out a hand, arched his back, and pinched the picture as if it would bite.

He stole a look, then quickly turned it away: this one depicted a thick rope cinching an anal swirl of fabric. He remembered tying that rope, pinching that flap, the stink of old fabric and musty basement.

The anger left him then, replaced by an acute distress previously unknown in his thirty-one years. His stature imploded with impressive speed: he was no longer a respected bank executive, nor young and handsome and rich; no longer the man who had bedded more women than most men would lay eyes on. Somehow, out of the clear blue—and on a Good Day, no less—his balls had found their way into the virulent hands of an Other.

"*I have money*!" he groveled, to the alley at large. "*Cash—I can get it now*!"

No response.

Barnaby floundered. "*Drugs! You want drugs? You name it, I got it*!" he lied.

Silence but for the city's far-off chatter.

His eyes continued their mad dance over the alleyway, searching for manshapes—or perhaps a note, something outlining the demands of his newfound despot. But there was only another of the baleful white pieces, within the depths of a connecting alley. It was just visible in the shadows, like a light terminating a very long tunnel.

Barnaby jogged down a half-there stairwell and into the cramped grotto. The cobbled passage spoke of Old New York, horses and carriages and oiled dirt, nickel whiskey and topper hats. The city noise drew even quieter with his advance, eventually tapering into a whispery hushing noise—*shush-h-h-h-h-h*. His loafers' clicks danced up the walls. Running water commentated from a stone-arched sewer grating. There was a dead animal, somewhere.

Barnaby went halfway in, but stopped before reaching the picture: eyes intruded.

He turned violently on his hips, tie chopping air—no one. But still he sensed eyes, watching.

"Hello?" he called feebly, arms raised in a surfer's-pose. The word echoed, died.

He swallowed, then went the short distance to the fourth picture and swiped it up, clammy sweat slicking his hands. The contact reprimanded him like before, making him flinch. He flipped the picture using two fingers—it weighed a fortune, no less than a hundred pounds—and eyed it eagerly, like a card shark turning a kitt...

Barnaby sucked wind and immediately used it for a scream. No aces there.

The picture fell to the trashy floor and Barnaby wilted with shock. Darkness devoured the crotch of his pants and spread adventurously outward. His jaw worked to no effect, opening and closing with piscine repetition. He shrunk against the alley's rigid wall, a lumpy mound of knees and shoulders.

Though showing only a burlap sack amidst a flash-obscured background, the picture dispelled any notion of coincidence or question, or fantasies of him being the butt of some bizarre joke: he was looking at It, the sack, that screaming thing planted in his Maine vacation home.

Lost in his cataclysm, Barnaby noticed neither the pinprick on his neck, nor the uncouth lips pressing there.

III

October 20th

A palatial chamber. Draconian firelight. A conspiracy of orange and shadow, a figure sketched in the gloom.

The figure stirs, and Buford returns to his body, tacit as a man boarding an automobile. His eyes report nothing, but smells of jasmine and rosemary confirm he is home. An anemic hand plays over the bare chest, a swell of oily sweat building at the sharp. The hand finds his face, and the fingers say he is smiling. Though Buford is old hat at astral travel—*aeons* old—the state never fails to fascinate: seeing left and right, up and down, past, present, and future, blended into a kaleidoscope of experience—marvelous.

His eyes adjust, the firelight displacing the void. Tendons creak, and he stands from the circle of glyphed stones. The harvest roils from within; if not expunged willingly, it will soon emerge on its own. He sways, balances on unshod feet, and traipses to the ancient table flanking the circle, vision blurred. He gropes wildly for the vial, fighting air, and his left hand meets glass, at once drawing it to his mouth. He braces legs barely felt, flanges his mouth firmly over the opening, and, with a watery belch, relinquishes the harvest to its destination.

The vial corked, he presents it to the babbling firelight: the viscous black liquid is perfectly opaque, a little column of night. Success. Buford commits the vial to a proud wooden rack, then collapses on a mountain of cushions, beyond exhausted.

Never gets any easier, he thinks wearily. Of all his black rites and sinister enterprise, ingesting and regurgitating another's energy is by far the most despicable. It goes down like a sewage roux, and its return is no smoother. The metallic flavor haunts his tongue; he sips from a demijohn, swishes, swallows.

Fatigue harasses him, the Languor of the Walker, and he moans into the flickering black. Once upon a time, such success would've awarded some satisfaction, a sense of accomplishment, but after defying the boundaries of reality itself, Buford finds his photographic shenanigans little more than a parlor trick. Though it *had* produced a fine result; he gives himself that. By the finale of his alleyway expedition, the poor Tasle had been practically *bleeding* the stuff. A mere prick of the nape had gushed the black energy down Buford's discarnate throat, so much struck oil.

Buford allows a painfully brief rest, then calls out, "Servant!"

A door opens in answer, bringing faraway light and, shortly, a man-shadow.

"Phone, now," Buford screeches, his accent inextricable.

The shadow retreats, and reappears in seconds flat, a bulk at its side. The servant sulks gracelessly into the chamber, morbidly tall, his shadow lengthening over the desert of floor. A phone hangs from one hand, its cord umbilicaled beyond the jamb.

The handset finds Buford's importune fingers. "The client, Mister Checker, dial him," he spits at the man-thing.

The rotary chatters; the line rings once. Click.

"I have found one chinked," Buford says, the words inflicting the cavernous room. "Expect the sample."

The earpiece speaks a single word—"Understood"—and the line dies.

IV

October 21st

Tat-tat-tat...tat-tat-tat...tat-tat-tat...

Barnaby rapped his outsize desk, echoing about the office like dripping stalagmites. The noise ceased, and he raised both hands to his face as if blow-drying a manicure. His nostrils flexed, and yes, his hands still smelled.

He cursed and sprinted to his private bathroom. Steam billowed as he soaped, rinsed, and repeated, abrading the skin in some places. His head lolled sensationally with each stroke, threatening to depart his shoulders.

He returned to his high-backed chair, waited, and took another tentative sniff—no dice. The stink of spent gasoline infected both hands, defying a dozen washings. After a defeated groan, he returned the hands to the desk.

Tat-tat-tat...tat-tat-tat...

Clumsy with fear, he'd splashed himself while burning the loathsome pictures last night. In retrospect, he was lucky not to have ignited his flesh with the photographs, but he remained ungrateful. A picture-snapping lunatic had his testicles in what felt like an industrial vise; his thanklessness was pardonable.

The phone chirped and Barnaby flounced in his seat. He regarded the handset dubiously, chewing his lip.

They's comin' for ya', Big Barn. Gonna lock you up fer sher. He'd heard that voice before, at the bar up north, where he'd met her. Barnaby's eyelid twitched.

Two rings. Three. He picked up.

Lock you up!

"*SHUT UP*!" Barnaby shouted, a static-laden echo of himself sounding from the handset.

"*Mister Tasle? Sir?*" said a tiny female voice. Charlene, his secretary.

He sandwiched the phone between his left ear and shoulder. "Sorry," he said, kneading his temples, "that wasn't for... for you." An awkward pause. "What's happening?"

"I was calling to remind you of your three-o'clock," she said; then, meekly, "with the board..."

Barnaby's hands stopped mid-knead, his eyes shooting to the digital desk clock. He read a three, a two...then looked away.

"They're...they're waiting for you, sir," Charlene said, frail as a child.

More kneading. "I'm sick. Tell them I'm sick," he croaked, hoarse. He'd been screaming a lot. "I'm leaving early." The receiver made an injurious *clack*, and Barnaby doubled over in his seat, squeezing his skull as if it might run away.

Lock you up, Big Barn...

He tried to scream again, but managed only a thready whimper.

***

The fifth unoccupied taxi passed without so much as a glance. Aghast, Barnaby tried for an outraged "*Hey*!" but his voice again bottomed out. *A cabby conspiracy*, he thought, dumbstruck. Since he'd hailed The Good Taxi the previous morning—an age past, it felt—every cabby in New York seemed to have gone blind.

He removed his corpulent billfold—a Moroccan Launer, nothing but the best for Big Barn—and produced two hundred-dollar notes. As if carrot-luring a horse, he extended the bills into the street, swishing audibly.

One cab passed. A second.

"*Come on*!" Barnaby whisper-screamed. His throat felt to have incurred first-degree burns.

He repeated the gesture to a third, and when this too failed, he cursed pitifully and slung his ornamental briefcase at the vehicle, deranged with spite. The case connected with the cab's rear window, strong enough for a solid *thunk* but not to break the glass. Beyond a flicker of brake lights, the cabby showed no response.

I'm invisible, Barnaby concluded. I could step out in front of one and it'd plow right over me.

He took the first reluctant step homeward.

***

Consumed by his sudden blacklisting by the city's cab syndicate, Barnaby didn't notice Maiden Lane until he was there. It lay between him and the subway, nothing less than a wall. The sight brought a traumatized chill, and he approached with the same dubiety he'd shown his office phone.

Lock you up, Big Barn...

"*Shut ... up*," he hissed, teeth in his voice. A passing woman shot him a vinegary look, and he returned one of his own—if looks could kill. The woman hooted and rounded Barnaby with a generous berth, her New York apathy temporarily suspended.

Barnaby spat in her general direction, then continued toward the alleyway, each step a study in self-control. After three, however, he went stock-still, his face screwing up: another brick-clutched picture, sprouting plantlike from the quoins. *Déjà vu*.

It sent the first swell of dementia through Barnaby Oswald Tasle, his mental picture-frame dipping askew. Feet from the brick, he did a double-take and cried out, earning him sidelong looks and raised eyebrows.

Instead of a Polaroid, this one was of flimsier stock, roughly the size and thickness of a four-by-six wallet photograph. Battling an urge to flee madly into the street, he reached out for the back-turned picture...then withdrew as if burned, having second thoughts.

He appealed a passing man in a black overcoat. "Who put this here?" Barnaby asked, indicating the alleyway. The passerby raised a frigid shoulder and kept on, not missing a step.

Undeterred, Barnaby turned to a peeved-looking young tough strutting from the opposite direction. "Who put this here?" he snapped, and when the other man failed to halt, Barnaby stepped impudently in front of him. "*Hey*, I'm talking to you—!"

Without prelude, the man brutally slung Barnaby from his path. "Screw off, ya' crazy jerk," he said, and went casually on his way as though this were a daily occurrence.

Taken by surprise, Barnaby careened over the sidewalk and went down hard, his head finding cold and hard, a shimmering white nebula splashing his vision. When he was again able, he touched the crown of his head, and the hand came back bloody. He tried to stand but his extremities were whatever is beyond heavy, returning him to the ground. The brick wall doubled across his vision, the glossy picture duplicating with it.

Seemingly by its own accord, the picture dislodged and pendulummed to the sidewalk, coming to rest harmlessly over Barnaby's knee. Face-up.

Barnaby's eyes fell to the picture, again victim to that strange magnetism endemic to Maiden Lane. There were three of them at first, a diaphanous triptych, and as the copies slowly merged, he made out a woman smiling from the picture's shiny surface. Long black hair, dark eyes, a button nose, lavender fingernails, a comely mole on her neck...

I know her, Barnaby thought through a punch-drunk haze. *It's just Zoe.*

His scream brought up blood.

V

October 21st

With one graceful heave, the black ichor spouts from Buford's mouth. The vial fills to capacity halfway through, and the overflow spatters the floorboards, heavy like dripping wax. He is initially infuriated by the spillage, but it doesn't matter: the chinked one had simply contained an overabundance of negativity. And a vialful is a mouthful, after all.

Buford's newly wet body falls to the mound of cushions, bathed in firelight. Sweating and shaking, he wonders over Tasle and the job at hand. It was remarkable: the crazed man had lain opened and vulnerable after only a single, pitiful stage of Buford's ploy—and by the picture of a fair young woman, no less. All things should be so easy.

Buford laughs lamely and thumbs a splotch of black from his chin. *Feeling a trifle guilty, are ye?* he thinks, envisioning the terror Tasle had worn as he was siphoned dry. Ripe this one is. And so malleable, clay to be molded, his defenses cracked like an egg. If Checker decides to go all the way—and is there any doubt he will?—a full harvest will be academic. Tasle is no

Alcatraz; the right prescription of torment will see him open with elementary ease, his goods for the taking.

"Servant!" Buford cries, and within moments the phone is at his ear.

A bedlam of dialing, a single ring, and the line clicks open.

"Pleased?" Buford asks, knowing the answer.

Thick breathing from the earpiece. "Yes." The wet smacking of lips, no doubt tasting of metal.

"Another?"

"Yes."

"Very good."

Click.

The alpine servant obediently retrieves the handset and mates it with the cradle. He removes himself without being asked.

VI

October 22nd

The Patterson terminated its sinuous gravel driveway, a sleeping giant in the verdant Maine wood. The name for Barnaby's vacation home had come as arbitrarily as ordering from a French restaurant; he'd never known a Patterson, and, in light of his nightmarish last visit, would probably run screaming from anyone donning the surname. Bearing the hallmark of wealth, the three-story Colonial boasted expensive shake and copper gutters, the porch arcaded by Doric columns. Watchful dormers. An idyllic picket fence. A carport. You would never think it a tomb.

In light of his shoulder-to-shoulder urban upbringing, Barnaby had sought seclusion when shopping for his home away from home, and the little plot in southern Maine had proved to be ideal. Following a single visit, he'd bought the place at the seasoned age of twenty-seven, with a six-digit check from his own bank. The property lay ten miles outside Randy, a homely one-stoplight town with more people in the ground than above it. He'd loved the place when he bought it, four years ago; now, he could see it burned to the ground.

A half mile down road, Barnaby killed the headlights and eased his rental car over the soft shoulder, a deadpan rain encasing the windows. The home's forlorn floodlight pronounced the end of the driveway, the rain distorting it into an achromatic blob. He stilled the engine and sat ruminatively in the car. The rain drummed.

A handgun from the center console, ammunition. He spilled bullets into the car's cup holder and fed the magazine full. His eyes were another man's.

The door creaked, opening to wet dark, and Barnaby was gone.

***

Buford's phone rings, as he knew it would. He scoops it up.

"Let's talk," says the choked voice on the other end.

"Yes."

"I'll buy."

Buford smiles a row of savage teeth. "Very well."

"When?"

More agonized silence. "Tonight."

The line goes dead.

Buford hangs up, his smile lingering. The million will be welcome.

***

Barnaby in a vitreous slicker of rain, the storm unrelenting, the house still.

The Patterson showed no visible signs of breach, but this placated Barnaby little. *Some*one had gotten in *some*how, as evidenced by those miasmic pictures. He thought it a thief, most likely, some rogue lowlife who crawled the countryside, ransacking vacation homes. But what a surprise Barnaby's must've been, with its gritty secret in the cellar, certainly more than the crook had bargained for. But this hadn't been any garden-variety burglar, those who commit their crimes black-faced and in a turtleneck and toboggan; this one had been wily enough to exploit his grisly find, had probably left afterward, researched the property, and found the owner to be none other than a wealthy bank executive. How fortuitous! And now he was terrorizing Barnaby, icing him with the pictures before making demands at the threat of disclosure—blackmail at its finest. But, pictures or no, they would prove nothing without a body. And the crook surely knew that, was probably sitting guard over the prized evidence like a Roman outside Christ's tomb.

Barnaby envisioned the scene, with the certainty of the insane: the degenerate blackmailer, camped out in The Patterson's basement, defending his find and smiling ear to ear, a Polaroid camera around his neck. It made perfect sense, tea and sugar.

Barnaby mounted the back porch, gun drawn as if robbing his own house. "*But I'm gonna spoil your party, old chap*," he whispered, his lips moving funny. His eyes had never been whiter. "*Poop it real good.*"

He tried the backdoor—locked. The key did its work, and Barnaby infiltrated the adjoining laundry, whispering the door to. He slipped from his shoes and, guided by a mental floor-plan, slithered through the rooms, rain dripping unseen trails. After a cautious survey of the two upper stories, everything proved just as he'd left it, free of camera-wielding invaders or their leavings.

To the basement, then.

The cellar door ended an indented hallway, unassuming in the gloom. The bar released with an iron groan, gritting Barnaby's teeth, and the door opened with a greater noise, altogether ruining his element of surprise. He cursed quietly and entered.

Barnaby tensed. "*I know you're down there*!" he cried from the stairhead, summoning the last of his voice. The words resonated from below: *Down there, down there, down there*.... It was his only answer.

A foul, rot-tinged wind struck him as he crossed the threshold, flooding both his mouth and nose, invasive like drowning. He engaged the stairwell's hanging bulb, shielding his eyes as they climatized. His feet shifted the decrepit risers.

"*I got a bullet with your name on it, son,*" he called down to his imaginary villain. "*Come on out and I'll make it quick.*"

No one came out.

He hunkered at the foot of the stairs, waiting. The carrion odor was stronger there, and Barnaby was tolerating it no better. "*I'm coming on five,*" he coughed, choking on the sour air. He grasped the doorknob with his free hand. "*One...two...three—*"

He burst into the basement proper, gun raised, eyes furious. He hit the lights, and his doddering shadow induced a knee-jerk squeeze of the trigger, two of the three necessary pounds of pressure. With an anxious look around, he registered the room as safe.

The wood-paneled apartment was almost unchanged from when he'd bought the place, empty of burglars. The walls crawled with yellowish lightning bolts of mildew. The ceiling was oppressively low, the tiles stained. An itinerant constellation of dust danced in the light. The sack lay spang center in the room, *in situ* from a month earlier.

The bulbous swell of burlap sat alone over the floor, like chintzy furniture, a fibrous hemp rope strangling the top into a flap. A map of terra-cotta discoloration ran through it, becoming a uniform stain near the bottom; the sack could've been a giant paper bag holding a greasy sandwich. It lay amidst a dried bed of blond liquid, the apparent source of its mottled complexion. There was a small hole near the very bottom, sprouting an inert sliver of lavender.

Tat-tat-tat...tat-tat-tat...

Barnaby shrunk into himself, as though there was a draft. "*Shut up, you prude little BITCH*!" he bugled into the little room, rattling the ceiling tiles. He dropped the gun and fell to his knees, muffing both hands over his ears.

The obnoxious rapping had haunted him in the guilty weeks following his thirty-first birthday, so much a tell-tale heart. He'd met Zoe at one of Randy's hick bars, all black hair, brown eyes, and bust in the beer signs' amber glow. He'd wanted her then, like a cat craving milk (or a mouse). The woman had appeared drunk as a skunk to the stone-sober Barnaby, rendering her the perfect birthday gift, and a single boilermaker had been all the persuasion necessary to lure her to his lonely vacation home. Later, however, as they canoodled in his den, his hands greedy as their master, she had proven not quite inebriated enough to undo her wrappings.

Her rejection had infuriated Barnaby, who'd been denied nothing in life, his lust transmuting into rage. "*What do you think you came here for*?" he'd half screamed, half whined, so much a tantrumming child, to which she had only shaken her head and gathered her things. After being curbed a second time, he had calmly backhanded her upside the head, knocking her out cold. It had happened with the spontaneity of a bodily function, entirely expedient in the moment.

Barnaby had molested her then, parting her limp legs like the bar's batwing doors. Afterward, stricken with a weird post-coital madness, he'd drug the defiant woman to the cellar and imprisoned her in a makeshift burlap sack, due punishment for her transgression, he'd thought. He had eventually sobered from this fit, but Zoe had remained in the sack, now in fear of reprisal. The first day, she'd screamed incredibly, murmuring floor-filtered cries as Barnaby cut into his birthday cake (chocolate, his favorite); the second day was marked by sickly negotiation, most involving sexual favors in exchange for release; the third brought only a droning "Please," moaned with broken-record tenacity; by day four, she could only smack the cement through the sack, her protest devolved into a series of muted thuds. By the end of Barnaby's week-long vacation, Zoe -- he'd never gotten her last name -- had gone quiet but for the brooding Morse code of her fingernail against the floor: *tat-tat-tat...tat-tat-tat... tat-tat-tat-tat.*

Snapping back to his present hell, Barnaby went to his haunches before the dappled sack, eyes Coke-can-cold, jaw lolling stupidly. A stringer of drool escaped his mouth and bungeed from his chin. He grabbed the gun from its nearby rest, dragging it languidly over the cement before flipping it butt-first in his hand. A grunt, and the butt came down, smashing the corpse-finger; it made a dry crack, like a roach meeting a boot heel. He stood provisionally, holstered the gun in his waistband, and hoisted the paper-light sack over his shoulder, his expression unchanged.

He turned to leave, but then saw the man standing nearby. The crook, his face terrible. Barnaby bleated with alarm and scrambled for the gun. He raised it, tightened on the trigger... then stilled: it was only his reflection in a wall-height mirror hung across the room. A movie cliché.

A puzzled look fell over him: nowhere was the dapper fellow he was accustomed to seeing in the mirror. That man had been replaced by a gaunt effigy, his auburn coif of hair reduced to a rain-matted slick painted over his skull, eyes dilated into bovine black globes in stress-ringed sockets. Mud and rain soaked his jeans and mackinaw jacket, reducing them to dowdy rags. Drool glazed his unhinged jaw. He smelled like he looked. With the tattered sack over his shoulder, he appeared a sardonic Santa Claus, perhaps the man who delivers the coal. And with the gun in his waistband, he looked like—

"*I'm not a murderer*!" he yelped at the Santa Claus look-alike, voice splintering. "*It was suicide! The cunt killed herself by keeping her pants on*!"

As fast as he'd smashed the finger, he levered the gun and emptied it into the mirror, arm pumping with each report. The glass detonated and the assembly fell face-first to the floor, where it would stay forever. Barnaby stood over it for a long time, fruitlessly squeezing the trigger. He then flung the gun like a rock and collapsed into a sobbing husk, the sack thudding beside him.

His eyes chanced over the exploded mirror, and he noticed something through his blear of tears: a square of white was secreted behind the glass, contrasting the tarred backing. A Polaroid. His eyes widened to the point of discomfort, threatening to leap from his head and dangle like macabre Christmas ornaments.

And then eyes punctured him from behind.

Barnaby snorted and wheeled around, but there was only yellowed paneling and barren cement. Alleyway *déjà vu.* He twirled back to the mirror, flinging a hand of drool to the floor. Dropping on all fours, he stuttered forward and timidly pulled the Polaroid from its roost, the stock warm in his hand—*From the shots*, he told himself, though the rounds had pierced the mirror's opposite end. He regarded the picture as though it were a living thing. *Losin' yer mind, Big Barn,* chimed that despicable Southern-fried voice.

Barnaby managed a sickbed "*Shut up.*" He stole another glance over his shoulder—clear—then deliberately flipped the picture, wincing ... and his pained expression dissolved: the exposure was pure white, a picture of milk. Before he could question this, a smear of brown interrupted the whiteness, followed by a lick of beige.

He squint his eyes and furled his brow, as if lifting something very heavy. "Still...developing?" he said, with a cretin slur. Still perched uncomfortably on all fours, he blew over the stock and flapped it in the air.

Beige poked through the creamy haze...a mote of black ...

Faraway recognition tickled his head, as it had while examining that first venomous picture two days earlier. *Impossible!* he cried inside, as if the rebuttal had previously derailed such phenomenon.

A jean-clad leg ... a bedraggled shock of hair ... more beige ...

"This isn't happening."

Losin' it, Big Barn ...

A silvered length of cement...a tangle of rope...a hunched shoulder...

"*Stop it! STOP IT*!" he commanded the picture, but it didn't stop.

Gonna lock you up, boy ...

A muddy plaid sleeve...a spindly hand...a bulge of chestnut weave—

Barnaby howled and the picture fell to the jigsaw of broken glass, developed to finality. It depicted a man at a wall-hung mirror, the little pane reflecting Barnaby's failing, stress-aged face.

***

For a heartbeat moment, an amorphous human shape is described within the small cellar tomb, standing eye to eye with Barnaby Tasle. He sees it as one would swine in flight, and his eyes would widen further if not drawn to capacity. The shape, keenly luminescent in the dark, staves its attack long enough for Barnaby to squeak in fear. Then it rabbits forward, inhumanly fast.

Barnaby's cry is cut short as the shape makes a third eye over his forehead. There follows a distinct sense of suction, as if a vacuum has been placed over the wound, and then all goes numb, the shock voiding his legs and laying him supine over the floor, the dried pool of Zoe's excrement haloing his head.

Unlike most of Buford's subjects, Barnaby survives the harvest of his soul—though his existence is far from substantial. Legs at crippled angles, arms akimbo, he can do little more than flutter his eyelids and think catatonic thoughts. With idiot's eyes, he sees the ghostly luminance implode on itself and disappear, leaving him terrifically alone. He wants to yell, scream, but all that comes are plosive grunts, those of a deaf-mute attempting speech. The nagging Southern voice in his head has gone quiet, along with most other sentient thought. But he is aware. Painfully, horribly aware.

A vegetable. The thought churns panic, and he struggles to the extent of his ability, willing himself to move an arm, shift a vertebrae, cough—*anything*. Blood flows, synapses fire, shrieks press on a dead tongue, and Barnaby at last senses movement: a single fingertip, leaping spastically from its resting place.

Splayed next to his victim's stinking bones, his body winding down like an old clock, Barnaby stares blankly as his cuticle raps over the cement. *Tat-tat-tat...tat-tat-tat...tat-tat-tat-tat....*

30 Minutes or Less

By: Matthew W. Williamson

I still remember a light snowfall outside of the cabin windows. The sun had started to set, washing the sky and ground with a vibrant pink, like the color of ribbons on boxes of Valentine's Day candies. It was a picture perfect moment for Kerra and I. The smell of simmering beef stew filled the cabin while the crackling fire mixed with our soft footsteps.

My legs shook as I approached her. Perhaps it was the full afternoon of skiing. But I suspected it was the engagement ring that I nervously thumbed in my pocket that was tripping me up.

Her slender figure hovered weightless and angelic in the outlining light of the fading day. She stood quietly in front of the sliding glass doors, taking in the view of the snow-capped trees surrounding us at our little hideaway.

The flowery smell of her shampoo and body wash encircled me as I pulled her body close. Feeling her damp, warm skin through my shirt and and pajama bottoms; I leaned in close to whisper the words that I had been rehearsing for weeks. The five words that would change my life and hers.

Forever.

She moaned contentedly as we embraced. My mind raced, filled with second guesses as my mouth prepared to speak without wavering, without a hint of hesitation or fear. I reassured myself that this was the moment I had been waiting for. If I let it slip by now, my life would never feel complete.

I held my breath for a moment before finally speaking. Now you're probably thinking my five words were: "Kerra, will you marry me?" And I wish that were so. That was my original intent.

But life doesn't always grant our wishes. My words were not spoken in a lovesick daydream.

They were grounded in a soupy, dark reality of conflict and tangled emotions.

My heart raced and adrenaline ran through me like a waterfall as I whispered into her ear softly; “I know what you are.”

It was in the moment between my words and her startled reaction that I shoved her away from me, intent on pushing her through the glass doors and over the outside deck.

The dream sometimes continued longer, but my alarm woke me from the retrospective nightmare. I slapped it silent, the red numbers blurry as the sweat stung my eyes. With two hours before work, I had enough time to finish my latest note to Detective Reese.

I should have gone to check on Lydia downstairs, but that would have to wait. My words were swimming in my head like a fish in a bowl too small, and I didn’t want to lose the momentum that had come to me.

Admittedly, I had not intended to share so much correspondence with him; but building trust takes time. Especially with work like ours. My first few letters to him were so that we could establish a baseline with each other. I needed him to understand my purpose—my calling—or else the apology would fall on deaf ears. I needed to write carefully, as each letter undoubtedly betrayed details about myself. I understood that my notes to him were slowly drawing him closer. Personal details would be engraved in the writing no matter how hard I may try to conceal it. I couldn’t afford to allow him to catch me until I was ready.

Dear Detective Todd Reese,

In April of 2005 you found a woman with 19 stab wounds (each of those wounds was filled with a cucumber) laying impaled on a methane vent at the city dump. I won’t lie, there were others before that chicken-legged disease spreader. And yet, I consider her to be the first true expression of my calling.

Her name was Jeanne Philmore wasn't it? An ironic last name don't you think? After years of selling herself, ruining lives and marriages, bearing several illegitimate children that ended up in foster homes, I and I alone ended her reign of despair.

She held out longer than I expected as I filled her new orifices with the vegetable, twisting it for maximum effect. I was impressed by the amount of penetrations she was able to take, but, after all, she did have years of practice.

She spat her past exploits at me without regret. She enjoyed being a pig. I watched as she succumbed to death, unrepentant for her sins.

I do not seek attention, and what I do is not a grand calling of a higher power.

But it is a calling.

Where you are bound and tangled by the red tape of the state and country you serve, I am not. In many respects we have similar goals. Yet the polar opposite ways that we approach that end has brought us together as adversaries.

I do not wish this in any way. Jeanne Philmore was a plague that the law you follow prevented from bringing to justice. I was able to bypass the constraints imposed upon you and make the world a better place.

My regards to you.

I didn't sign the letter. I never did and never would. There was no reason to. I had proven who I was to Todd in previous and graphically detailed writings. And he never used a name for me—not publicly yet—during his televised replies to me. Nor did he feed the media scavengers any details about my letters or my work. With little given from him they lacked a clever splash page to sell their rags with.

I believe he did this to show mutual respect. It's pleasing to see that I'm not endangering the work of my calling for nothing.

I sent the letter in email form from a laptop that I had acquired months ago. Most drive-in restaurants around here had wi-fi, so I could park nearby and still get a signal. Ironic isn't it? We live in the age of cell phones and street light mounted cameras; and yet the more eyes they have, the less they see.

I can't say that I enjoyed the tasks I carried out. They simply needed to be done. As for the variance of my executions, that was mostly decided by the crimes of the offender.

Some were taken quickly, but when circumstances worked in my favor I was sure to make an example of them. Others still were offered a chance to repent and change their ways. Although, more often than not, their pleas and promises were false.

In the second floor bathroom, I considered how this house and I were alike: barren and empty, yet not without purpose despite our hollowed innards.

A man stared back at me from the medicine cabinet. His name was Cale Vincent to the outside world, but not to me. With a pinch of regret and hypocrisy I was forced to occasionally rely on the dated idea of personal identification. I accepted nicknames when offered; as I felt they were the sum of another individual's perception of me. Does that sound so ludicrous? I think not. Especially when some version of golden wisdom passed down through generations went something like: "If you want to know about yourself, ask someone else."

Our eyes did not blink or wander as I washed the vital regions of my body and ran a few ounces of hair gel into my blond mop. Last night's white tee and khakis were mostly clean and relatively unwrinkled. They would suffice. After all, I wasn't expected to dress that well considering my job.

I replayed my past and the expectations of my future while driving deeper into the city. The green grass of the suburbs was slowly smothered by uneven pavement as the neon lights of downtown replaced the daylight.

I worked as a deliveryman for a crowded little pizza shop called Justin D's. It may not sound impressive, but it was a great aid in my calling. I was able to be somewhere new every night. That made me harder to track by the police, and I intentionally took alternate routes to my destinations in order to search out more degenerates.

I didn't actually need the job. Father had been a smart investor after returning from Vietnam and had tilled strong financial ground for our family. He had put up the money for my medical schooling, and would have for Kerra's had I asked.

I would have asked…had she confided more in me before making the rash, foolish decisions that ended our relationship.

As I entered the back door of the kitchen, Justin thrust several pepperoni pies in my hands with addresses scribbled on top. He gave me a light cuff up the side of my head—his way of saying hello—and hurried off to light his next cigarette.

Amanda waited for me by the door as I left. She set two freshly baked pumpkin muffins atop the pizza boxes with a smile. I dared to give her a small kiss on the cheek as I exited. I was withdrawn from the world and quiet by nature. I watched and listened, but rarely contributed to the general conversation of the kitchen staff. Justin and Amanda understood and respected my privacy, while at the same time treating me like a family member. It wasn't a feeling that one often got from a workplace environment and I was deeply grateful for it. Although my reactions to them were calculated and not truly based in any available emotion.

The work night was frantic, yet uneventful. I returned home at 12:30 with two turkey subs and sticky fingers from two more pumpkin muffins. Muffins are best when eaten warm after all. They would be a nice treat for my house guest Lydia.

Lydia, like Jeanne before her, was a prostitute. And yet, as I closed in on her, I realized she was a kind soul lost in a world of depravity. I chose to rescue her instead of delivering vengeance.

After I castrated her married customer and sewed his genitals into his mouth, I tore her from the cheap motel room and brought her home with me.

It wasn't an easy adjustment for either of us. There were a few escape attempts before I was forced to remove both her legs and one arm; not to be sadistic, but, rather to aid in her rehabilitation. It would take her some time to undo a lifetime of poor guidance.

She has been with me for a few months now, and we have a routine worked out. After her sponge bath and bed change I offered the sandwich. I knew she was still angry with me for bringing her here, yet she took the offering with full trust and began eating right away.

While she ate I began reading to her. It was called *The Giving Tree* by Shel Silverstien…a lovely story. Simple yet ingenious as it reached it's moral outcome.

I traded off with children's stories and some psychology books from my own collection every night. I had hoped to retrain her way of thinking so that she wouldn't make the same mistakes again. One had to nurture as well as teach. I knew I simply couldn't preach to her and expect a miracle rehabilitation. We were two separate individuals, coming from different experiences and upbringings.

I had done things to her that she didn't couldn't comprehend or agree with, but she knew I didn't want to kill her. She understood that much.

Her blue eyes tracked me as I circled the bed, tucking her in. I spoke softly about the story and asked her questions about it. Tears streamed down her cheeks yet she did not speak. Perhaps anticipating a punishment if answering incorrectly.

Make no mistake; I never violated her insides. Nor would I hurt her intentionally or out of spite. She was a student...a child to me. My only goal was her rebirth.

I lamented and dropped the discussion. She seemed to be working herself up tonight. I could almost see her heart pumping underneath her skin. Perhaps my readings were working, or she was forcibly rejecting them. I would need more time to determine my success rate. I pulled a syringe of liquid hydrocodone and injected it into the IV well I had placed in her neck.

Her eyes rolled back as she fell into euphoria. I watched her taut body shudder as the drug took her over. She was fed, changed, and now high. Her sutures were healing nicely, although she must have still felt a great deal of discomfort. I didn't enjoy drugging her nearly as much as she enjoyed it. It would be something we would have to work out in her future. But for now I had to be understanding of her pain and her needs.

Her senses skewed, I left her to writhe in pleasure while I retreated to my room to double check my satchel for tomorrow's event.

It rested on the floor next to my desk, overstuffed and stretched at awkward angles. I was mildly concerned that I may have packed it too heavily: twenty feet of barbed wire (pre-clipped at five-foot lengths), a hammer, my rain slicker, and a toy crossbow.

The crossbow was my favorite. I purchased it at a flea market ages ago and recently constructed a wooden replica of a small pizza box to conceal it. I had already given it several tests and learned how to tip the bottom slightly enough to keep the handle and trigger out of sight.

Good for one shot only, but a nice silent shot.

I tangled the sheets all night, my anxiousness keeping me awake. Home invasions were always tricky and filled with variables. Granted, I delivered justice to several of my targets while in their homes, but I had never forced entry the way I intended to this time.

My previous targets had been more out of convenience and occasionally a spur of the moment decision. But if Thursday night went well for me it would open up new doors for me.

No pun intended.

But I reassured myself that I had been carefully studying the streets, neighbors, and most importantly, the building layout for weeks. With my targets schedule and habits memorized well enough. Justice and I would prevail.

Next morning, I awoke earlier than usual to the sound of a lawnmower chugging outside. Groggily shuffling to the window, I peered out into the blue haze of early afternoon. I felt my lips pull back into a snarl watching the neighbor Keith steadily pushing the gas powered beast over damp grass—dad's old mower. I spent my share of summers pushing it when I was younger.

Keith had taken advantage of father's generosity while he was alive. And now, after father's recent death, he had no obligation to return the borrowed property to our family. I wondered how much else this bastard had pilfered as father's health and senses crumbled away.

My eyes strayed to the front of the yard where Keith's wife knelt planting flowers in window boxes. And behind, at the edge of the walkway, a realtor sign stood tall, belligerently announcing the sale of the house.

"Motherfucker," I said aloud.

Keith was an arrogant, mindless, self-serving drone, always in competition with our family. Always trying to one-up any event, gift, or accomplishment father had been part of. And now he wanted to race us in selling houses. How absolutely pathetic.

I did have a spot for Keith in my grand plan. He would be punished while I absolved myself. I would not allow him to get away with robbing our family.

I know what you're thinking, but no I'm not doing that.

Killing the neighbor would lead Reese right to me. Keith was a lanky, googly-eyed asshole, but selfishness was a minor infraction in the grand scheme.

And over a lawnmower? Well…that would be just plain crazy.

My deliveries seemed to pass by in fast forward as I awaited the end of my shift. But I think the few hours after work were by far the most rewarding and renewing moments of my life.

Returning home by 3 am, I checked on Lydia while I threw my soiled clothes into the basement furnace. It was a good thing I shop at thrift stores. I found my wardrobe dwindling more often every month.

After kissing her forehead goodnight, I nearly ran to my room to begin writing Reese of my exploits tonight. You see, my act tonight was meant as a peace offering to him. I was hopeful he would understand. His acceptance of my gift was crucial for us both to reconcile.

Dear Detective Todd Reese,

I had heard through whispers that Ronald Watson was a drug dealer and unprosecuted rapist. The man had a name that was feared by victims and peers alike. I'm writing this to tell you he is no longer a threat.

Truth be told, I had a harder time getting past his roommate/cousin than I did breaking him.

She was about to slam the door on me, when my arrow pierced her collarbone. A lucky shot considering she left the door chain attached. But the building was a rotting hole and I easily rammed my way through.

Rap music blared from upstairs, apparently someone starting their weekend party early…or never ended last weeks.

But I was grateful for it; their noise hid the sound of our interaction. I kept a hammer tucked in my belt behind me. As she tried to pull the arrow out and crawl away, I straddled her grabbing her hair to hold her head still. I removed the tool and smashed both of her eye sockets in. I continued to hold her down, even until after her bowels released themselves, soiling both of us.

Still alive but unconscious from the shock, she continued to breathe in shallow rasps as I dragged her to the bathroom.

What should have been the cleanest room in the house was littered with syringes, spoons, and stained clothes.

After I saw the marks on her arms I knew she was nothing more than an addict. Likely used to sell drugs and to be used for sex while she was on them.

I dropped her into the bathtub and de-veined her like a shrimp. She came around one time only with a piercing scream as I pulled the heroine clogged roots from her once fine ebony body.

No one above seemed to hear or care.

She was used as a tool in life. A puppet even. So I strung her insides to the shower bar and faucet as a metaphor.

Once I was satisfied with my message—my heroine marionette—I turned the shower on and went to the kitchen. The fridge was well stocked with beer and beef jerk,y so it took me a few fevered minutes to hide the contents and racks. I knew Ronald would be home soon. And I knew he always checked the refrigerator first thing.

I was waiting for him inside. As soon as he opened the door I sprung at him.

Long story short, Detective, you will find the names of his suppliers, fellow dealers, and customers written in blood on his walls. He tried to play hardball at first. But after I displayed his female companion to him and forced him to swallow a few of her teeth he opened right up to me.

Unfortunately my pen was broken during our struggle, so after subduing him, I improvised and used one of his fingers.

One of several that I removed.

My Regards to you.

I had rewritten the note several times as the bags under my eyes darkened. It didn't feel complete to me. I had written too much of the woman and not enough about my interrogation of Ronald. I was on my fifth draft before passing out at the desk.

As I lay unconscious and drooling onto the keyboard, the fateful dream returned to me. This time however I was a third person watching the scenario unfold. I felt even more helpless than usual as it all replayed before me:

Kerra smashed through the glass…screaming. Her shrill cry cut short as her abdomen smashed into the guardrail of the balcony. The wood scraping her skin and holding her in place for that one moment. The zero moment. The last moment available for one to choose between the paths that would direct their future.

I saw the look on Cale's grimacing face as he watched her teeter like a playground see-saw. He approached and grabbed her flailing ankle. With a flick of his wrist, she was hurled over the edge.

We both rushed to the railing and peered down. We reached the edge in time to see the rocks below bounce her body around like a rubber ball. Her fine skin pulled apart with each impact until landing in the snow below like a discarded toy. The last beats of her heart pumping a velvety red outline around her.

A mist from her cooling body wafted up to our tearing eyes.

Cale turned to me. "It didn't have to be this way. She could have told us she was selling her body to pay for medical school. She just had to ask us for the money. We could have paid her tuition and all lived happily. Father told us to live humbly with our money. Not to flaunt it. But he didn't say that we couldn't use it at all."

I found myself nodding agreement as the cold wind embraced our hearts.

It was because of Kerra that I lost interest in school, love, and eventually life. I spiraled for weeks when I found out about her indiscretions. Tearing myself up inside before I found the Calling. My Calling. I came to understand the reason that life had dealt me the hand it had. I was being prepared for this. Forged from pain and loss into an avenger—rectifier of moral wrongs—and I was strong enough to realize it and embrace my fate.

I awoke with the usual shakes and cold sweat. The reaction was becoming less frequent and certainly more controllable. The dream while still disturbing was losing its potency on me. Soon I would erase it completely.

Sunday night I broke into Keith's tool shed. The pre-fab building was easy enough to breach. The deadbolt was easy to cut away, and the hinges swung quietly.

Inside, I found the lawnmower neatly parked next to father's air compressor.

I hauled them both back under the silence of a starlit sky and full moon. Father's garage was mostly barren at this point. Most of his estate was already distributed among the remaining family. Only the humble house itself remained undecided on.

For now.

I knew I wouldn't be able to remain here forever. Nor would I want too, even if I could find a way to stay. Father's quaint three-story house was nice, but it wasn't my birth home. It held no precious memories that I longed to cling to. And while I missed him, I didn't feel alone. I could keep Lydia for as long as I wanted for company, but that would be selfish of me. And keeping her at this point wasn't an option to carry out my end-game with Reese.

With our property returned, I had only to move Lydia.

I had little time left. My own preset schedule was catching up to me.

Contemplating her fate I once again sat at my desk. I deleted the last note for Reese from the laptop and drafted a new one. I had meant to drag the notes out a bit so that I could describe my calling and hopefully garner his acceptance of my apology. However with things moving this smoothly, and for them to continue to fall into place, I would have to just get to the point.

The final version of this note would not be sent from email. I intended to print it out and seal it in a postmarked envelope.

I wanted a new beginning; nto rewrite myself again. And for that to happen, Detective Reese would need closure.

Dear Detective Todd Reese,

I want you to know that I deeply respect and admire you for not taking any time off from the police force in light of the tragedy that befell you several months ago. I know you are fe-

verishly looking for me. And I understand why you feel the need to hunt me down and deliver justice as the legal system dictates

I'm sorry I killed your girlfriend. I know now that she was working an undercover sting as a street walker. I had spoken to her several times, but always drove away. She was very attractive—a little too attractive and clean looking to pass as one of the disease-spreading tramps that plague our city. After I met and passed her by, I grew curious, thinking that perhaps she was new to the profession. Perhaps being drawn in out of stupidity and desperation. I had seen that happen before. And I thought I could help her.

So I continued to watch her as best I could.

I followed her home several nights, calculating the best way to reach out and save her. I admit I didn't feel fully prepared when I confronted her on the steps to her apartment. It was a balmy Wednesday night and quite uncomfortable to wait in. I could see that it was taking its toll on her as well. So I used it as a conversation starter.

She was taken off guard by my topic of humid sweat and street grit. I could see that.

As was I when I saw the glint of her police badge in the flickering streetlight.

I reacted. I couldn't let my Calling be cut short. I had made a terrible mistake introducing myself to her, and I couldn't afford to be placed on a suspect list.

I charged her and punched her in the chest, dragging her inside and demanding she take me to her apartment. Fighting for her every breath she obliged. But not out of fear. I could see it on her face and feel it in her tensed muscles that she meant to turn the tables soon.

As she fumbled with the keys to apartment eight I smashed her head into the doorjamb. I needed to keep her disoriented as we entered. We would be on her turf after all. I had no reason to doubt that it wasn't her apartment. After all, a police officer wouldn't intentionally endanger the lives of others.

Likely fighting the approaching blackout, she still managed to escape me. She crossed the room and clawed at the shotgun mounted inside her broom closet. I grabbed her by the neck and underarm, spinning her down onto the faux hardwood floor.

My weight was on her with my knee in her back. I had the advantage.

Sadly, the situation called for me to end her life. I wish it hadn't turned out this way. She was a fellow peacemaker, and innocent by my standards. Yet she had clearly seen my face. The best I could do for her now was to make it quick and painless.

I plunged the knife into the base of her skull and upward. It was a quick death and would allow for an open casket during her funeral service.

It was while I was cleaning up my traces around the apartment that I found framed pictures of you two together. I checked the machine and heard the last message you left for her.

I was even more shocked to discover this. What were the odds that I would kill someone you were involved with by accident? I could only imagine how this would infuriate you. How could you think what had just transpired here was anything other than an attack against you? After all, you had already been assigned to my cases for months.

I figured that you would be reassigned elsewhere after the accident. Then I realized that your relationship was kept secret from your peers at the force. There was no way they would let you continue the case if they knew how personally involved I had made you become.

I am sorry, Detective Reese. I can't return what I took from you, but I can try to help you put your life back together.

It is time to make it right. It is time to end this torment in both of our lives.

I surrender.

My Regards to you.

I was very pleased with my work at this point. Although I also understood that despite my righteousness and dedication, I was a sloppy executioner. My deeds up to this point began to feel like labor pains; knotting my stomach in serpentine coils.

Perhaps I was in labor. A new me was being born at this very moment.

I looked forward to my time away, to giving myself some rest and relaxation while I re-prioritized my goals. As I rocked back and forth in my desk chair I felt something. Something I hadn't experienced in a long time.

Relief.

Just a few days and this would all be over. I smiled and headed to the basement. I would have one last chance to read to Lydia.

Timing was crucial. I knew this as a medical student and as a pizza deliveryman. Rushing led to mistakes, while taking too long would lead to unpleasant outcomes.

I sealed the letter in a manilla envelope and mailed it Monday afternoon. Reese would get it the next morning and come for me. I had one night to put everything in place for my surrender.

Keith had not noticed his shed was missing some borrowed equipment yet—which I was grateful for. If he had summoned the police too soon, it would ruin my surrender before I was ready.

Lydia was harder to move than I had hoped, and I sacrificed father's medical equipment along with her. I was saddened at letting her go without fully rehabilitating her, but she needed to be released into others' care for my fresh start.

I knew my last act with her may haunt me. Perhaps in dreams like Kerra did. But time would tell. It was certainly a lesson that I could learn from: Keeping a pet project is a bad idea.

By Tuesday morning I was seated in the attic. My neck hairs bristled as I stared out the window expectantly. Anytime today they would show up. Excited and scared as I was, I looked forward to seeing this through.

I grew restless by mid-morning, perking up only when I saw Keith strut out to his tool shed. Perhaps he was going to get more tools to prune his yard for the realtor.

I laughed as I heard his scream.

I didn't peg him as a swift of mind individual. Minutes passed after the scream and he remained in the shed. I imagined he was fumbling with all the "evidence" I had placed. *Stupid bastard.* I wondered if he was frozen still with shock, or perhaps had tripped over the pile of medical textbooks I left on the floor.

Better yet, as if on queue, the first of several police cruisers sped up to and over his precious lawn. The 'for sale' sign was run down onto the finely primped lawn in a flurry of dislodged grass blades and dirt tufts.

Keith fell out of the tool shed as the officers drew their guns and encircled the house. My breath was taken from me as they bared down on him. He was in a state of panic and confusion. To my delight, he resisted arrest and was Tazed several times before being hauled away. I giggled like a child as he flopped on the ground like a fish.

The street began to fill quickly with curious onlookers who were soon parted by the approaching medical personnel.

The EMTs remained in the shed for twenty minutes before wheeling Lydia out into the daylight. Her remaining arm flailed in the air as if she were waving goodbye to me. But it wasn't possible that she knew where she was or that I was watching her now.

Letting her go was difficult. I felt a sense of failure. And more-so, I felt I was unfairly punishing her when I severed her tongue and burned her retinas away. But I could not allow her to be able to identify me from Keith. Despite that, I remained pleased that I had given her a new home where she could be better taken care of.

Tears of joy and relief spilled from my dark circled eyes while I watched the remaining evidence I planted being hauled away.

My exit plan was working!

I had recovered my father's belongings, made Keith suffer (without death) for his transgressions against my family, and managed to settle things between Reese and myself. Now I could re-apply and train myself to be more efficient and methodical in my future endeavors. My learning curve had ended. My labor was over.

I practiced sorrowful and shocked facial expressions in the bathroom mirror as the event next door wrapped up. I would need a suitable story in case the police knocked on my door, and I was ready to deliver. But, if possible, I would lay low and disappear after quitting my job tonight.

There were other cities that needed cleansing of the growing human waste.

And there were other pizza shops to work in.

My regards to you.

Silence in the Court

By: Chantal Boudreau

I had always believed this day would come; where I would be confronting my daughter's common law husband, Jakob Fischer, in the courtroom. I had thought it would be for the sake of a bitter custody battle over my granddaughter, Stephanie, or even minor battery charges—perhaps even vandalism as a result of some temperamental backlash when Shelly chose to finally leave him. I had known that he was wrong for her from the first day we met, but I had also known that if I tried to convince Shelly of this, she would never listen to reason, and I had been worried that if I had voiced this opinion I would have just alienated her. Perhaps I should have swallowed my fears, and tried. Now, I have no voice at all—and she is lost to me nevertheless.

My eldest son, Grant, brought me here, at my request. He's the only one who listens to me anymore, and trusts what I say. Since the stroke, I can no longer speak, and my mobility is seriously limited. I can't walk, so he had to wheel me into the gallery in my wheelchair, and my only means of communication is by gently squeezing his hand; one squeeze for yes, and two for no.

I want to testify, but they won't let me. Because of my stroke and my inability to speak, they claim that they can't properly confirm my mental acuity. I may not be able to move very well, I may not be able to form the words I want to say, but I can think them just fine, and my memory is entirely intact. Grant believes this. That's why he brought me, hoping that I might find my voice at the right moment to make it count. He can't testify on my behalf. He wants to. It pains him, and I can see that pain in his brown eyes every time that he looks at me.

He wants to see justice for his sister as much as I do. If only that were our sole concern...

I can't twist my head to see Jakob enter, but I know when he has arrived by the buzz that emerges from the onlookers and the flurry of footsteps that echo over the tiled floor. Grant jerks upright and swivels in his seat on the bench. His expression goes from one of anguish to revulsion and restrained fury. His fingers tighten on my hand as well.

With several very shaky efforts, I finally manage to shift my view just enough to see where Jakob sits with his defence attorney. He has a good one, one of those fellows in the fancy Italian suits wearing a genuine Rolex. Jakob had a joint account with my daughter and, ironically, it means that he is using her money to pay for that lawyer. Jakob had insisted on controlling their finances, despite the fact that my daughter had earned the lion's share of their money. She had always yielded to his demands, until Stephanie had come along. I was surprised that Shelly had been willing to bend to his will so easily before that—I had always considered her to be the strongest of my children, the most wilful. She had been a responsible, well-educated professional woman, and had seemed to have her life in perfect order. But Jakob had had an inexplicable strangle hold on her emotionally, and for some reason, she couldn't find it within herself to fight him, at least not until Stephanie's arrival. Stephanie was what had changed everything. That was why things had ended the way that they had.

I know now that Shelly had been horribly lonely. She had never shared that with me. She had been a very private woman who was always too busy to talk. It was that human contact that she was craving that had initially made her easy prey to Jakob's artificial charms. He had hoped to live the easy life, coasting along as a kept man, and playing puppet-master from behind the scenes, pulling Shelly's strings. I don't think he ever wanted to be a parent. Stephanie was an accident, one who had interfered with his leisurely life and who had stirred up trouble.

Unintentionally, our eyes meet, Jakob's and mine. There is a malicious smile lurking in that cold, gray steel, even though his expression is vacant and slightly mournful. I know that his display is just a mask to try and capture the sympathies of the jurors. He is laughing inside, mocking me and my pain, and he is already celebrating victory. That bothers me as much as anything else. He hasn't won yet. I still have hope, as misguided as that may be.

Watching him stare into me like that brings me back to the day that I had last seen him- the episode that had led up to this moment. My final view of him had been as I had looked up into that chilling stare, while I lay prone and paralyzed on the floor. That was before the excruciating pain in my head had caused my eyesight to blur and had funnelled me into the blackness. He had smirked at that time, raising the chair to strike me. I suppose he was intending to claim that I had struck my head on it when I fell, just like he had claimed that Shelly had fallen down those stairs and had not been pushed. Had the sirens and flashing lights not arrived at that very moment, a result of my frantic and garbled call to 911 before I lost all ability to move or speak, I'm sure I would have joined Shelly in that cold bed of earth, rather than being sealed within the prison of my unresponsive body.

"Are you okay, Mom," Grant asked, following my trembling gaze.

I squeeze his fingers once, the barest of pressure—yes.

"Do you want to go?"

I squeeze his fingers twice. I want to leap to my feet. I want to point at Jakob and scream: "Murderer!" I want to grab the closest chair and pummel the man who killed my only daughter into a bloody pulp, wiping the memory of those hateful eyes and that triumphant evil smirk out of my mind forever. But I don't want to go. I won't let go of that hope that I can find my voice, and make sure that he pays.

I can tell that Grant wants to leave. I can hear it in his disheartened tone. He has given up and believes that Jakob has already won as well. He thinks that this will just be an event of self-torture, and he would rather not play witness to a judicial travesty, another marring of his sister's memory. I've told him what I saw that day through a series of questions with yes/no squeezes, and he believes me, even if nobody else is willing to accept my testimony. He knows that Jakob was abusive, and that Shelly was leaving him and taking Stephanie with her. He knows that I had arrived, harangued by one of my terrible stress headaches, to pick them up and take them home with me. He knows that Jakob confronted us, and that was when everything had gone wrong.

The trial today is a result of accusations that Shelly had been pushed and not fallen, but the physical evidence could not support one over the other, and while there were people willing to claim that they had seen Jakob mistreat Shelly in the past, the only witnesses to the actual crime was a two-year-old child and an older, stroke-afflicted woman considered incompetent by the court. Jakob's defence lawyer dances a pretty dance, one to the tune of circumstantial evidence, the normal day-to-day minor conflict that all couples experience, and the societal prejudgement towards men who choose to be stay at home parents. Yes, there had been arguments, he attests, but Shelly was actually the abusive one. She had the money, and therefore, the power in the relationship. She devalued Jakob, the lawyer claims. She questioned his manhood and robbed him of all esteem. She left Jakob too submissive to initiate a physical altercation, and caused her own accidental death by allowing herself to be distracted by obsessive little details—her typical state of mind—as she had been approaching the top of the stairs.

All the while, Jakob hangs his head, his gaze downcast. He is playing the victim, and he does so quite convincingly. There is none of his usual swagger, his jaw is not set, and his customarily tensed form is relaxed and non-threatening. Despite the charade, he cannot resist shooting me an icy look, the corner of his lips curling almost imperceptibly. I think he knows that I'm still fully aware, and the sadistic bastard finds my circumstances gratifyingly amusing.

I still recall the phone call from Shelly that day, the last real conversation that I had had with her—the last real conversation that I'd had with anyone.

"Mom, I want to leave him. I know he won't go, he'll insist on staying in the house, so Steph and I have to find some place new. Can we come stay with you, just until we can arrange something else?"

My heart had jumped for joy at the thought that she was finally ready to free herself from the ties that bound her to that cruel, cruel man. I had also felt a panic building in me as well. I knew that I was supposed to keep my stress-levels down, that I had been suffering from high blood pressure, and the attempts to lower it using medication had not been as successful as my doctor would have liked, but I could not shake the anxiety in face of my daughter's decision. There had to be a reason why she had changed her mind about sticking it out with him, and that thought alone had been enough to make my stomach churn with dread.

"Of course you can, sweetheart," I had told her. "You and Stephanie will always be welcome here." I had known that there was little she would be able to squeeze into her tiny compact car, and they would want to bring as much of their home with them as possible to allow them some comfort and familiarity. "Pack up what you need and I'll be over in the SUV to pick up you and your things." I had paused, reluctant to ask my next question, but needing to hear the truth. "I have to ask, Shelly, what finally did it? What made you decide that it was time? This isn't just a temporary thing, and you won't be going back as soon as the air clears?"

She had been as reluctant to answer as I had been to ask, but I had known that something had prompted her actions. She had put up with Jakob's mistreatment for years. There had to be purpose to this stand

"I won't be going back, Mom. He hurt Steph. I won't let him do that again." Her words had been blunt and firm. That was the Shelly I had known—the part of her that Jakob had suffocated into near non-existence. The idea that he had somehow harmed my granddaughter had been enough to cause a second sickening wave of anxiety to wash over me, bringing with it a horrible, head-spinning headache, one that had persisted when I had climbed into my vehicle and had made a beeline to Shelly's home.

"Steph? Is she okay?"

"I think she'll be fine, Mom. It wasn't much; I intervened quickly. He had never touched her in a violent way before today. He had shouted at her for little things in the past, typical things you would expect from a two-year-old, but I never thought he would let his frustration get the best of him. She spilled food on the carpet and he just lost it. He grabbed her and started shaking her really hard and yelling, with his eyes wild and bugging out and his face turning red. I stopped him—you aren't supposed to shake little kids like that. Everyone knows that, but he didn't seem to care. I'm worried he'll do something like that again, and next time I won't be around to stop him. He didn't even show any remorse."

He never had with Shelly, either, and when she had said that she had stopped him, I had understood what she meant. She had gotten in the way to protect Stephanie, and had allowed herself to be the target instead. I had wondered what new bruises she would be bearing as a result of that intervention.

I had raced over to their house, hoping to get there and leave with her before Jakob had time to notice the departure and protest in some aggressive manner. I had been aware that Shelly had overcome her greatest obstacle to shedding that destructive parasite, which had been her own personal reservations, but that did not mean he would allow her to go without a fight. My head had been pounding as I drove—a piercing agony that screamed at me as the road swam in front of my eyes. I had the window rolled down, so I could already hear their enraged screams as I was pulling into the driveway. I had stumbled out of the car, my right side numb and unresponsive to some degree, and after I had managed to make it to their door in record time, despite my sluggish movements, I had staggered inside. When I had found them perched at the top of the stairs, locked in a hostile embrace, I had tried to cry out for them to stop, but my tongue did not want to do what my mind wanted it to do.

Jakob had made no attempt to disguise the fact that he was willing to prevent Shelly's departure at any cost. Those cold gray eyes had been filled with hate and maliciousness, and his grip on the sleeves of her heavy coat had been relentless. Shelly had been trying to escape him towards Stephanie's bedroom door on the upper landing. He was the one who had actually been dragging her in the direction of the stairway, ignoring her efforts to escape him. His jaw had been set with determined ire, a natural pose for the mean-spirited man. He had always been dissatisfied with his lot in life, the perpetual bully foisting blame for his unhappiness on everyone else.

I had reached for Shelly's landline—my cell phone still in the SUV—and with great difficulty, I had dialled 911; gripping the receiver in my frozen claw of a right hand and shakily pressing the buttons with my left hand, then equally as numb as the right had initially been. That was when Jakob had thrown Shelly down the stairs.

It had not been a graceful fall. Her head had struck the wall, then the lower part of the banister and finally the stairs proper. There had been a grotesque crunch, with each blow, and when she finally lay limp on the floor of the lower landing, her neck had been contorted at an impossible angle and her wide green eyes had been staring lifelessly up at the ceiling.

I jolt upright in my chair with the memory, more of a spasm than a controlled reaction. Grant's eyes widen.

"Are you alright, Mom?"

He thinks I'm responding to something that was said on the stand, but I was lost in my reverie, still trying to pull the words out of the bottomless pit within me—the one that had swallowed them and refused to spit them out again. I actually want to scream, but I can't even manage that. I don't bother to squeeze Grant's hand. What's the point? I'm not alright, but if I tell him "no," he'll try to insist that we leave again.

He covers his face with his free hand in misery. He doesn't want to watch this train-wreck. The testimony before us continues and, unable to bear listening to the lies, I return to my memories.

When I had caught sight of Shelly lying there, dead, that had been the point when something inside my brain had literally exploded—the stress, the shock, the heartache—all culminating to bring about my downfall. I had tried to tell the 911 operator that my son-in-law had just murdered my daughter, but all that came out was a garbled: "Shelly...stairs...help." Then the receiver had toppled from my hand and I had followed it to the floor.

My head had shrieked with pain, my body refusing to do anything that I wanted it to. I had heard scraping, shifting sounds as Jakob repositioned her body, so it looked more likely that she had fallen. Then he had wandered over to stand above me, staring at me prone and helpless on the floor before bending down to pick up the chair.

Seven minutes—it had taken the paramedics seven minutes to respond to the call. If it had been eight, I likely would not have lived to see this day in court. If Jakob had not paused long enough to leer at me with that despicable smile and those soul-dead eyes, he would have had the opportunity to knock me into oblivion. He had only intended that for me, however, because he saw me as a potential witness who could testify against him in court. He had not realized that those words to the 911 operator would be my last. I wish that one of those words recorded on that call had been "murder" or even "push", but my voice had already started to fail me and I had not managed to give them even that much ammunition against him.

Jakob eyes me on the sly again, and I can tell that he is laughing inside. I think he's glad I'm not dead. He prefers it this way, with him on the outside, watching me suffer within my prison while fate is suggesting that it will spare him from his own.

The trial takes forever, and yet, despite the endless hours of torture, it seems to pass too quickly; because every second that ticks by without my words is another second where I might have been able to provide Shelly with justice, irretrievably lost. Towards the end I finally feel it, the desperate urge to point and accuse welling up within me. I find new strength, a second wind, a chance to finally hold that murderous bastard accountable. I know I can find that voice and break my silence. I draw in a ragged breath, and I open my mouth, preparing to speak.

"J –j –j –j- j- j- j- j- j..."

And that is it—that is all I can manage. I am crushed. Jakob had heard the attempt and had tensed, turning to watch me as I laboured to force the sounds from my lips. I was trying to say: "Jakob killed her; I saw him do it. I saw him push her intentionally," or "Jakob is a murderer; he killed my Shelly right in front of me." Instead, I am betrayed by an unwilling connection of brain to mouth, and a rebellious tongue. No matter how significant the need, it will not work for me. Hope evaporates for good this time.

My little outburst has not only drawn Jakob's attention, but that of the majority of those in the courtroom. Jakob's hand flies to his mouth, to conceal the mocking smile that he now wears. I am an entertaining sideshow—nothing more. He corrects for this quickly in case anyone else notices, turning the gesture into the suggestion of withholding shock, most of his face reflecting false pity—all but his eyes. Those cold, hard stones lose their dullness long enough to flash a gleam of mirth in my direction, a mark of triumph. I have failed. Shelly has lost. He has won.

As they find him not guilty, there is a final injury, one other loss as a result of my inability to speak. Stephanie had been a ward of the court, but once her father is declared innocent, they have no cause to keep her from him. Sure, there will be social workers and other people keeping tabs on him for a little while. Jakob will present the charade for them while they are there, a man in mourning who clings to the one thing he has left. He'll make sure not to leave bruises until the visits stop.

Grant is unable to watch as she is returned to Jakob, but I have the misfortune of not being able to turn away anymore than I can rush forward and wrest her from the doom that she will find in his abusive arms. She cries a little, and resists his hugs. He smiles wearily, playing the role of the doting father, grateful at the return of his pride and joy, but I sense the underlying frustration. There will be hell to pay for her display of reluctance later, and he will unleash his evil upon her in some manner that won't leave visible marks. There will be no one there to stand in his way then, just as there is no one to speak for her now, although not for the lack of trying.

As Grant rolls me out of the courtroom, his shoulders sagging and his heart heavy, a single tear spills noiselessly down my cheek. Stephanie will be as much a victim of this silence that keeps me prisoner as I am, while the real criminal walks.

And I am screaming inside.

Abraham of Harlon

By: Harley Pitts

Twenty or thirty colossal red ants are raising hell across Lyle's canvas issue shoes. He launches to standing and tears at his jumpsuit, lungs ablaze from a sprint through the dry November air. Lyle sheds the suit and slaps it against a tree like it's a rug that needs beating. He thinks about the ant bites that put him in the hospital the day of his fourth birthday party—one hell of a way to discover an allergy, but it seemed to set a certain tone for the rest of Lyle Aybear's life.

There's a clearing further into the woods, due east. The treeless gap glows a sick blue. Lyle peers through the tree-line at the interstate draped in the same cryptic cobalt. The white van lies on its side with one headlight snuffed and the other reduced to a feeble burn, similar to that of a flashlight covered in sand. The taillights spread a patch of red between the grass and the edge of the road. He lets his narrow eyes slide out of focus; it looks like the van is bleeding.

Everyone else is still inside. Maybe they're alive; Lyle doesn't care. They aren't moving, and he's no doctor.

The last road sign placed him ten miles outside of Roberts, but that was five or six minutes before the van skidded off the road and flipped. Escape was a daydream, not anything Lyle had given serious thought. He was still alive when the tumbling stopped, and running just *happened.* He had looked back at the toppled van and known he'd feel like a failure just standing there, waiting to go back and finish up his eight year bit.

He slides into the white jumpsuit and pauses: It'd be better for someone to see a shirtless guy running through the woods than a convict with a 'Department of Corrections' stamp on his back. He rolls down the upper and makes it into a kind of waistband.

Lyle takes a deep breath and sprints across the open field. The cold air stings his bare chest. He cuts through the woods and makes out a small house beyond the tree line—no lights inside and no vehicles in sight. An old metal trash can rises from a pile of empty beer bottles near the back door.

Lyle creeps out of the woods and scoops a rock. He wraps his hand around it and feels its weight, then takes a few steps and throws the rock at a side window. The stone nicks the frame and sounds like a line drive glancing off a bat, but the window explodes. Nothing else moves. Lyle crouches behind a bush and waits a full minute before deciding the place is vacant.

The homeowner is at least four sizes larger. Lyle shrugs. Anything is better than the jumpsuit. He puts on a baggy shirt and huge pants, then he checks the fridge for beer, instead finding expired lunch meat. He thinks of the trash can overflowing with tallboys and figures the homeowner is out doing some shopping.

He looks at some mail near the door. An envelope reads 'Mosley Steels – RR 4 Box 121, Harlon, TX.'

Lyle wades into the woods on the opposite side of the house. He rolls his jumpsuit into a basketball-sized wad and lofts it into the trees, where it catches on a thick branch. He needs a car, fast—the dogs will be loose as soon as they know Lyle's missing. He isn't a car thief, so he'll have to find a ride with keys—or rob someone and hope they stay tied up until he leaves Texas; he's hundreds of miles from any city large enough to accommodate a disappearing act.

Lyle walks two long miles. The patch of woods spits him out at the crest of a small hill overlooking downtown Harlon. Were the town an impressionist painting, it'd be called *Nausea Incarnate*. The tight mass of steel buildings, ramshackle houses and churches radiate a soulless dread.

He descends the hill and sprints between a machine shop and a hulking, steel garage. The city is bare and leaves nowhere to hide outdoors. Lyle sneaks around, skulking like a cartoon bandit from hedges to broken down cars to shabby buildings. The Harlon Police Department looks like the guard station at a strip mall. There's a black-and-white parked out front and a light in the window. Lyle figures the night shift cop is drunk or asleep—probably both. Harlon PD isn't the problem: his fear is being spotted by an insomniac resident.

He looks around the corner of yet another garage and evaluates a squat building across the street. It's the town's only gas station, and the pumps have been abandoned for some time. The picture windows release enough interior light to make the intersection seem metropolitan against its surroundings.

Lyle walks towards the store and eyes the fifteen-year-old truck parked out front. The sign over the station's door reads "Little Son's – Gas-Cold Beer-Cigarettes."

A haggard bell clanks against the glass when he goes inside. There's a small but powerful looking man behind the counter in an old cap and work clothes—-mid-fifties, looks like he belongs behind a tractor's steering wheel, not a cash register. His skin has a weathered, dirty look. His gaze holds the pique of someone who grew up working outside and likes to fix things for fun—-whatever definition of "fun" still exists for an aging man in this town.

"Hello," he regards Lyle the way you would a door-to-door salesman.

"Hey," Lyle says. "I…"

"You *walked* up here." The man looks Lyle up and down and snickers at the clothes hanging from his frame.

"Yeah, I did."

"Passin' through?"

"Trying to."

"But you don't have a car."

"You just saw me walk up here, so what do you think?"

The man chuckles through his nostrils. "No need to get rude. I'm just tryin' to make sense of this. Where'd you come from?"

"Waco," Lyle says. "Visiting my mother." He feels like a fool for letting the man waste his time with questions. "Look, sir…"

"No, *you* look, mister," he drawls, pointing a thick finger at Lyle's throat, "you didn't come from any Waco. You didn't visit any mother, and I *know* you ain't from Harlon. Now this here," he taps a radio next to him. Lyle's stomach bunches at the sight, "is a police scanner. I turned it off when I saw that you was comin' inside. A few minutes before that, I heard a bulletin come across, said someone who looked one hell of a lot like *you* had escaped the scene of a prison transport accident."

Lyle's fists clench. He's two blinks away from hitting the old coot in his ear, but the man puts a large revolver on the counter and turns it toward Lyle. Lyle's legs try to run, but his body won't move.

"Now I *seen* that look in your eye, and I don't want to see it again. You try for me and I'll empty this gun into you. Now if you want to listen for a little bit, things could turn out different."

Lyle's eyes are fixed on the gun. This is only the third time he'd seen a barrel from this end, and it's no easier than it had been on the other occasions. "Go on," he says.

"My name's Ezekiel," says the man. "People call me Ez, Zeke, whatever. Now, I know you're just a burg'lur—s'what they said on the dispatch, anyways—and judgin' by the way you're eyeballin' my pistol, I don't think you've been in too many vi'lent situations. I did five years on armed rob'ry myself, and I cain't stand cops. Now, you add those all things up, multiply them by this gun pointed at you, and you'll find that I may be the best friend you have at the moment."

Lyle's silence admitted the stalemate. "What do you want from me, Ez?"

"You ain't got nothin' to give," he says. "What I want is for you to abandon any notion to try and rob me, beat me up or take my gun. I'll help you get out of here. You prob'ly won't get away, but that's your problem. If you try anything on *me*, I'll put a bullet in each of your kneecaps and tell the cops up here you know the exact where'bouts of Doctor Cecil Hall his-own-self."

The mention of Cecil Hall fit into Lyle's mind like a piece of wire opening a circuit; Harlon, TX had rung bells when he saw it. The story of Doctor Hall—"The Abraham of Harlon," the media had called him—was one of the most sordid legends in the state's history. Even in the Houston suburbs where Lyle grew up, his parents would tell him the story as a kind of jesting, "I brought you into this world, and I can take you out" threat.

Cecil Hall had been a Baptist preacher in Harlon more than three decades back when the town had only one Baptist church. Hall had a vision and decided he was a prophet. His nickname came from the crime that brought him to infamy.

Hall's wife died under cryptic circumstances, and he was raising his two sons on his own. When one of the boys was fourteen and the other around nine or ten, Hall took his sons into their barn and offered them as sacrifices to God. He said God asked him to do this, and he proceeded without hesitation while asking the Lord to intercede if His will would allow.

God remained silent, and the church secretary—who later admitted to being one of Hall's several mistresses—came forward saying that Doctor Hall left a ten page letter on her desk, explaining the ordeal and the locations of the boy's sliced open bodies. He'd gone on the run, fearing his sacrifice would be misinterpreted as murder.

It had been almost forty years since the murders. Hall would be in his mid-seventies and was believed dead by all except the bored small-town cops in Texas, every last one of them harboring his own fantasy about finding the Abraham of Harlon alive.

"Okay," Lyle says to Ezekiel. "What do we do now?"

"You gonna rob me?"

"No."

"You gonna try *anything* funny?"

"Nope."

"In that case, we don't do anything for a while. I gotta finish this shift." He slides the gun back under the counter. "My employee comes in at five in the a.m. We can go to my house, get you some clothes that don't fit like bed sheets, see about findin' you a car that'll get you across the state lines. Meantime, you ought to get some sleep." Ezekiel points to a door at his left.

"Go back in the office and lay on the floor behind the desk. I'll come and get you when it's time to leave."

"How do I know you aren't going to lock me in and call the police?"

"Guy," Ezekiel says, "the only thing I call the law is a bunch of nippleheads. If you'd rather take your chances in the woods, go right ahead."

Ezekiel shows Lyle into the office, hands him a musty emergency blanket, then locks the door from outside. Lyle has never been further from feeling tired, but there doesn't seem to be any harm in lying down for a while.

***

"*Cuh-zin. Get up, cuhhh-zin.*"

Lyle's eyelids begin to peel open. The fluorescent light wakes him with a start. Seconds pass before he remembers lying down in the office.

"I told Chuck that you were a cousin visitin' from out of town," Ezekiel whispers. "Get up and be nice."

Lyle stands into a painful stretch—rising from the cold tile is excruciating. Nothing drives home the inevitability of aging quite like sleeping on a floor. He folds the blanket and places it on a stack of old phone books.

Ezekiel stands near the cash register and briefs Chuck on some hunting news. Chuck is Ezekiel's size except he has flab in place of the latter's explosive muscle.

"Hey," the chubby man extends his hand, "I'm Chuck."

"Hey, Chuck." Lyle doesn't mention a name, unsure what Ezekiel has said about him.

"Well, Malachi," Chuck says. Lyle thinks Ezekiel may as well have said his name was John the Baptist, "Zeke tells me you're visiting from…Nacogdoches, is that it?"

Ezekiel is nodding, and Lyle goes along. "Yeah, a lot of our family lives up around there."

"Really?" Chuck seems vexed. "Ez always told me he didn't have much family left."

Lyle's jaw clenches. "Well, ol' Zeke is a cousin, but he's really more of a brother."

Chuck laughs as though hokey sentiment explains everything.

"Enough chit chat," Ezekiel says, clapping his hand onto Chuck's shoulder. "We gotta get to the house, get you settled in."

"Good meetin' you," Chuck says with a wave. Lyle nods and follows Ezekiel to the truck.

They drive through snaking backroads for more than twenty minutes before turning into a long, rocky driveway onto a huge property. Lyle can see an old barn off to the side and the lip of a pond deep in the backyard. They park alongside the massive early 20th century manor.

"This was my daddy's house," Ezekiel says.

"Big place," Lyle says. "What'd your daddy do?"

"A whoooole lot of baaaad things." Ezekiel looks off into the vast field behind the house. "But he asked the Lord's forgiveness before he passed, and I believe it was granted him."

Ezekiel leads them into the massive house. The foyer has a grand staircase at its center with white balustrades against walnut steps. Both of the rugs flanking the staircase had once been elegant and expensive, but were now caked with dirt and curling at the corners. The air in the house holds a hollow rottenness, the way your arm smells when you let dog saliva dry on your skin. Heavy curtains smother the morning sunlight and leave the room with an even darkness. There are fake plants and real plants in equal number, though all of the real plants look to have been dead for some time.

Ezekiel gives Lyle's elbow a jovial slap. "C'mon down to the basement. I got a bunch of clothes down there'll fit you better'n those you're wearing. Looks like you robbed Mr. Steels or somethin'." Lyle's nerves spike before it occurs to him there can only be one man of Mosley Steels' size in a town like Harlon.

He follows Ezekiel down the staircase. Each board wobbles and creaks. Ezekiel flips a switch halfway to the bottom and two low-hanging lights flicker and settle on a pale yellow. The basement is cleaner and more lived-in than the foyer. It's filled with tools and knick-knacks organized on three tiered steel shelves and in trunks stacked against the walls. A wooden partition is constructed at the far end of the room. Its large door looks like one you'd see on a walk-in freezer and wears a huge padlock like a belt buckle.

"Clothes're in here." Ezekiel slaps the top of a battered red trunk.

Lyle flips the latches on the case and coughs when a stale, mothball odor floats into his face. Ezekiel chuckles and rearranges some things across the room. He pulls down a small toolbox and takes inventory of its contents.

Lyle grabs a flannel shirt and corduroy pants. He slams the lid and fumbles with the latches while he notices a foreign smell cut through the lingering dankness, something he can't identify. It's more medicinal than the rest of the house's scents and smells like tequila mixed with rubbing alcohol.

Lyle opens his mouth to ask Ezekiel about it, but a plastic bag falls over his head and cinches at the base of his skull. A wet rag slaps Lyle in the chin and comes to rest near his ear, sitting there like they're companions inside a balloon just large enough for the two of them.

***

Lyle's head feels split down the middle. Opening his eyes triggers a sensation that might have otherwise come from pulling out a fistful of his own hair—something that would be impossible, since his hands are tied behind his back by what feels like piano wire.

His chest feels as though it were on fire. Lyle tucks his chin and looks down. A scream bursts from his throat when he sees his chest has been shaven, blood running from the words carved into his torso and pooling in his naked lap. Lyle doesn't try to read them. His feet seem deformed—they've been broken throughout. It's a small blessing that he can't feel them at all.

Lyle is no longer in the basement. He looks around and guesses he's behind the wooden partition. The room is candlelit and there's an intricate mural on the concrete wall in front of him. It's a scene of the crucifixion of Christ, one that captures the event at its dramatic apex. The mob is in the foreground, cheering and weeping. Solders are milling around on the hill beneath the crosses. Jesus seems out of proportion, a bit too large, perhaps to better show the detail of his suffering. A large table sits between Lyle and the mural. It's a hybrid between a hospital bed and wooden altar.

The walls alongside are blank as the day they were built. He turns his head as far as it will go and can't see anything behind him.

The heavy door clanks open. Ezekiel strides through and pulls the door closed. He's wearing a three-piece, hunter-green suit from sometime around 1970, but one that looks as new as if it'd just left the store. It fits like he's had it since 1970—his bulging frame stretches the seams and the vest looks as though it'll fire a button across the room any second.

"What're you doing?" Lyle yelps. "What is this?"

"This is the most important day of your life," Ezekiel says with a gentle smile.

"What? What're you talking about?" Lyle struggles against the restraints. They dig deeper into his skin.

"You should save yourself the trouble of all that," Ezekiel says. "You seemed to know the story I mentioned at the station…the one about Doctor Hall. Do you?"

Lyle can't believe he's being questioned. He can't believe *any* of this, but being asked arbitrary questions seems an exceptional cruelty.

"Well," Ezekiel eases into a storyteller guise, "let me tell you the part of the story that no one else knows but me." He walks around in front of Lyle and stands next to the table, clapping his hands together like a preacher at a potluck.

He begins: "Cecil Hall had two sons on record, but he had three. The third one he delivered himself in the basement of his own house." Ezekiel motions around the room as though offering an example. "Mrs. Hall died during childbirth, rest her, and Cecil took this as a sign that this child was not like his other two boys. He buried his wife in the back of the property; told his flock that her mind had become sick and that she'd abandoned him.

Ezekiel unbuttons his coat and reveals the pressed white shirt beneath. "Doctor Hall prayed and decided the boy should remain in the basement, separate from the treach'ry and immoral influence of our world. He believed the child was ordained to do great things—though he had no idea what those things might be—and by keeping the birth unofficial, he knew he'd be givin' the boy a special freedom."

Ezekiel removes his coat, folds it, and sets it at a corner of the wooden altar. Lyle sees a short machete strapped against Ezekiel's chest, resting under his left arm.

Ezekiel's voice finds new volume. "Doctor Cecil Hall's revelation that his oldest sons was to be sacrificed to the Lord came to him when the youngest was fifteen years old. The boy lived his life in the basement. He was occasionally let outside in the interest of good health. His brothers swore on the Bible to never speak of their sibling and Doctor Hall was sure no one else knew of the boy's existence.

"The child was not bitter about his burden. His daddy explained, from the time he was old enough to understand, that the boy's path in this world would be a unique one chosen by Jehovah Himself.

"When the time came to sacrifice the older boys, Doctor Hall told the boy of what God had asked of him. He wished he could wait until the boy was fully grown, but he'd soon be sixteen, and that was old enough to start making decisions.

"He gave the boy his life savings—a modest amount, just to help him get started—and sent him to West Texas. Once the public outcry over the sacrifice had died down, the property would go up for sale. The boy was to return and use a separate, larger sum to ensure he won the auction of Doctor Hall's estate. He was then to live a quiet life, until the Lord delivered the opportunity to fulfill His will for the boy.

"Doctor Hall said he would climb into the well at the back of his property following the sacrifice, and he instructed his youngest son to set him on fire, so that he could see Heaven. He believed he would return on his eightieth birthday, at which time he would bring an eyewitness account of the glory of God's kingdom and save every soul who heard his amazing story.

"The boy did just that, and when he was in his mid-twenties, he had nearly ruint his mind and body pleadin' with God to reveal His plan. The boy hadn't grown much since the age of sixteen, but he had taken to exercise and healthy livin', workin' outside whenever possible. He used the remainder of the Doctor's money to purchase a corner store in town.

"One night, as his thirtieth birthday approached, the boy was praying, and the Lord spoke softly to him. God said he'd visit in a dream and reveal His will.

"The boy waited, night after night, and for a whole month had no dreams he remembered. Then he had a dream that a man visited him—a man who wasn't good but wasn't terribly evil, perhaps a petty thief like the one's crucified next to Christ." Ezekiel motions at the mural behind him with a wide sweep of his hand. "The boy dreamed that he and this man were suddenly at Calvary, and his daddy—Doctor Hall—was there waiting to return to save the sick and hopeless world.

"In the dream, Doctor Hall gave the boy a large knife," Ezekiel draws the machete from its sheath and holds it in the palms of his hands like he's offering it to Lyle, "and he said to his son, 'The life you take from this unworthy man will enter me and return my soul to the world where you and I will begin our ministry.' And the boy took the knife and laid the man at the base of the cross, where he took his life."

Ezekiel walks to Lyle and lifts him onto his shoulder. Lyle's broken feet shift and send waves of revulsion through his body. He lays Lyle on the altar and moves the folded coat to the bloody seat of the chair. He pulls a silk handkerchief from his pocket. His eyes are full of pure joy, and he pushes the cloth deep into Lyle's mouth. He holds the machete in his right hand and steadies Lyle's writhing torso with his strong left arm.

Lyle looks up at the jagged, homemade blade, and tears burn the corners of his bulging eyes.

"Today is Cecil's birthday...*my father's birthday.* I am thankful to the Lord for you."

Lyle's scream hits the back of the handkerchief and returns to his throat. He feels it die mere inches above the spot where the machete falls, smashing into bone. His body goes limp, and his head spins. Ezekiel Hall runs the blade back and forth across Lyle's spine, and though hearing has failed Lyle, the sawing resonates through Lyle's jaw before it echoes into silence.

The Caged Doll

By: Adam Millard

The car drifted slowly through the darkness. Trees passed on either side, so slowly that Annabel could see ancient carvings, etched by star-crossed lovers in an era gone by. Romance was certainly dead; the closest you could get now to a tree-carving expressing love for another was a graffiti tag on the side of a supermarket billboard.

"Are we nearly there?" Kelly yawned from the passenger seat of the clapped-out Metro. "Julie, do you even know if this is the right way?'

Julie, who was the only blonde girl in the car—and definitely blonde in the stereotypical manner of the word—glanced across to her friend in disbelief.

"Of course this is the right way," she spat. "It's a shortcut, and one that'll get us to the party in plenty of time for you to try and drink the place dry and drop your knickers."

Annabel laughed from the back seat. "Yeah. I've heard all about that last party you were at."

Kelly shrugged her shoulders. "What can I say? I like to have fun."

"There's fun," Julie said, "and there's offering yourself up for gang-banging or religious sacrifice."

Kelly began to laugh so hard that a coughing fit ensued.

"See!" Julie said. "She can't even defend herself. She's actually gagging now in practice for some lucky stud later."

"Annabel," Kelly coughed, "take no notice of her. She's got a stick up her arse the size of Nelson's Column."

"What? The black guy who was in jail?" Julie shook her head. "I have no idea how that is even an insult."

All three of them burst into laughter.

It was going to be an amazing night. Julie—the blonde idiot who thinks Nelson Mandela fought in the Battle of Trafalgar—had managed to swindle tickets to the event of the year. Only the coolest students from Newport University were attending; sure, a few muppets would slip below the radar, but the place would mostly be heaving with the popular people; the beautiful people. If the rumours were to be believed, there would be a few special attendees.

Annabel had heard through the grapevine that Locusts of Doom were going to be playing. She'd almost wet herself upon hearing the news; they were one of her favourite rock bands. She had seen them more times than she could remember.

The tickets had been a gift from Kelvin Burns, whom Julie had slept with a blue-moon ago. She had used her sly and somewhat evil methods to extract the tickets, merely promising poor Kelvin more sex in exchange. Once the tickets were in hand, though, Julie had let Kelvin down gently…or something along those lines. In fact, she had blackmailed him, threatening to expose his strange fetish for balloons to the entire campus. Strangely, he hadn't mentioned the cruel ploy to anyone. Weird that.

"Do you think they'll have good food?" Kelly asked, rubbing her belly. "I swear to God, I could eat a fucking horse over here."

"There'll be plenty of food," Julie sighed. "Kelly, I have no idea how you keep the weight off. You eat more than my kid-brother, and he's a proper fat bastard."

"I work out," Kelly smiled.

"Threesomes with Johnnie Katt and his buddies does not equal working out," Julie laughed. "Neither does walking to the shop for more fags and vodka."

"There should be a law against you talking so much," Kelly retorted.

"Truth hurts."

They drove in silence for a few minutes. The hole where a radio had once sat looked quite sad. Annabel stared at it from the back seat, and wondered why Julie had never replaced the one that had been stolen. What was the point? None of the locks worked in the car; a shiny new, top-of-the-range car radio would last a matter of minutes in Newport.

Turning her attention to the passing night, Annabel felt herself falling slowly to sleep. Great, I'll be the life and soul of the party at this rate...

Then, suddenly, Annabel said, "Julie stop!"

Both girls in the front of the car almost jumped out of their skins. Kelly spun her head around to her friend as Julie slammed on the brakes.

The car screeched to a sudden halt. Dust from the trail whipped up a miasma behind it.

"What? What is it?" Julie was wide-eyed, but talking to Kelly. The seatbelt prevented her from turning to face Annabel. "Did I hit something?"

Annabel grabbed onto the headrest and pulled herself through the gap in the seats. "I saw something," she said. "I think I saw something."

"Well, of course you saw something," Kelly laughed, nervously. "The whole entire universe does not just exist within this piece-of-shit car."

"I'm not joking," Annabel said with a seriousness that required attention, despite her friends' banter. "I think I saw a baby."

Julie unbuckled her seatbelt and twisted to face Annabel. "A baby?" she said. "Is it possible that you saw some kind of animal, or—"

"I know what I saw!" Annabel interrupted with a lot more intention than even she had anticipated. Julie was taken aback, and Annabel sensed that she had to placate the situation with a calmer statement. "I'm pretty sure I saw a baby, but it was in a cage between the trees."

"Oh great," Kelly offered, sardonically. "Not only is there a baby in the fucking woods, but it's been caged as well."

Annabel reached for the door handle and pulled, half-expecting the thing to either snap off in her grasp or not open at all. When it did open, allowing the cool, calm breeze of the night in, she was astonished.

"Wait, Annie!" Kelly said. "I was only joking, but you aren"t seriously thinking about going out there."

Annabel swung her legs across, almost laddering one of her fishnet stockings on the seatbelt clip, and said "I'm going to take a look. You guys can wait here if you like; I'm just going to make sure that I'm not going completely insane."

"Good luck with that," Julie said.

As Annabel exited the car on the one side, a door slammed shut on the other. She whirled to find Kelly trying desperately to light a cigarette. The breeze, it seemed, was a recalcitrant little shit.

The engine died, which Annabel mistook for an accident at first, until Julie's door swung open and she clambered out, almost tripping over a vine. Julie looked to her friends and smiled. "I sure as shit ain't waiting around while you two go off into the darkness. I've seen way too many horror films for that."

The three of them began to walk away from the car; Kelly was still trying to light her cigarette with increasing frustration. After a few more steps, and seven or eight more failed attempts to spark up, she cursed and tucked the unlit cigarette into her jacket pocket.

"So this shortcut of yours?" Annabel said. "Anybody ever been killed out here?"

Julie smiled. "Not that I know of. Not yet, anyway." She pushed Annabel, who in turn almost fell into a particularly nasty patch of something-or-other; the darkness made it visually indeterminate, but the smell suggested it was better not to go rolling around in it, whatever it was.

"Asshole," Annabel said. "I think that was horse shit."

"I think what you've got us doing out here is horse shit," Julie said. "We should be at the party by now. Instead, were out in the middle of nowhere looking for a baby in a cage that may or may not be a figment of your imagination."

"There," Annabel said, pointing into a clearing between the trees. "Told you."

There it was, just as Annabel had described it. Roughly twenty metres into the woods—visible only by the fraction of moonlight hitting its bars through the gaps in the trees—sat a cage. Inside the cage, facing away from the girls, sat a baby. It was completely naked, except for a nappy.

"I don't believe it," Kelly said. "Who the fuck would put a baby in the middle of the woods with just a nappy on?"

"Who would put a baby in the middle of the woods at all?" Annabel said. "See, I told you I saw something. I was right."

"Unfortunately," Julie said as she began to walk towards the cage, "you were."

The three girls walked slowly across the clearing; twigs and dead leaves crunching beneath their stilettos which were, Kelly couldn't help thinking, the worst shoes for navigating through the woods. In fact, this was possibly the first time that Kelly had ever stepped into the woods without being dragged by her father, who was a self-confessed "survivor" of the Bear Grylls ilk. If it grew, according to her father, you could eat it, and if you got sick from eating it, then there was always something nearby that you could scoff down—providing you weren't retching too harshly—that would make it better.

Julie reached the cage first, and took a step around to the front. "Oh my God! That is one of the sickest things I have ever seen!"

Annabel and Kelly weren't in as much of a rush to reach the cage. "What?" Annabel gasped. "Is it dead? Holy fuck! Is it dead?"

And then, Julie burst into hysterics. "It was never alive in the first place, you douche." She sniggered. "It's a fucking doll!"

The two girls joined Julie on the opposite side of the cage, who patted each of them on the back as she continued to chuckle helplessly at the strange sight.

It was. It was just a doll, sitting upright. Not only was it just a doll, but it was one of the ugliest dolls any of them had ever seen before, the kind that you would see at a thrift-sale for a few pennies and still walk by in disgust. In its mouth was a pacifier too large for any real baby; its eyebrows looked like they had been etched on with permanent marker, leaving the doll with a constant expression of anger.

"That is just wrong," Kelly said, not sure whether to be relieved or downright abhorred. "I've seen some sick shit in my time, but that's just soooo fucking wrong."

Julie laughed. "We know all about the sick shit you've seen, baby-girl. I'm sure some of it's on the internet."

Annabel ignored the banter and gazed down at the monstrosity. *Who in their right mind would leave a doll in the middle of the woods, in a cage big enough for a tiger?* It made no sense. Something was amiss.

"Open it," Julie said, laughing so intensely that she actually drooled a little.

Kelly shook her head. "Uh-huh, not me. If my father taught me one thing with his stupid expeditions, it was that if something looked like a trap, then it probably was."

"Fine," Julie said, retaining an air of seriousness. "I'll just tell everyone at the party that you were frightened of a little doll."

"I'm not frightened of the doll," Kelly said, pointing to the toy. "I'm frightened of the bastard that put it there. I mean, whoever puts a doll in a cage, then drags it out into the woods is probably slightly unhinged; either that or completely insane."

Julie snickered and reached for the bolt. Annabel wanted to stop her, but she knew that if she did so, she would become the butt of the jokes at the party, if indeed they ever arrived.

The shortcut had turned out to be a bad idea.

As Julie slid the bolt across, rust scraped off; there was a terrible squeak as she yanked it all the way across.

"I can't believe we're doing this," Kelly said, taking a step back as if it would somehow eliminate her from the proceedings. "I mean, this is just silly. It's a doll, for crying out loud. We should be at the party pounding booze and eyeing guys, instead—"

Julie pulled the door, which opened with a low-pitched creak loud enough to make the end of Kelly's sentence inaudible.

When the door was fully open, Julie took a step forward; into the cage.

"Are you fucking crazy, girl?" Annabel said, this time unable to silence herself. "You're just gonna step into a cage in the middle of the woods?"

"Yep," Julie said, reaching down for the doll. "You know why? Because there's nothing to be afraid of; this is just something some kids have been playing with out here."

Kelly shook her head. "Sick kids. Have you seen those angry eyebrows on that thing."

Julie raised the doll to her face so that they were eye-to-eye. The oversized pacifier fell out of its mouth and landed with a thump on the leaves below.

"I think it's cute," Julie said in a voice reserved for the first time you meet a newborn baby. "Whoever did this to you is a sick puppy. Yes they are. Yes they aaaaaare."

Now Annabel felt sick. The thought of attending the party of the year seemed to be little more than a memory now; standing in the middle of nowhere, surrounded by trees, cooing at a child's plaything as if it were a real baby, now that was the in thing to be doing.

"Can we go now?" Kelly asked, clearly bored by the charade. "I'd like to be drunk right now."

She turned; Annabel followed. "Show's over folks, nothing to see..."

"I don't think that's a very good idea," a voice said.

Kelly and Annabel turned back to find Julie staring dumbfounded towards the doll, which she still clung with both hands, eye-to-eye.

"What did you say?" Annabel asked.

Julie looked petrified; she was visibly shaking, and although it was cold—the breeze was showing no signs of settling—it wasn't that which made her tremble so.

Julie mumbled something.

"What?" Kelly said, taking a step back towards the cage.

"I said…I didn't say anything. It did." She emphasised the '*it*' with a nod in the direction of the doll.

There was a second of silence, and then came the laughter; Kelly was almost doubled over, holding her side as if they threatened to spill out all over the ground. Throughout, Julie remained absolutely still, her face contorted into an expression of fear. Annabel spotted it first, and when Kelly straightened up and wiped the tears from her eyes, she saw it, too.

"We're all going to be playing a little game tonight," the voice said. It came from within the doll; a tinny male voice that sounded the way a person does on the other end of a phone-line.

This time, after the voice spoke, Julie dropped the doll to the ground and lunged for the cage door.

"I don't think that's a very good idea," came the voice again, a split second before she reached the exit. "JULIE..."

As soon as she heard her name echo out from the innards of the plastic doll, she stopped dead. Fear, it seemed, had taken control of her motorm functions. The next thing to go would be her bowels...

Annabel looked across to Kelly, who pushed her hand up to her open mouth in an attempt to stop from screaming. Things had taken a turn for the worse; the doll—no, not the doll, but whoever was talking through the fucking thing—knew Julie's name. Whatever was happening had been staged, to what purpose remained to be seen, yet Annabel knew that it sure as hell wasn't going to be good.

"If any of you try to run," the voice said, "all three of you will die without even playing the game."

It was that word that did it for Julie: Die. The way in which it rolled from his lips, too, with such ease and unquestionable intent; he meant every word of it.

"I am giving all three of you a chance to live through the night. All you have to do is play the game, and if you win, then you go free, but I'm afraid you won't be making it to any party tonight."

Shit! He knows about the party, too! Annabel thought. A party which they would all be at by now if she hadn't been staring aimlessly out of the window of the shit-heap Metro. They would be drinking vodka and rubbing up against complete strangers on makeshift dancefloors. Instead, they were out in the dark, in the middle of the woods, playing some crazy game with a complete psychopath intent on killing them if they dared to make a run for it.

Strange how things alter so quickly.

"How does he know my name?" Julie asked, nervously running a hand through her hair. Somewhere, off in the distance, an owl hooted as if to break the silence that followed her question.

A few painful seconds passed, then the voice said, "I know all of your names. I know where you all live, and I know that you all want to be popular." He paused, seemingly for dramatic effect. "I will make you very popular here tonight, since it means so much to you. You will be the talk of the town for years to come. How do you like that?"

Annabel suddenly felt the most isolated she had ever been. A chill ran through her spine making her shudder; it was as if someone had gouged a hole at the nape of her neck and poured ice water into it. How was this possible? Things like this didn't happen to her; things like this only happened in movies, or to unfortunate souls out in the sticks.

"What do you want?" Julie screamed. She hadn't intended to, but she couldn"t help it; the thought of being set up like this was almost too much for her to take. Somebody—some sick fucker with nothing better to do—had planned this out, probably sketching every last detail whilst sitting alone in their bedroom. The thought made her physically sick, and it was all she could do not to upchuck.

"There is absolutely no need to shout," the voice calmly replied. "The doll has a receiver housed inside. It also has a camera, so I can see every move you make, and since we're on the subject, would you be so kind to straighten the poor little doll up? A spider has just crawled across the lens. I assure you that any attempt to run, or trick me, will result in all three of you dying very painful deaths," the voice cackled…witch-like, demonic. "Do you understand?"

Kelly took a step back from the cage. "I think he's bluffing," she whispered to Annabel, who was shaking her head frantically. Loudly, she said, "I don't think he's anywhere close enough to hurt us. In fact, I think he's at home right now, jacking off to this stunt."

Annabel couldn't believe what Kelly was saying. She did, however, have a valid point. What if this maniac was just some kid with a webcam and a penchant for silly games? Sure, that was it; there were thousands of them out there: spotty, greasy little kids who play computer games about dragons and orcs for eighteen hours a day, only this one wasn't playing games with avatars anymore; he had caught himself a couple of live ones.

Inside the cage, Julie nodded along with Kelly's theory. It made perfect sense now. Some geek had taken a shine to her, set up the whole ridiculous scenario on the off-chance he would catch a glimpse of a tit or some ass.

"I don't know about you two," Kelly said, spinning on the spot with emphatic grace, "but I am going to the party."

"I wouldn't do that if I were you."

Kelly began to walk away from the cage. She didn't get more than three steps, though, as the report of a gun sounded. Kelly squealed as she fell to the ground, clutching at her shin. Annabel dove for cover, only to find that there was none. Inside the cage, Julie pushed herself up against the side, her mouth wide open in a fearful O.

"Now look what you made me do," the voice from the doll said. "I told you not to do it."

Kelly was writhing around, grunting between clenched teeth. Her eyes were clamped shut. She was in absolute agony.

"What do you want from us?" Annabel screamed from the ground. It seemed like a good idea to stay put for a while, at least until she knew the maniac wasn't just going to execute them for the fun of it. "We'll do it! We'll play your stupid game!"

The owl hooted once more, as if in agreement with Annabel's decision—although, what other choice did they have?

The doll lay silent for a moment, perhaps in deep thought; maybe he was trying to figure out if they would indeed play along, like the good little girls he expected them to be.

Kelly sat up, holding her knee tightly. Her fingers were dripping with blood, but in the darkness it looked more like tar. Her eyes remained shut; it was better not to see the wound, or so her father had taught her. A wound only really starts to hurt once you realise just how bad it is. *Words of a fucking idiot*, Kelly thought, as it hurt like a sonofabitch and she hadn't opened her eyes since getting shot.

Finally, he spoke. "I need all three of you to climb inside the cage."

Now Kelly opened her eyes, wide. Was he seriously asking Annabel and herself to voluntarily entrap themselves in the cage? For what purpose? It would remain unbolted, which kind of defeated the object of caging somebody; unless of course he made a personal appearance and locked the thing himself. In which case, they were positively screwed and probably wouldn't live to see dawn.

"Are you out of your mind?" Annabel said, speaking into the darkness. Since she had no way of determining his general whereabouts, the next best thing was to simply aim words off in every direction.

"Ever so slightly," the voice laughed. "But I'm trying to get a referral. It's just taking soooo damn long."

He laughed again. The hairs on the back of Julie's neck rose once more. The guy was a creep; a creep with a shotgun; a creep with a shotgun who had no qualms with using it.

"What are you going to do with us once we're in your little cage?" Kelly asked, obviously in pain from her wound; her hand was dark all over, completely covered with blood.

"I don't think you are in the position to ask any questions," he said, crackling through the doll. "In fact, I'm starting the game right now by putting a time-limit on it. You have fifteen seconds to get in the cage. Otherwise, the next shot will mess up that pretty little face of yours."

The three girls barely had time to exchange terrified glances before the countdown began.

"One..."

Holy shit! Annabel thought. He's gonna do this; he's gonna count to fifteen and then start shooting.

"…Two…"

There was no way that she was just going to lie there, cowering for cover, waiting for the lunatic to count to fifteen before he came a-blasting. She pushed herself up onto her haunches and lunged towards the cage. Julie was signalling for her to hurry—

"…Three…"

—which she couldn't even if she wanted to; she was at full-pelt. She took a quick look across her shoulder to find that Kelly was dragging herself along the ground, pushing leaves and dirt aside with every movement she made.

"…Four…"

"Hurry!" Julie cried from the safety of the cage—which, under any other context, would never make sense. "Get to your feet!"

"…Five…"

"Easier said than done, bitch," Kelly grimaced as she dragged herself another few feet. "When was the last time you got shot?"

"...Six..."

Annabel reached the cage and stumbled in through the open door, clipping her head on one of the bars. It hurt like hell, and began to bleed almost immediately, but she ignored the pain and continued to encourage Kelly.

"...Seven..."

Of course, she should have grabbed Kelly and dragged her to safety, but she had just seemed too far away at the time. She had panicked, making sure that her head wasn't going to be separated from her body first and foremost; it was survival instinct. Plus, she wasn't too sure that the count would go all the way to fifteen, like the freak promised.

"...Eight...Nine...Ten...Eleven." The voice seemed to speed up, as if he wanted to shoot Kelly. Maybe he did, if only to prove a point or make an example of her.

As she got close enough, though, the arms of her friends reached out and dragged her the last few feet. Exhausted, bleeding like a stuck pig, Kelly collapsed.

After a few seconds, which felt like an eternity to the incarcerated—was that the right word for it when the door remained wide open?— girls, the doll crackled back into life.

"Aaaaahhh, that wasn't so bad, was it?"

"Fuck you, you crazy bastard!" Julie screamed into the night. "You won't get away with this.'

"Oh, I will," he said. "I'm very popular around these parts. Nobody would ever suspect little ol' me of anything so sick and twisted."

That made Annabel's stomach turn over. Sick and twisted? That meant that whatever he had planned, it wasn't going to result in a happy-ending.

"Why don't you just let us go?" Kelly said through gritted teeth. "We promise we'll never mention any of—"

"Promises, promises, promises." He paused, as if thinking something over in his head. When he finally returned, his voice sounded different, more composed. "Now, Julie, I want you to close the cage door. Do you understand me?"

Julie gave cursory glances to her friends, trying to gauge their opinions, but neither of them were looking at her. Annabel was staring at the toppled doll on the ground, and Kelly was staring down at her bloodied shin.

Without speaking, Julie stepped closer to the cage door; she felt so unguarded as she yanked it closed, its creaking hinges cried out in what could have been pain. With that done, she moved back into the centre of the cage and held her arms aloft: what next?

"Very good," the doll spat. Kelly wanted to kick the patronising fuck in the face, but it wouldn't make a difference except piss of the man behind the voice—the man with the hand-cannon. "Now, I want you to take the nappy off the dolly and open it out in the centre of the cage."

"What? Why?" Julie pushed the hair away from her face. "This is crazy."

"Yes it is, and I'd just like to add that if you don't take the nappy off and unravel the fucking thing in the next five seconds I will shoot one of you in the face."

Annabel dropped to her feet next to the doll and began grappling with the cloth. Their captor's countdowns had thus far been honoured, and she didn't fancy calling his bluff about this one. The voice didn't have time to reach number one before the nappy was removed and laid out on the ground. The three girls stared down at the items that had been concealed within it. Three daggers, identical in size and design; the handles seemed to be made out of ivory, but Kelly wasn't so sure about that. Ivory, bone, wasn't it all the same.

"What are these for?" Julie asked. "Giving us a fighting chance? Tell, you what: if you run off now, and we chase you with these little knives of yours, will that make you happy?"

"Silly girl," the doll – which was now completely naked and looking even more sinister than ever – sniggered. "The knives are for you, and I suggest you start using them if you want to live."

At first, Annabel didn't understand; *use the knives on what?* Julie knew immediately what he meant.

"You want us to use them on each other?" Julie said, glancing from the bone-handled daggers to her friends. "You think we're going to stab each other for you, you sick fuck?"

"I think that you don't have a choice," the voice said. "Whoever is alive at the end can go free, but there will be only one survivor. If you refuse to partake, then that's just cock-a-doodle-dandy with me. It gives me more target practice, not that I need it."

Annabel couldn't believe what she was hearing; he wanted them to kill each other, the winner going free, otherwise all three of them would be executed right there and then. It was a nightmare scenario. She didn't feel real as she glanced down at the knives; it was as if she was having an out-of-body experience. Her head began to throb, and her heart was bouncing around in her chest like she'd consumed nothing but caffeine for days. This was crazy. It was crazy, and ridiculous, and they should have been dancing and drinking at a fucking party by now....

"We have no choice," Julie said. "He'll kill us all if we don't."

Kelly shook her head. "We do have a choice," she said, pushing herself up onto her haunches. "I'm not going to fight you or Annabel, and I certainly ain't gonna stab you."

Julie thought for a moment. The owl that had hooted twice before was suddenly welcome as the silence was unbearable. Annabel watched as Julie glanced around the cage; there was never a more appropriate moment to ask: Penny for your thoughts.

"Then that'll leave me and Annabel, won't it." Julie dropped to the floor and plucked up one of the knives. She pushed the other two away with her free hand, and they clanged against the other side of the cage.

It all happened so fast that Annabel was standing motionless when Julie jabbed the knife into Kelly's stomach. The hilt —human bone?—was all that remained visible of the dagger, sticking from Kelly's gut, one of her best friend's treacherous hands still wrapped tightly around it.

Kelly screamed, but only momentarily. Once the realisation of what had happened kicked in, she fell silent, glancing down at the protruding weapon with terror. Her face contorted, and she stumbled backwards hitting the side of the cage with a thud. The blade pulled out of her as easily as it had entered. Kelly slumped to the ground; a thick rivulet of blood seeped from the corners of her mouth. A second later, her head lolled to one side, as lifeless as the doll that had gotten them into this situation.

And that was that; one down, one to go. Julie didn't spend a second mourning her friend. She seemed to be possessed, a woman with an agenda, as she turned to face Annabel.

"That's it. That was wonderful, Julie. Kill the other one."

Annabel couldn't speak. She had just witnessed one of the most brutal things imaginable, and the woman staring at her now, with eyes that suggested pure hatred and intent, was going to do exactly the same to her.

"What the fuck!" Annabel cried, knowing that nothing she could say would placate Julie, who had already done enough damage to spend the rest of her life in jail.

"I'm not dying tonight," Julie gasped. In the moonlight, Annabel saw a tear streak down one of her cheeks, leaving a glistening trail behind it. "I'm sorry."

She lunged forward, kicking the doll out of the way. Annabel tried to reach the knives that Julie had kicked away, but she was too fast. She grabbed Annabel around the throat and squeezed. Annabel's scream was pushed back down, and she was left with only a whimper as Julie's grip tightened.

Julie lifted up the knife and screeched. She brought it down, but was met with resistance from Annabel's left hand. They stood like that, grunting and struggling, for a few seconds, just long enough for Annabel to wonder what she would have been doing at the party right now.

"Why won't you just...DIE?" Julie took a step forward and pushed Annabel over her extended leg. She went down with such force that her head cracked open on impact; her eyes rolled up into her head, the whites the only parts visible. Julie was prepared for a bit of rolling around, scuffling, trying to survive, but Annabel had had the fight knocked out of her and just lay there, breathing laboriously.

Julie pushed the hair away from her eyes before plunging the knife into Annabel's heart.

***

He walked across to the cage, a smile stretching from one side of his face to the other. He'd done it; he'd actually done something worthwhile with his life. He would be the most talked about killer in the town and, although nobody would know it was him, he would buy every newspaper, tape every radio broadcast, and record every news channel. Yet, he hadn't been the one to kill them. That little present was Julie's; a gift from him.

He saw her sitting in the cage, and she looked beautiful. The way her hair stuck to her face with blood and sweat; the way her eyes were half-closed with fatigue; she was amazing beneath the glow of the moon. She must have stabbed that last bitch a hundred times, maybe more. He lost count after the first ten.

He leant the shotgun carefully against the cage and opened the door. She looked up at him, expressionless at first, and then she smiled.

"Did I do good?" she asked.

"Oh, baby, you did very good," Kelvin Burns replied. He held his hands out, and she took them and pulled herself to her feet. They embraced. "Honestly, that was the sexiest damn thing I ever seen in my life."

"You need to get out more," Julie said, and then kissed him passionately on the lips.

Kelvin pulled away. With one hand he wiped blood from Julie's cheek. "Shall we go to the party now?"

She nodded. "I could do with a few drinks."

They started towards the car, holding hands as they went. What a perfect end to a perfect night.

Candy Apple Red

By: Rebecca Snow

Raif slid his calloused hand across the worn letters of the entrance sign. He'd been running the funhouse for the carnival nigh on thirty years. They'd been the best years of his life except for the summer weeks they'd set up near DC when that sniper was loose. Nothing murdered business like a random killing spree.

Tonight he'd be packing up and moving out along with the other carneys. Their two weeks in the Fredericksburg summer heat dwindled to hours. Raif thumbed a piece of flaking paint as he watched a couple of giggling teenage girls approach. Touching his battered fedora, he nodded at the pair and took their tickets. They gripped each other's arms and smiled as he swung open the metal gate, bowed, and made a sweeping gesture with his free arm toward the funhouse entrance. Their mismatched tiptoe steps made him smile as he wandered down memory lane with all the others who had crept through the entrance in years past.

Hearing the squeals and shrieks as the girls made their way through the twisting hallways and mirrored paths, Raif reached for the next tickets. He tore them in two, handed the stubs back to the father and the three children, and pointed toward the entrance. Two of the chaser lights circling the red arrow had gone dark. Three others sputtered as they tried to keep up the pretense of drawing patrons to his remote corner of the fairgrounds. He'd have to replace the bulbs in the next town.

A smile spread over Raif's face as he heard the smallest of the man's three children start to cry as they traversed the balcony outside the mummy room. The two teenage girls tumbled out of the exit into the darkness near a pair of portable toilets.

"Wanna do it again?" one girl said.

Raif strained to hear an answer over the din of the midway. Instead, he saw the other girl shake her head and drag her friend toward the games of chance.

"I hope Marty takes you for all you've got," Raif mumbled as he turned to take tickets from a group of frat boys.

"These things are so lame," the tallest one said. "It's false advertising to call it a funhouse. There's nothing fun about it."

Raif tore the ticket and looked up from under the brim of his hat. The tall boy's face was pale. Handing the stub back, Raif dragged a finger over the boy's clammy palm. Sheer terror filled the air around this one.

"Me thinks thou dost protest too much," Raif said, lifting an eyebrow as the rowdy group disappeared through the black-lit tunnel. Chuckling to himself, he listened as the others in the group thumped and quieted only to boom in deep laughter as they tormented their tall friend.

"Time to go home," the father said carrying his still crying child toward the fairground exit.

Raif checked his watch, 9:45. Shaking his head, he wondered what kind of father would take then three kids through a funhouse so close to bedtime. His best guess had the man divorced with no idea what to do with his offspring on custody weekends.

Raif took a stained rag from his back pocket and wiped his face. Not much longer. All the attractions would close at 10 pm. The games and food stands stayed open until 10:30 in order to swindle the stragglers as they wandered to the exits. He watched the Ferris wheel roll, its carriages swinging as it coughed up its last passengers of the night.

Years ago, before the management banished the funhouse to the back lot, a steady stream of customers had filtered through Raif's line. He'd always been next to the crowd-pleasing freak show before it was deemed politically incorrect. But as long as the administration kept him on board, he didn't care where they put him. Raif sighed. He missed Zelda, the bearded lady.

The frat boys lurched from the exit. Their tall friend, head lolling to the side, was supported between two of them.

"I can't believe the loser passed out," one of them said.

"I can't believe he's the only one of us with a car," another grunted as he jostled the taller one for a better grip.

The group faded into the final clanks of the tilt-a-whirl's last spin. Five minutes left.

Turning back to the gate, Raif saw a woman standing in front of him, thrusting a ticket into his arm. Her dyed black hair, growing out reddish at the roots, had gone through an attempted straightening. The humidity of the late July night had it resembling a burnt haystack.

"Here," she said jabbing him with the ticket she clutched between her outstretched fingers. Her bright red nails glistened in the flickering light.

Raif rubbed the spot where she'd just poked him. He knew he'd have a bruise in the morning.

"Angela, wait!" a stocky, balding man said as he jogged up panting. "We need to talk about this."

The man slumped over, pressed his hands on his knees, and gasped for breath.

"We've got nothing to talk about," Angela screeched in a voice that scraped goose bumps down the length of Raif's spine. "You accused me of sleeping with your brother AND your father." She pressed the ticket into Raif's shoulder a second time.

The balding man blew out a quick breath and stood.

"That's because you did," he said. "I saw the pictures of you and Joe."

Angela stared back at what Raif hoped was just an acquaintance. Her mouth opened and shut like a fish on a dock before the biggest, fakest tear Raif had ever seen welled in her eye and threatened to crease a valley through her makeup.

Raif took a sidelong glance at his watch. Three minutes to go.

"How could you?" she shrilled. "You never loved me."

Raif shook his head as if to clear the cobwebs. His brow creased as he tried to follow the woman's fuzzy train of thought.

Looking over at the other man, Raif saw him slump his shoulders and open his arms for the woman.

She sobbed and slapped the man. Her simpering pout flashed to a menacing scowl.

"Don't come near me," she said in a dog's growl. "It's all your fault."

Angela grabbed Raif's hand by the wrist, turned his hand palm up, and crushed her ticket into it. Reaching through the bars of the gate, she lifted the latch and ran through the opening to the funhouse door. Both men watched as she disappeared inside the spinning tunnel.

"Pardon me for askin'," Raif said after a heartbeat of silence. "But what in the Sam Hill was that?"

The man's shoulders sagged, and he leaned against the rattling gate. With the flattened palm of his hand, he rubbed the blush from Angela's slap.

"That's my fiancé," he said. "Think I should go after her?"

Raif checked his watch.

"You've only got a minute to do it," he said. "In my personal opinion, I think you should cut bait and run. She's just gonna give you a heap more trouble later on."

The man let out another sigh as a pinched smirk bloomed on his face. He pressed his hands to his shirt pockets and looked up at Raif.

"I don't have another ticket," the man said still holding his palms to his chest. "She'll kill me if I don't go after her."

Raif shrugged and ripped Angela's ticket in half. Handing the stub back to the man, he unlatched the gate.

"Your funeral," Raif said with a shrug. "One way or the 'nother."

A loud clatter sounded as the man tumbled and fell in the spinning tunnel. Grinning, Raif stretched his arms above his head and yawned. It had been a long two weeks. It was almost time for his treat.

He tilted his head as he heard the man in the funhouse crash into the first hall of mirrors. A multitude of clunks signaled the man's collisions with the walls. Raif heard the woman's footsteps clipping up the corner stairwell. He slipped to the back of the funhouse and pulled a lever. After a shrill shout and a thud, he pushed the lever back to its original position.

"Wait up, Ann," the man yelled. "I'm coming."

Raif picked up a piece of straw and listened as the man's quick yells and stomps drew closer to the exit. Leaning against the gate, he saw the man stumble from the funhouse into the darkness of the night.

"Did you see her?" the man shouted. "I couldn't catch her."

Raif nodded and chewed the straw. After uncrossing his arms and adjusting his hat, he pointed in the direction of the carnival's main gate.

"She was shoutin' somethin' about callin' somebody to come get her."

"Oh, great. Now I won't be able to find her for days," the man said.

Raif watched as the man shrank into the distant crowd before turning off the main switch that mechanized most of the funhouse. He pulled up the front ramp and barricaded the entrance before he traversed the now stationary tube. The rollers on the floor clattered as he shuffled his dusty work boots over them. Reaching into a dark corner, he twisted a small knob near the ceiling. The background music and sound effects echoed louder through the cramped space. Body bags swung as he pushed them from his path. Had the funhouse been active, a number of pneumatic forms would have hissed to life at every turn.

Striding to the uneven back staircase, Raif bent down and felt the edge of the top step. His fingers found the well-worn lip of wood. He grunted with the effort of lifting the trap door. He unclipped his flashlight from his belt and lit the opening he'd revealed. Angela's hands flew to her eyes, and she howled.

"Let me out of here!" she said.

"Now, why would I do a silly thing like that?" Raif asked pushing his hat back from his forehead.

"Because my fiancé will kill you if you don't."

Raif snorted.

"I don't think he'll do any such thing."

"Ben!" the hysterical woman yelled. "Ben, I'm in here!"

"He can't hear you," Raif said as he smiled down at her.

Angela took a deep breath and let out a scream that would have shattered a glass eye.

"Don't waste your breath. He thinks you went home with Joe."

Bubbling, hiccupped sobs rose from the woman in the padded trap.

"Aw, c'mon. If there's one thing I can't stand, it's a cryin' psycho." Raif shook the flashlight beam to make it dance in the woman's face. "Now, stop that, or you'll make me do somethin' drastic."

The blubbering faded to snuffles.

"That's better," Raif said as he opened a small metal panel in the wall. He pulled a Snoopy thermos from a crooked shelf and tossed in into the hole. "Drink up. I've got a lot of work to do up here."

"Wait, please…"

Ignoring her plea, Raif swung the top step back into place and kicked it with a boot-clad foot. He made his way through the mummy room, stepped onto the small balcony, and began to pull the pins and remove the panels. The festive lights began to wink out around the carnival as a few larger work lights gave their best impersonation of daylight. The front gates had been closed, and the breakdown had begun. The trucks were scheduled to pull out near dawn.

With the balcony dismantled and stowed, Raif moved through the mirror maze. He enjoyed the shocks his special surprises gave the customers. To Raif, a scream was worth a thousand words. His creations would have amounted to trillions of words if he'd been counting.

Raif wound his way through the funhouse maze and walked through the exit into the steamy summer night. He strolled to the gate and removed the old hand-painted rules and slid them just inside the exit door. The carnival's maintenance men took care of the portable steel barricades. All he had to do was fold the ramps up and lock the exit door. The semi would haul the funhouse to its next destination. He would ride with Marty in his battered station wagon. Before the exodus, Raif had a little celebrating to do.

Stepping back through the exit door into the relative darkness of the corridor, Raif meandered back to Angela's holding pen. He lifted the top step and shined his light on her unconscious form. It amazed him how they always drank his thermos cocktail. He lifted the panel that had held the container and pressed a smooth, red button. The padded floor beneath the woman rose to a foot below the top step. Raif reached down and grabbed the woman underneath her arms and dragged her back into the vampire room. He hefted her to the flat surface of the closed coffin before he strapped her wrists and ankles with some leather straps designed to look like intricate scrollwork. Reaching into his back pocket, he produced a ball gag and strapped it around Angela's neck. He tried to finger comb her hair into some semblance of beauty, but each attempt made the rat's nest look more rodent-friendly.

As he waited, Raif listened to the sirens and door slams that repeated every five minutes on the sound effects loop. His favorite was the yowling cat. It always made the girls jump. Deep, maniacal laughter filled the funhouse, and Angela's eyes fluttered.

Raif sat on an upturned crate and watched her struggle against her restraints and grunt in desperation. Beads of sweat bloomed on her forehead as real tears trickled down the sides of her face. Muffled squeals eked out from underneath the rubber ball gag.

"Ain't no use thrashin' 'round like that," Raif said as Angela's resistance lessened.

The woman froze and mewled through her binding.

"Nobody can hear you, and nobody's lookin' for you."

Angela's eyes widened as Raif stood and stepped from the shadowy corner. Her head whipped from side to side. Stifled intonations filtered around the gag.

"No, I won't let you go," he said as he brightened the lights.

Angela let out more staccato mumbles.

"Why are you here?" Raif said raising one eyebrow and watching Angela nod. "Because you were in the wrong place at the wrong time, and because you're a shameful waste of skin."

The woman stopped struggling. After a moment, she raised her eyebrows and stared into Raif's eyes. Motioning with her head, she attempted to draw him toward her. The corners of her mouth twitched around the gag into the semblance of a distorted smile. She lowered her gaze to his belt buckle before returning to his eyes. She raised her knees and parted them as much as the restraints would allow. Watching her tilt her head in what he assumed was an attempt at flirtation, Raif laughed.

"Let me get this straight," he said. "You want to service me in return for me lettin' you go?"

He saw her fingers reach out for him as her eyelids drooped into what some would have called a bedroom gaze.

"Sorry, sweetie. That ain't happenin'."

The woman on the coffin shrieked and thrashed. Raif shrugged and took a step toward her. She struggled against her bonds as he leaned down and inhaled near her ear. The scent of cotton candy mingling with funnel cake lingered with a touch of mustard. Drawing in another breath at the base of her neck, Raif coughed. She had worn enough perfume to incapacitate a herd of elephants; the cologne was an effective mask of her fear.

"Looks like we're gonna have to clean you up a little," he said before he turned off the light and made his way back into the ratcheting tear down of the carnival.

A black bag rested on the ground under one of the trailer wheels. He waved at one of the gate crew before hefting the bag onto a shoulder. Backtracking until he was back with the writhing woman, he turned the light back on and unzipped the bag. He emptied half a small bottle of rubbing alcohol into an empty

Cool-Whip tub. Dipping a scrub sponge into the bowl, he saturated it and began to scrub Angela's neck as she tried to twist away from him. Once her flesh was rubbed a sufficient scoured-pink, Raif sniffed. Some of the scent lingered on her shirt collar, but her skin was devoid of the stench.

Angela flailed when Raif lifted a pair of scissors from the bag.

"I don't want to have to knock you out again, but I will," Raif said as he snipped the seams of Angela's shirt and pulled the worthless fabric from beneath her squirming body.

Even in the stuffy, humid air, goose bumps dotted her arms and stomach. Raif wasn't impressed with the waifish form that wiggled on the coffin. With a few more snips, he'd dismantled her useless bra. When he sliced her skirt to her waist and released the elastic, he wasn't surprised she hadn't been wearing panties.

"I got a question for you," Raif said pausing over his black bag. "Are you scared of sharp objects?"

When he held up a gleaming scalpel, Raif saw Angela's eyes flutter closed and her head fall limp. He shook his head and began to cut. As the first candy apple drops of blood seeped from underneath his blade, Angela jerked sideways causing Raif's hand to falter.

"Great," he said. "Now I have to start over. Try not to move this time."

He began to slice in a different spot, but Angela's incessant quivering made the line uneven.

"I didn't want to do this, but I guess I'll have to," Raif said.

He reached into one of the black bag's zippered pockets and retrieved a syringe. After flicking out any air bubbles, he plunged the needle into her arm and drove the sedative home. In a few moments, Angela's head drooped. Her eyes remained open with their lids at half-mast.

"Won't be as much fun, but it'll look a mite sight better."

Raif returned to his work and carved various faces over every inch of the woman's canvas-like skin. When he was through, he stepped back and gazed down at her bloody body. Her chest rose and fell with each breath she took. He reached for a gallon bottle of bleach and poured it over her hair. Passing over her face, he continued to trickle the bleach onto the oozing wounds. The smell of the liquid stung Raif's eyes and nose, but she had to be clean before drying. Over the next hour, he watched as her black mess of hair turned almost white, looking like a distressed cotton ball. The skin around the cuts had puckered before he loosened the straps around her limbs. He lifted her arm, dropped it, and smiled as it flopped to her chest. Angela's body thumped to the floor when Raif pushed her off of the coffin. Pulling a key from his belt, he fit it into the lock under the edge of the lid. Raif burrowed his hand through the beads of desiccant and pressed his palm to the base of the casket.

He turned to the miserable wretch on the floor and sighed. If someone had taken care of the women in his life for him like he had just done for Ben, the world would have been a better place. Lifting Angela's wilted form, he nestled her into the coffin. He strapped her ankles and wrists with leather ties just inside the lid and covered her mouth and nose with several strips of duct tape. Raif scooped handfuls of desiccant over his whittled works of art and shut the coffin lid. The lock engaged, and he turned to negotiate his way to the exit. He wouldn't see Angela until the carnival reached the next city. By then, his carvings would resemble a hundred shrunken apple heads.

As Raif ambled around the hall of mirrors, he glanced through the Plexiglas walls. Behind a piece of clear plastic, a man's face stared back with its mouth stretched beyond the limits of a normal scream. Eyes bulged from sockets as if smacked by a cartoon mallet. Raif remembered the man punching his girlfriend in the carousel line when the carnival had traveled through Baton Rouge. Another skeletal corpse swung above the room's exit. The finger bones hung low enough to graze the scalps of anyone over six-feet tall. The man who'd lost his bones had lured a girl into the woods behind the carnival in Austin, Texas. Standing beyond the skeletal reach, Raif turned to survey the room. At least fifteen men stared back at him.

"Don't worry, guys," he said. "I know the mummy room got the last one; and the vampires before that. It's your turn to get the girl."

Detour

By: Bennie L. Newsome

1

"Stop riding my ass!" I screamed at the vehicle in my rearview mirror.

Blinding headlights filled the interior of my car, making it nearly impossible for me to see. The automobile to my rear was driving so close that it was practically in my backseat! Worry began to surface amidst my anger. If I was forced to brake for any reason, the moron behind me would plow right into my vehicle. I had to do something.

I let up on the gas to drop my speed, letting the driver behind me know that I would not be intimidated and their best bet would be to go around. Sure, I was in the fast lane, but there was clear traffic on the right. Why not go around?

Instead of doing the reasonable thing, the car continued its extremely close pursuit.

"Tonight is not the night!" I growled to myself.

After eight hours of standing on my feet, I found out at the last minute that I had to stay at work two more hours. When I was finally able to clock out, I stepped outside to see that darkness had descended, which meant that my wife had already cooked dinner and it was getting cold. Yeah, I could warm it up when I got home, but everyone knows that food is best when it's fresh off the stove.

If missing dinner is enough to light the fuse to my explosive anger, how do you think I would respond to an ignorant asshole riding on my bumper? I'll tell you how I felt. I felt like the jerk-off was unknowingly huffing and puffing on my short, lit fuse.

If you were to ask anyone that knows me, they would tell you that Darryl Wallace is a docile person—which I normally am—but there are four things that I just can not tolerate; four events that can only take place when I'm behind the wheel of a car.

Pedestrians crossing the street while the light is green happens to be a big pet peeve of mine. In the end, your ignorance is going to ruin two lives. Your life is going to be messed up when I knock you out of your shoes, and my life is over if I can not provide the police with a legitimate explanation.

Drivers getting over at the last minute when they *know* the lane is going to end really gets my blood boiling. Get in at the back! What makes you so special that you have to go all the way to the front?

People cutting me off is a quick way to get me on the horn and flipping the bird, but there is something that infuriates me more than anything in the world. Tailgating.

My eyes continued to shift from the road in front of me, to my rearview mirror which showed me that the car to my rear had not receded one bit.

You're going to make me lose my motherfucking mind! I screamed internally.

My brow was creased with so much anger that my head hurt. I could hear my veins pulsating along my skull. *Thu-thump! Thu-thump!* The thumping sound was like a wailing siren, signaling that a reactor was overheating and on the verge of an explosion. I did not need a siren to tell me that I was overheating, I knew I was overheating. My body felt like it was on fire. My light colored skin was probably glowing red by that point.

All of a sudden, the car behind me jumped into the right lane.

Strike one! I thought. I am not fond of outward aggression being directed at me.

Squealing tires filled the night air as the driver recklessly sped up. Me being the aggressor is totally fine, so I turned my head and glared at the vehicle as it passed me on the right.

The car was a rusty blue, 1986 Cadillac Eldorado and I thought I saw five individuals stuffed inside. One of which, had the nerves to mouth some foul words and shoot me the bird.

"Strike motherfucking two!" I yelled at the brazen young man.

Calm down before you have a stroke, or an aneurism.

The Eldorado blasted past, causing my white Pontiac Sunfire to shudder from the sudden windstream. That was disrespectful enough, but whoever was in the driver seat had the audacity to hop over in front of me, cutting it dangerously close before shooting off into the distance.

Strike three, I calmly said to myself.

My fuse was gone; the flame had reached its destination. I exploded, but not in the typical fashion that a normal, sane individual would have done. No. I am an atomic bomb compared to the rest of humanity, and at that point, I was in my peaceful stage. I was portraying the very same peace that overcomes a land when that infamous flash of light suddenly appears in the distance. That very same peace that one feels just before they are caught up in the devastating blast radius and immediately has their existence ripped from them.

2

The '86 Eldorado swerved right and pulled up alongside the broken curb. The rust bucket came to a brake-squealing halt, instantly causing the immediate area to become engulfed in the smell of burning rubber. The driver killed the engine and quickly unbuckled his seatbelt. Both doors on the car swung open loudly and everyone began hopping out.

The driver, Daniel Barnes, ran toward the house that belonged to his youngest sister and her sorry excuse for a husband. "Tamika, I want you to hang back while we go in first!"

"Why do I have to—"

"Now is not the time to argue with me!"

When she showed no signs of disagreeing any further, Daniel turned to his three brothers. "Justin, you come around to the back with me. That son of a bitch is probably gonna dip out the back. I wanna be there when he does. Chris and Charles, I want y'all to start beating on the front door. Flush him out."

Everyone acknowledged that they understood their orders and moved to their positions. Right away, Chris and Charles started kicking and punching the front door while screaming for their sister's husband to come outside.

After only a few seconds of waiting on the back porch, the kitchen door opened and Tyrone—the husband—bolted out the door only to find that he had ran straight into a trap. Daniel's powerful arm came up and knocked the frightened man down.

Tyrone landed on his back with an "Oof!"

"Let me explain—" THWACK!

Justin met Tyrone's explanation with a booted foot to the side of his face. The wounded man howled from the excruciating pain.

"Come on," Daniel said after looking around at the surrounding houses. All the noise they were making was sure to draw potential witnesses. "Let's get him inside."

Justin and Daniel bent down and grabbed Tyrone roughly. They dragged the protesting man into the house and slammed the kitchen door shut behind them.

Daniel looked over at Justin then tilted his head to indicate the front door. "Go let them in!"

"Gotcha!"

While his little brother went to open the door for the other two, Daniel balled his hand up into a huge fist and smashed Tyrone in the face.

The grown man started crying. "Please just let me go! Please!"

"When my little sister begs you to stop hitting her, do you listen to her?"

"I didn't hit your sister this time," Tyrone whined. "She got mad at me 'cause I came in late. Said I smelled like another female, so she called y'all and told y'all I hit her. I ain't touch her this time! I swear on my momma's grave!"

Daniel stared at the bruised man. Fresh blood fell from Tyrone's now crooked nose and trickled down the front of his face. "You cheating on my sister, Tyrone?"

"Man, I ain't cheating on your sister!"

CRACK!

Daniel's solid fist connected with Tyrone's face again. The battered man resumed his whimpering.

"Get your punk ass up!" Daniel yelled as he snatched Tyrone up by his collar.

"Just let me go!" Tyrone pleaded as he was forced to stumble through the kitchen.

Chris met Tyrone at the doorway and greeted him with a jab to his stomach. Tyrone simultaneously farted, let out a groan, and doubled over. Charles walked up and gave the poor man a swift, fierce kick to the ribs.

"Let me get a lick," Tamika said as she walked over to the fallen man.

"STOP! What are y'all doing?" Latrice, their youngest sibling, screamed as she came running down the stairs. She looked past her brothers and sister to see her bloody husband laying on the floor. "Stop beating him!"

"Did he hit you again?" Daniel wanted to know.

"No!"

"Why would you call us and lie about him hitting you? You knew he had an ass whooping coming!" Tamika yelled.

"He…he made me mad!" Latrice screamed back. "He had been out with his homeboys again and I thought he had been with some female. So I called Daniel and told him he hit me."

"I told yo' dumb ass," Tyrone said from the floor.

"What did you say to me?" Daniel asked in an incredulous tone. He took his big foot and stomped on the man's back.

"Oh God!" Tyrone yelled as he rolled around in pain.

"Hey Chris…Justin, dump this moron out on the porch!" Daniel commanded.

Without hesitation, the two young men grabbed Tyrone and did as their big brother asked.

Daniel turned to his baby sister. “And you oughta know better than calling me with a false alarm. We nearly killed ourselves trying to get over here, and we could’ve hurt somebody else in the process.”

“I know,” Latrice said meekly.

Daniel was about to scold her some more, but he heard yelling come from the front porch. The four siblings that were still in the house rushed outside to see what the commotion was all about.

“I’m gonna killed all of y’all!” Tyrone screamed from the sidewalk. Somehow the fraught man broke loose when he felt fresh air on his face.

Curtains were pulled back as the neighbors looked out their windows. Front doors opened, and some came outside to stand on their porches. Even the smallest bit of excitement was sure to draw attention.

“Y’all motherfuckers are going to pay for what you did to me!”

Justin, the youngest male, stomped his feet on the wooden porch and Tyrone jumped back a bit even though he was halfway in the street by that point.

“Get your retarded ass outta here!” Tamika shouted.

“Imma kill all you motherfuckers!” Tyrone yelled as he escaped down the street.

3

I flexed my fingers in my black leather glove.

There they go right there! I told myself while watching the six figures on the front porch.

There were originally five. I knew this because I followed them ten miles before they came to a screeching stop in front of the house they currently occupied. Four men and one woman hopped out of that piece of shit they called an automobile. Now there were four men and two women. No matter. They would all die soon enough.

I turned my attention to the small man who fled down the street while hurling curses back at the ones on the porch. He was of no concern to me. If anything, the man was a Godsend. Everyone on the street witnessed him threatening the lives of the individuals on the porch. Every finger would be pointed at him.

I'll teach you motherfuckers not to ride on my ass!

I slid my right hand into my second leather glove and flexed those fingers as well; cannot afford to have any kind of hindrance when killing people.

4

Once they returned inside the house, everyone grabbed a place to sit in the living room. Daniel looked at his youngest sister. Her head was in her small hands and tears rolled down her delicate features. Latrice was obviously worried about her husband's well-being.

She only has herself to blame, he thought before saying, "Well, since you made us come all the way out here, I guess we might as well chill out a bit."

Latrice shrugged her tiny shoulders. "That's fine. Tyrone won't be coming home tonight anyway. Probably over at his ho's house by now."

"Why do you put up with his bullshit?" Tamika asked. "I would leave him if I knew he was cheating, and the first time he hit me would've been the last time. I would've killed him."

"I love him."

"You a fool," Daniel said as if it was a simple fact. He turned to Justin and said, "Aye, move the car to the back of the house. I don't want that dumbass to come back and slash my tires. And after you park the car in the backyard, get that case of beer out the trunk. I need something to drink."

5

"Shit!" I exclaimed when I saw one of my targets hop into the driver's seat of the Eldorado.

I returned my car key to the ignition and turned, an act that brought my Sunfire rumbling to life. I wanted every last one of them to die and it would be easier if they all stayed in one spot. However, one of the guys looked as if he was getting away.

If that person was the original driver, then he was the most important one.

I'll just have to follow him, kill him, then come back for the rest.

I watched angrily as the car reversed a bit then drove through the yard, making its way to the back of the house. A sinister grin replaced my frown. The guy was not leaving; he was just moving the car to a more remote location.

I don't know how much time I have. I need to stop stalling.

I turned my car off and hopped out. After manually opening the trunk, I took off my work shirt and threw it into the back of the car. My black undershirt stayed on, and the denim jeans I wore would have to suffice. I was not one for the theatrics. No ghoulish mask or creepy robe for me.

I kicked my sneakers off, tossed them into the trunk with my work shirt, and removed a pair of old, battered boots. I purchased them from a homeless guy a long time ago after I saw on a television show that police can find culprits by their shoe prints.

When I was satisfied with my attire, I removed my machete from beneath the clutter in my trunk. The tool was primarily used for gardening, but every once and a while it served another purpose—a deadlier purpose.

I stared admiringly at the sharp, glistening blade. "Let's do this," I said while slamming the trunk shut.

I hurried down the cracked sidewalk with long, purposeful strides. My arms swung angrily at my sides. The machete seemed to glow with a life of its own as it reflected the light of the full moon.

There was no one out on the porches, and I did not see anyone in their windows. It would not have mattered if there had been anyone watching. It was too dark to get an accurate description, and even in broad daylight people were bad at remembering details.

I made a sharp right turn and hurried through the high grown grass. The blades of vegetation rustled loudly as I went along. Within no time, I made it to the back of the house where I spotted the Eldorado and a person standing at the trunk. My quickened steps alerted the man to my presence.

He spun around and shock with a twinge of fear registered on his face. "Who the hell are you?"

The only reply he got was my blade being rammed through his sternum. Whatever he was about to say next became lodged in his throat. The blade sliced deeper as I stepped closer. I stared into his eyes and was elated to see a mixture of fear and pain dance across his facial features.

"Is this your car?" I asked in a nonchalant manner.

His mouth opened, but he did not speak. He just stared at me with wide eyes.

"Is this your car? Were you the one driving earlier?"

The young man slowly turned his head to face the house. He looked as if he was about to scream for help. I snatched the machete from his torso and with one swift motion I sliced his throat open. A gurgling sound emerged from the horizontal hole in his neck. Before he could fall to the ground, I pushed him into the trunk and tucked his limbs inside.

"Y'all fucked with the wrong motorist on the wrong night."

6

"What the hell is taking Justin so long?" Daniel asked as he flipped through the television channels.

Chris, the second oldest sibling, stood and headed for the kitchen. "Let me go see what's keeping him."

The man waltzed into the poorly kept kitchen. Dishes were piled high in the sink and lined the small counter. Two large, full trash bags sat near the back door, and a case of beer sat on the kitchen table.

"He brought the beer inside!" Chris yelled back to his kinfolk in the living room. His next few words were meant for his ears only. "So where the hell is he?"

Chris walked over to the back door and pulled the short curtains aside so he could stare out into the backyard. The car had been moved, the beer had been brought in, but there was no sign of Justin.

"Is that your car?"

Chris whirled around to find a strange man glaring at him. "What the fu—"

The man grabbed his face with strong, gloved fingers and shoved his head through the door's small window. The sound of breaking glass filled the house.

7

"Chris! Is everything okay in there?"

It only took a minute for me to slash the startled man's throat and stuff his body into the stale smelling cabinets beneath the kitchen sink. My heart was beating fast, adrenaline coursed through my veins. I had to quell the joy I felt and summon the rage that had brought me to that house. Happiness would make me sloppy, anger would keep me alive.

"Chris!"

I heard the sound of frantic footsteps heading in my direction. With no other option in sight, I went to stand near the doorway that connected the living room and the kitchen. I pressed my body against the wall just as the remaining four came running into the kitchen. Their breakneck speed combined with their intent focus on the broken window made them oblivious to my presence.

A big guy ran in first. *One,* I counted.

There was another, smaller guy and a female. *Two, three…*

Just as the fourth person was coming through the doorway, I waylaid her. I ran her through with my machete and muffled her cry of pain and surprise with my gloved hand. I used the blade to lift her small body, carried her into the living room, and slammed her onto the carpeted floor. I snatched the blade out and plunged it into her gut again. While she whined into the palm of my hand, I retracted the weapon and ended her struggles by slicing her throat.

8

"Is that blood?" Tamika asked. She had never seen so much spilled blood before.

Daniel and Charles, who had more experience with such things, slowly made their way over to the door where the puddle lay. Charles looked away from the thick substance and went to examine the broken the window, while Daniel followed a trail made of smeared blood to the kitchen cabinet.

The man took a deep breath, afraid of what he was most likely to find, and pulled the door open. "Umph!" Daniel dry heaved and quickly slammed the cabinet door shut.

"Hey, bruh, what's wrong?" Charles asked as he and Tamika hurried over to a kneeling Daniel.

"Chris…Chris is…dead."

Tamika let out a frightened gasp. Unconvinced, Charles reached for the cabinet door.

Daniel knocked his brother's hand away. "He's dead!"

"Do you think…Tyrone…did it?" Tamika asked as her tears fell onto her shirt.

Daniel shook his head in disbelief. "He said…that he would, but I thought…I thought he was just mouthing off. Latrice, do you think—"

"Where is Latrice?" Charles asked.

Tamika looked around the filthy kitchen, but their sister was nowhere in sight. "She was right behind me!"

Daniel jumped up from the floor and hurried for the living room. Charles and Tamika quickly fell in step behind their big brother.

"Latrice!" Daniel yelled when he walked into the living room and failed to see his little sister. "Latrice!"

"OH MY GOD!" Tamika screamed before putting her hands to her mouth.

The brothers followed her wide-eyed gaze and saw another trail of blood leading up the stairs.

"MOTHERFUCKER!" Daniel bellowed. He turned to his terrified sister. "Go call the police!"

Tamika was too paralyzed with fear to move.

"Tamika! Go!"

"Okay!" Tamika screamed as she ran to the couch and picked up the telephone from the side table.

"Charles, let's go and see if we can find Latrice. If I find Tyrone, I'm going to kill the son of a bitch myself!"

9

From my hiding place in the living room closet, I heard the woman cry, "9-1-1, my brothers and sister have been killed. Yes! I'm sure. They've been murdered. Blood is all over the place…and…."

The closet door creaked as I slowly pushed it open and scanned the room. The woman was on the phone and she was all alone. The other two had went upstairs. When the door was opened wide enough, I stepped out and carefully shut it behind me. I was standing behind the couch, the woman's back was to me.

She turned her head to the side and yelled, "Daniel! What's the address?"

"I think they can figure that out for themselves," I said as I raised my machete and immediately dragged it across her throat. There was a quick gasp then a wet murmuring sound before she slouched over. I let her fall to the cushions and moved around to the front of the couch. I picked up the phone's receiver from the floor.

"Hello! Hello, ma'am, are you still there? Hello!"

"And then there were two," I whispered as I returned the phone to its cradle, thereby ending the call.

10

Without saying a word to one another, Daniel and Charles hastily followed the path of blood all the way to the master bedroom. Daniel, being the first one to arrive at the room, shoved the door open and instantly reached for the light switch. After fumbling along the wall for a few seconds, he found the small protrusion and turned the light on.

"Nooooooooooooooo!"

The two men wailed in anguish when they discovered their baby sister's dead body sprawled out on the bed. Latrice's neck was severely cut, her once lively brown eyes had a vacant look about them.

Daniel staggered over to the bed, plopped down on the bloodstained comforter, and proceeded to cradle Latrice's corpse. He had been both his brothers and sisters' keeper, and he had failed miserably.

"Why, Lord?" the man cried out. He pulled her body closer to his and screamed, "Why?"

Brimming with anger and helplessness, Charles punched a hole into the wall. "I'm gonna kill him!"

He stormed from the room and rushed down the hallway. "Tyrone! Come out you motherfucking coward!" The irate man made it to the top of the staircase and froze. His anger was instantly drained and his body was refilled with fear.

Standing in the middle of the stairs was a crazed looking individual. His black gloves were stained red, and he held a gigantic knife that dripped blood. The dangerous looking man's clothing was also covered in blood, but that was not what held Charles' attention. Charles recognized the man's face.

"Oh shit!" he muttered. It was the slow driver from the white car. The man he cursed at while flipping him the bird.

"So you do recognize me. Good. Now it's time I give you a lesson in driving etiquette."

Charles turned around and made an attempt to flee. "Daniel! It's that—"

The words he wanted to say were cut off. Charles looked down to see the tip of a blade sticking out of his stomach. He grunted as the blade was twisted then jerked from his back. The killer grabbed him by his shirt collar and pushed the man over the stair railing.

11

I watched my fifth victim's body fall through the air and hit the living room floor. BOOM! The man landed with a house shaking thud. I stared at the motionless body until I was satisfied that he was not going to move ever again. I was never really sure unless I slit their throats.

"Who the hell are you?"

I looked up to see a big, muscular man standing in the hallway. My sixth and final victim. The driver.

I felt a tickling sensation on my face and reached up with my free hand to wipe it away, unknowingly smearing blood across my face. With my bloody machete, I pointed toward the rear of the house. "I guess that's your car in the back."

The furious man let out a bestial roar and charged at me. A man wielded by rage versus a man wielding rage; the man wielding rage wins every time and I knew this. That's why I stood without flinching, grinning at my approaching foe. When he had come close enough, I dodged to the right and went low. As he stumbled past me, I sliced his left calf open.

"Aaaaaaah!" he screamed as he fell to one knee.

"You know what's so sad?" I asked as I stood up straight. "Your friend down there recognized me and he did not even try to apologize. That's okay. He wasn't sorry when he saw my face, but I bet you he's sorry now."

As soon as I began to approach the man, he somehow managed to stand up and flipped over the hallway banister. *Pure desperation.* With a muffled thud, he landed atop his fallen comrade.

I walked over to the railing and yelled, "There's no point in you trying to escape!"

12

Daniel cried briefly for his dead brother as he crawled over the young man's fresh corpse. He promised himself that if he managed to escape he would mourn properly, but just then was not the time and that certainly was not the place. He could hear the psychopath's heavy footsteps coming down the stairs.

I have to get out of here!

Daniel gritted through the intense pain and managed to climb to his feet again. The back of his leg was slashed open and the rest of his body ached from his fall. Despite his injuries, the man began to slowly but steadily hobble out of the living room and through the kitchen.

He reached the back door which was still unlocked. Daniel quickly yanked the door open and glanced over his shoulder as he staggered through the doorway. The killer was only a few feet away.

"Yeah, I'm still here," the man said. "Just trying to see what you're up to. You're not planning on escaping in your shit mobile are you? I slashed the tires."

Daniel looked at his tires as he limped out into the yard. The man was right. The tires on the left hand side of the vehicle were totally deflated. He assumed that the tires on the right were the same.

"HEEEEELLLLLLLP!" Daniel screamed. "HELP ME SOMEBODY!"

"We can't be having that now can we?" the killer asked as he hurried over to his distressed quarry.

Seeing that help was not going to come anytime soon, Daniel decided to try fighting again. He was a lot bigger than his adversary. If he just concentrated, he should emerge victorious. Daniel spun around, trying to catch his opponent off guard, and swung his right fist.

The stranger ducked while cutting open the man's forearm.

"AHHHHHHHHHHH!" Daniel screamed out.

"Shut the fuck up!" the murderer said as he came up and stabbed Daniel in the neck.

13

I yanked the sharp machete from his neck and watched as he slid down the side of his car. The man slumped to the ground, his life giving substance bleeding out onto the dry lawn.

"One less terrible driver on the road," I said as I prepared to depart, but a rustling sound caused me to spin to my right. My latest victim's screams had attracted unwanted attention.

I shouldn't have been fooling around! I initially thought. I began to wonder if I should kill the new arrival or just run off, but I soon realized that neither choice was necessary. The good Samaritan turned out to be the man that I had seen running down the street earlier. My patsy.

Could things get any better?

The bruised man looked as if he was about to bolt, but I yelled, "If you run I'll throw this blade and pierce your heart!" I was bluffing of course, but there was no way that he knew that.

"Please! Please…don't kill me!" the man pleaded.

"I'm not going to kill you, Tyrone," I said as I walked over to cowering individual.

"You … you know my… name?"

Tyrone flinched when I began wiping my bloody blade on the front of his shirt. He probably thought I was cleaning off my machete in an intimidating manner, but I was actually making sure he looked the part.

"Of course I know your name," I said while placing my blood covered glove on the side of his face in a comforting gesture. They had been screaming the man's name as they ran throughout the house and I just assumed it belonged to him.

"I saw how they assaulted you and I just had to do something. Hold this for me."

Tyrone unwittingly grabbed the handle of the machete. When he realized what he had done, he let the blade fall to the ground.

"If that's where you want to leave it, that's fine with me," I said with a shrug. I turned away from the man and began making my way through the backyard.

"What…what about my wife?" Tyrone asked in a meek tone.

I turned around and asked, "What did she look like?"

"Small, light skin—"

I nodded my head without having to hear anymore. "Yeah, she's dead. Upstairs in the bedroom if you wanna go and say goodbye." I was not feeling remorseful. I just thought it would be beneficial to me if the cops found him holding her body.

I heard police sirens in the distance so I ended the conversation and started sprinting across the backyards. It only took me two minutes to make it to the end of the street, jump into my car, and drive away.

WHOOSH! Several police cars and two ambulances whizzed by as I did my best to navigate out of the neighborhood. I had been too angry and focused on the Eldorado to pay attention to my surroundings when I entered the area.

After a couple of dead ends and a lot of backtracking, I found my way to the interstate. “Ugh! Thank God!” I exclaimed when I was on route to my home. Getting lost always scared the crap out of me.

As I sped down the dimly lit road, my cellphone began vibrating in the cupholder. “Shit!” I said when I retrieved the phone and saw my wife’s name on the caller id. I had totally forgotten that I was already running late before I made my side trip. Now I was *extremely* late and it did not look good on my end.

I pressed the green button on the cellphone and said, “Hey, sweetheart!”

“Why aren’t you home yet?” she asked angrily. She was in no mood for my antics.

“I’m sorry baby,” I said as if it was no big deal. “I got off work late, then there was an incident on the interstate that caused me to make a detour. I’m back on track now, and I’ll be there shortly.”

A Twisted Garden

By: Joe DiBuduo and Kate Robinson

Jardin des Peupliers
or *Trees in the Garden of St. Paul's Hospital IV*
Vincent van Gogh 1889

My father, Jean-Luc Maurice André Audet, moved to the Netherlands from France soon after I was born. Thank God he christened me with the simple name of André Audet. An influential poet, he stopped writing after he took refuge in Amsterdam. As the years passed we lived on his savings, and as he aged, the money dwindled and he fell ill. I always wondered at the loneliness in our lives caused by the disappearance of my mother. As he lay on his deathbed, my burning questions finally broke his silence.

"I felt compelled to leave Saint Rémy de Provence so the curse wouldn't affect you."

"Curse, what curse? Why did you not bring my mother with you when we left?"

He sighed deeply, resigned to his lonely life and an inevitable death. "It's not in your best interest to know. You were born under a dark star. Just stay away from your birthplace."

I found it hard to believe a learned man would utter such a silly warning. Then he coughed just once, a deep hacking gag that caused blood to flow from his nose, and he fell silent.

As I washed the blood from his face, I knew Death would soon take him. Irritated at his reluctance to share the circumstances of my mother's disappearance, I tried several more times, each time more urgently than the last, to coax him to reveal the nature of this supposed curse and what had happened to my mother. I continued pressing him with questions even as he went out of his head, questions he seemed clearly unable to answer.

But in his final hour, he fell in and out of a delirium and mentioned the Monastery Saint-Paul de Mausole in Saint Rémy de Provence. He spoke of it just once, perhaps by mistake. He wouldn't discuss it further and as life leaked from him, he took his secrets to the grave.

One day soon after my father's death, I came across an old woman dressed in the manner of a gypsy, a fortune teller who wandered along the banks of the River Rhine. For a guilder, she told me that my birth under a dark star meant that a generational curse was upon me because of some sin perpetuated by an ancestor.

"How could I be cursed?" I asked. "Up to this point, except for the absence of my mother and the loneliness of my father, my life has been exemplary."

"A curse is a curse, and one can never know when it will befall them. The good news is that I can lift the curse for only ten guilders."

What hogwash. This hag was using old-fashioned superstitions to extort ten guilders from me. When I was born in 1853, most superstitions were long abandoned, spoken of only by country folk. Only the ones so common they had become universal were repeated, such as seven years bad luck for breaking a looking glass, or that a black cat brought gossip and bad news. I knew these were nonsense because my boyhood kitten Minnie was midnight black and sweet as could be. A curious child, I'd broken more than one looking glass to see if my luck would change. Nothing ever changed, despite these folk superstitions.

After my father's funeral and a proper period of mourning, a burning desire overcame me to see the village where I was born to the mother I had little memory of. I returned to Saint Rémy de Provence, traveling along the River Rhine from Amsterdam. Immediately, I fell in love with the village, feeling as if I had truly come home. At my first opportunity, I hired a carriage and told the driver to take me to the neighborhood of the Monastery Saint-Paul de Mausole.

The driver slowed the horses as we approached the lane where the monastery rose like a great fortress over fields and cottages nearby. He informed me that the old refuge now held a hospital, an asylum for the mentally afflicted. At a distance, I saw a garden nestled against the old monastery, dotted with twisted, deformed-looking trees composed of many colors. These hues grew throughout not only the dagger-shaped leaves, elongated much like willow or eucalyptus leaves, but the shades of red, yellow, green, brown and a peculiar blue-gray were also present in the bark. I might call these trees beautiful because of their subtle and variegated colors, but they also appeared tormented because of their deformities.

Beyond this bizarre garden and just down the lane from it, stood an ordinary cottage with a small garden of its own. Rather plain, but this garden radiated such an eerie feeling that I understood why my father spoke with dismay about the neighborhood. The modest cottage was barely visible from the lane, but a stone path wound through the garden toward it.

I immediately forgot my quest to see my birthplace, which possibly lay nearby. As the carriage passed the monastery, we came upon an artist standing on a knoll, and as we drew beside him, I saw he was dressed in a drab but paint-stained suit. One would inquire, of course, about this artist who recorded this bizarre garden – was he also strange? But no, he was not twisted or colorful like the garden. Despite his ginger-colored hair, he appeared straight-laced and drab because of his passive demeanor and his somber clothes.

The artist painted upon a canvas held by a rickety wooden easel. I told the carriage driver to stop and watched as the artist worked in an unusual fashion. He picked up a bit of vermillion on his brush, dabbed it here and there on the canvas, and with quick movements of his hand, spread the small bits into many small lines with a palette knife. Then he repeated the process with the other colors on his palette. To my surprise, this technique gave his painting a layered, impressionistic texture that dazzled the eye with movement.

I gazed at the painting and then at the garden again. Even before I learned more about the cottage and its garden, I began to consider the colors of this twisted foliage as the shades of insanity and the trees' twisted branches as the result of some revulsion.

"Excuse me, sir. Why did you choose this particular garden to paint?" I called to the artist.

"Can't you see? Are you blind?" he shouted.

Intimidated by this outburst I calmly asked, "See what?"

"See what sort of twisted individual must live near these gardens!"

"I can't understand how you can tell who lives there by looking at a garden. Look, the cottage has the same trees in its garden as the Monastery Saint-Paul de Mausole." I pointed at the large garden and then at the smaller one.

The artist stared at me. "Yes. You. You could live here."

"Me! Why me, Monsieur?"

"You with your colorful attire and tidy coiffure – just like those gardens, you're perfect and twisted at the same time."

No one had ever spoken to me in this manner before, and I wanted to slap the artist's face for his impudence until I realized he must have seen a special beauty in the gardens or he wouldn't be painting them. Though I felt uneasy about the gardens and especially the cottage, I could extrapolate that because he perceived a similar quality in me meant that his remark was complimentary.

"How much do you want for this painting? Tell me what you want; your price is immaterial to me."

His face registered surprise. "I've only sold one painting before," he said, signing it "Vincent van Gogh" with a flourish of his brush. "A few guilders are enough."

I didn't recognize the name when he signed the painting, but I easily produced the petty cash he requested. As soon as I returned to my newly leased home, I poured a glass of wine and hung the painting in my bedroom where I gazed at it by candle-light, appreciating the colors and the artist's unusual brush strokes. My attention was drawn for the first time beyond the twisted garden and to the barely visible cottage. When I saw movement in the painting, it caused me to question first my eye-sight and then my sanity. Then my skin tingled with the excited sensation of a voyeur, as if I were peeking at things not meant for my eyes.

As I looked closer, the front door of the cottage opened, and a gentleman and a lady walked along the stone pathway to the gate. They stood talking at the gate, and I watched in horror as the man performed an act upon the woman so dreadful, so horrible that I can hardly bear to describe it—he drew something from his pocket, a thin wire, and wrapped it around her throat and strangled her, nearly severing her head. I watched her eyes grow wide in surprise and then glaze over with fear as he twisted the wire around her neck. Finally, the light dimmed in her eyes and she slumped to the ground.

Chilled with horror, I wished I'd never encountered the painting or the artist. Why did this twisted garden even exist? I blew out the candle and lay in the dark wondering how I might fall asleep.

But fall asleep I did, and at dawn's first light I believed either I dreamed all that I had seen in the painting or that my wine was tainted. My day progressed normally, and after a day of sorting my belongings out, I endeavored to fall asleep without gazing upon the painting. But after quaffing my evening glass of wine, the painting had a nearly magnetic effect upon me. When I gazed upon it again and it came alive once more, I knew it wasn't a dream or the wine. How that plain Mr. van Gogh could put such life into this macabre painting was unfathomable.

I watched as the gentleman from the cottage came outside again to shovel dirt into a hole where he planted a sapling. There was nothing sinister at all about his labor until the tree slowly twisted into a misshapen form that mimicked the other twisted and deformed trees. Confused and intrigued, I could only conclude that he must have buried the girl there after his heinous act, and that the tree must have tried to twist itself from her grave in disgust. I recoiled in horror. Did this mean someone was buried under every tree in the garden?

If so, why? For what reason did this gentleman kill so many? Night after night, I felt inexorably drawn to scrutinize the painting, to look for some clue that would answer my questions. I resolved to do a bit of detective work, but how could I discuss what I saw with anyone? I thought if I went to the library and researched supernatural phenomena that I might find a clue as to what transpired at the yellow cottage.

I dressed and proceeded to the village square. My inquiries led me to the library of the hotel I'd stayed in for a few nights upon reaching St. Rémy. Not knowing where to begin looking in the modest room dimly lit by gas lamps, I approached a young woman reading at a desk.

"What can I do for you?" she said in a soft voice, looking up from her book.

The light from a nearby lamp flickered across her lovely face. Charmed by the Provence mademoiselle, I introduced myself. "André Audet at your service," I said, "or rather, I'm badly in need of yours. I don't quite know what I'm looking for. I observed a very strange happening…a waking nightmare, perhaps. I'm wondering if you have any books on the supernatural?"

The way she smiled told me that my either my admiration was returned or that she had no belief in the supernatural.

"Msr. Audet, as you can see, this library is quite limited. There are one or two such books located along that wall." She pointed a slim finger at a shelf across the room. "If you're looking for something about a recent event, you won't find anything but old classics in this library. You'll have better luck at the newspaper office. They have a morgue where they file clippings of reports about such things."

"Thank you, Mademoiselle…"

"DuBois," she said, blushing, "Danielle DuBois."

"May I visit with you again tomorrow, Mlle. DuBois?"

"Ah, I'm afraid not—"

Embarrassed, I took this to be a rejection. "Forgive me, I'm sorry for assuming—"

Danielle blushed again. "I'm afraid I only work her on Mondays. On Wednesday and Thursdays, I assist my father at the newspaper."

"Oh? And that's why you know so much about it, then."

"Yes, my father is a news editor. I write a column critiquing new art and literature in Provence."

"I shall look forward to reading it then. May I call on you there sometime? Perhaps we could dine after your work." I was encouraged when her cheeks bloomed with color again and her eyes sparkled with her consent.

I walked from the hotel to the weekly newspaper office across the square, and requested permission to peruse their files. After an intensive search, I came across an article from two years prior that described a cottage in St. Rémy where wicked and hateful things had happened for over two centuries. It was located in the very same neighborhood as the Monastery Saint-Paul de Mausole that my father had mentioned in his delirium. Shocked, I never considered that a cottage might be wicked or hateful. After watching my painting come alive night after night, I realized there might be some truth to this story. I scanned through the article for details.

Back in 1680, the authorities discovered six bodies buried under the garden of what I now knew for certain was the yellow cottage. The owner, a sculptor by the name of Yves Gagnon, claimed he was forced by an unknown entity to perform murderous acts. He testified he had to kill anyone who couldn't appreciate the beauty of his work. What the madman did exactly to his victims was not detailed, but he was hung for his efforts. I left the newspaper mentally exhausted by my search, but endeavored to walk to the courthouse located on the far side of the city square. Perhaps I could find out more about the Gagnon case in records of the murder trial.

I looked up the incident in court records. These revealed that the stone path of the yellow cottage was the length of many "last walks", a metaphor for the walk of a condemned prisoner to the gallows, and later, the guillotine. As in my painting, Gagnon felt compelled to walk his guests along his stone path to the gate and choke them to death. He methodically buried his victims in the garden, planting a sapling over each one. Naturally, his sanity was questioned by the court, and physicians and clergymen were consulted. One suggested a diagnosis of melancholia leading to insanity, and two declared Gagnon to be possessed by demons.

I asked the clerk if there were any more criminal cases concerning the cottage near the monastery. He thought for a moment and left his desk for a cabinet, where he located and extracted three more documents.

Exactly one hundred years later, in 1780, nine bodies were found buried in the garden of the yellow cottage. Eugenie Beaulieu, by all descriptions, a beautiful creature, was a writer of epic poems and tragedies. She also gained infamy as the first female serial murderer in French history. That a poetess so dainty and cultured could commit such ghastly crimes was unbelievable to many until the garden was dug up. She said she was forced by an unseen entity to poison her victims because they couldn't appreciate her poetry.

The next court document went on to describe how the new owner of the cottage hired painters to change its color to a drab brown that blended into the woodsy surroundings. Within a few months, the hue supposedly faded back to a soft butter yellow, but I suspected this was an old wives' tale.

The final incident was exactly twenty-seven years later. The body of a young woman had been buried without her head and hands. The authorities dug up the entire garden at the yellow cottage after her husband reported her missing, but never did find her severed parts. Both the legal record and the trail grew vague. The decomposed body couldn't be adequately identified and it appeared that the owner of the cottage, who was issued a summons to appear before authorities, and the young woman's grieving husband had both left the country. Or were they one and the same man? The case had closed in confusion.

This happened the year I was born. *Could it have been my mother's body*, I wondered? Impossible. If she had been a victim of the owner of the cottage, how had she come to be there? Why would my father not relate this terrible tale to me so that I might resolve the issue? My mind reeled with exhaustion and macabre thoughts. If the garden were dug up today, how many bodies would be found?

I resolved to do more direct detective work. On the next moonless night, I walked through the village and to the lane past the monastery. I crept through those twisted trees and hid in the cottage garden. I had a clear view into a window, fortuitously left open. A dim light shone through this open window and the voices of those inside floated into the garden. The gentleman living there had a lady guest and they conversed about art.

"My friend is an artist," he said, "would you care to see his latest painting?"

"Yes, please show me his work," the lady replied.

The room went silent for a moment, and I crept into the lowest branch of one of the twisted trees to get a look. The gentleman carried a painting covered with a sheet into the room. He set the painting on a table and uncovered it with a flourish. She gasped, I gasped. It was exactly like the painting I had purchased, save for an additional tree.

"How hideous! Whoever painted this monstrosity belongs in an asylum," she said hastily, then covered her mouth with a dainty hand, remembering that the artist was the gentleman's friend.

Calmly, the gentleman drew the sheet over the painting and took it from the room.

"I apologize for my outburst…it is getting late—" the woman stammered when the gentleman returned.

"Have no fear," he said cordially. "May I walk you to the gate?"

She stood and offered him her arm. They strolled down the yellow brick path, arm in arm, chatting softly. When they arrived near the gate he did to her what I had witnessed him do to the other girl in the painting.

I remained where I hid. How I shivered as he fetched a shovel and measured an exact five paces from the latest tree he had planted, a mere sapling. He dug a new hole, placed her body into it, and placed another sapling on top of her. Once he shoveled the pile of turned earth onto the roots, he watched as the tree twisted and turned as if in horror at being placed atop a newly murdered woman.

The next day I couldn't resist returning to the scene of the crime. I strolled past the cottage and the artist stood exactly where he had before, daubing at an exact replica of the painting I had purchased. This painting, upon observation, had a small difference: there were two more trees in it. Absorbed in his work, the artist said nothing to me as I passed.

Why a man would kill someone because they didn't like a painting intrigued me, to say the least. Should I go to the police? I felt disinclined to and simultaneously felt disgusted with myself for not doing the right thing. I decided to contemplate the murderer's behavior and my own motivation. The most direct way to solve both mysteries would be to engage the killer in an interview and try to discern his motivation.

Upon the pretext of being interested in purchasing the property, I strode confidently to the front door of the yellow cottage. The name plaque above the bell said Tristan Duhamel, whom I recalled as an art dealer who worked from the business districts of both Paris and Amsterdam. I was curious that the plain Mr. van Gogh was a friend of such a prominent man, and I wondered how much he knew about the businessman's nefarious activities.

The distinguished-looking gentleman answered the door. "May I help you?" he said briskly.

"Please pardon my intrusion, Monsieur Duhamel." I quickly mentioned a feigned interest in buying the property, and he promptly attempted to close the door in my face.

"You had better listen to my proposition, because I know what you did last night."

At these words, an incredulous look spread across his face. "I don't know what you're talking about."

"I know why your new trees are twisted and growing so quickly," I said, secretly quivering in my heart of hearts.

At this, he knew that I knew his secrets and invited me inside.

I stepped through the doorway with my hand on the grip of the snub-nosed pistol I concealed in my greatcoat. My jaw dropped in amazement at the interior of the cottage. From the outside, it appeared to be an ordinary two-story house, but inside I discovered it had only one floor and very high ceilings.

The walls were painted a creamy white that seemed to both absorb and reflect light, and the floors fashioned of polished, multi-colored marble. The hand-carved ebony woodwork had massive proportions, much larger than a cottage called for, with doors nearly ten feet high and the frames reaching nearly two feet higher. What amazed me even more were the paintings, all hung in perfect sequence. There were landscapes of the cottage with no trees, with one tree standing beside it, two trees, and so forth. Each painting added one more tree to the twisted garden. The gentleman stood silently watching as I rushed from painting to painting, counting the trees. The final painting looked and smelled damp. This one held over a dozen trees, reflecting the number of bodies that must be buried in the garden.

An empty space on the wall marked the spot where my painting would have hung if I hadn't purchased it from his friend. I felt the pull of that space exerting itself. The spot beckoned for my painting. I was nearly overcome by the same irresistible force that coursed through me when I felt compelled to view the painting at my home. I felt that I needed to rush home and bring the painting to hang in the reserved space, but I managed to resist the impulse. I judged it foolish that I had not alerted the authorities because surely I had discovered a serial murderer in our midst.

Truly this cottage was evil and beyond reproach. Did the thing that possessed this cottage need the paintings to survive? Was I drawn here so it could recover the one painting it didn't have? Or was it because my mother had perished here?

Feeling faint, I pulled my pistol from my breast pocket and leveled it at Msr. Duhamel.

He met the barrel of my pistol with a brazen smile. "Ever since van Gogh told me you purchased one of his paintings, I've been expecting you, Monsieur Audet. He told me your demeanor matched my garden, so it was easy to recognize you. After he sold the painting, I was prepared to offer you a generous sum, so I recently hired a detective to find you. I learned that once you graduated from your university studies, you became a writer, but your work was harshly criticized. Once I read your literary stories, I knew you were a kindred spirit and would understand."

I raised my pistol higher. "Understand?"

"I know you're trying to understand me, or you would have taken this matter to the authorities. You know that I'm intent upon making the world a better place."

I tightened my hand on the pistol grip. "How can you possibly imagine that killing anyone makes the world a better place?"

"Do you know how many are buried out there and who they are?" He pointed in the direction of the twisted trees.

"I know there are fifteen, but I don't know who they are." All I had to do was look at the trees, even in the paintings, and know every tree meant a body buried beneath it.

Duhamel tossed his head back in an eerie laugh. "Art critics, each and every one of them a critic! I gave them all a chance, just for once, to appreciate true genius by showing them these paintings. Not a one grasped their beauty or their significance. That's why I waited for you. I know your soul believes in artistic beauty, be it painting, sculpture, or letters."

When he told me all he killed were art critics, I put my pistol away.

"A job well done," I heard myself say as though someone else spoke through me.

Duhamel, looking relieved, retrieved a bottle of fine whiskey from his kitchen.

He poured two fingers of the amber liquid in each glass, handed me one, and held his aloft in a toast. "To your new home," he said.

I raised my glass as well, thinking of Duhamel's drab friend, Vincent, and his fancy that I could be the owner. How strange this was happening so quickly!

As we warmed ourselves with the whiskey, we agreed on a purchase price for the cottage. A satisfying price, exceedingly low, because I solemnly promised I'd take very good care of his garden – and continue with the planting!

After we shook hands on our deal and discussed the particulars of the banking issues that would allow Msr. Duhamel to slip out of St. Remy, I glanced up at the paintings again. *My paintings, all my lovely paintings.*

Then a movement in the first caught my eye – the one with no trees at all. A young woman, dressed in the fashion of ladies three decades before, walked toward the gate with a dark-haired gentleman dressed in an old-fashioned but new greatcoat. For a moment, they stopped and looked over their shoulders at me and smiled. My mother. My father. We were now all together and home at last!

I could hardly wait to invite Mademoiselle DuBois to dinner and share my good
fortune . . .

All Things Being Equal

By: Ian Brazee-Cannon

"Here we are again," Clay said in a mockingly cheerful tone. "Our last session together. These last couple of years, we have spent much time together and have not always agreed on what is best for me. But all of that ends today.

"With all that has happened I need to make it clear to you why things have had to end up the way they have.

"I never told you about the first murder I ever committed."

Dr. Price shifted in his chair as though he had come fully alert for the first time.

"I was but four at the time. I know that will get your attention. I was sitting on the couch with my father. It was a hot summer evening. Our screen door had a big hole in it from me falling through it several days before. A large number of flies had moved in.

"For some reason those flies scared me. I kept asking my dad to tell them to leave. He laughed at me and tried to get a few with his fly swatter. At one point I broke into tears. My father hit me with the fly swatter and said 'Kill the bugs yourself, they ain't nothing to be scared of, you little sissy'.

"Fourteen years later and I still remember what he said word for word.

"I took the fly swatter from him. I was not about to let anyone call me a sissy you see.

"For several hours it was like a dance. The flies slowly flew around, from time to time landing in front of me. As I lowered my weapon upon them, for I knew what I held in my hands was something more than a household utility, they took to the air. They were mocking me and I knew it.

"Then I got one. There was a loud crack as the swatter hit the table with the fly caught under it. A death scream. I raised my weapon from the table. The twitching body of the fly still stuck within the groves of plastic. I watched as the last ounce of life slowly faded from the harmless insect. I found poetry there.

"I murdered twenty-seven flies that night. Thirty-two the night after that. Forty the third night. Each night, I had to outdo myself. I kept count in a notebook, which I still have if you're interested in looking up my body count, this way I would know how good I had become. With each fly I felt less afraid. With each fly I gained a better understanding of what life was and how easy it comes and goes. Yet none were as interesting as that first kill."

Clay took note of the disbelieving look in Dr. Price's eyes.

"I know a four-year-old is not normally dexterous enough to swat flies, or at the level to keep a journal, but I assure you, I was. I have no reason to lie to you now. I will only lie once today, and it will not be to you. I would think you would know me better than that by now.

"After that I showed off to friends or anyone else who would watch by going after bees with my bare hands. I got stung more times than I can remember, but it never truly hurt. My fears of insects had vanished, same for spiders. As soon as I saw something small and insignificant, a term I used a lot during that time to explain a mistaken attitude towards smaller creatures, I killed it. There were oh so many ways to kill.

"Then I moved on to larger creatures. We did have a mouse problem after all.

"I loved setting the mouse traps and waiting to hear the spring's snap as the mouse's neck was broken in an instant. I rarely got to see the mice as they died, but I always examined the bodies afterwards. I wanted to know what happened in their bodies to cause death.

"Then when I was six years old, a cousin of mine, who was a few years older, got a BB gun for his birthday. The gun was the most interesting instrument to me. It was capable of doing so much. It was a powerful BB gun, not just your run-of-the-mill toy.

"There was a field out back of my uncle's farm house. My cousin liked going out there and killing the prairie dogs. I would come and watch day after day.

"Then one day he let me have a shot.

"I got one with my first try. It was a gut hit. I watched as it slowly died. I could see the panic on its face as it hurt and it knew that something was wrong. It knew it was dying, but it did not understand the cause. I could see the eyes asking 'Why?' It wanted to know what it had done to deserve to die in such a slow, painful way.

"I had never before had the chance to truly watch death. It was a moment that I shall treasure always. Everything before had died without showing any emotions that I could understand. It was during this moment that I realized something important. I was wrong when I called insects insignificant. It occurred to me that everything that lived must have a use. Every piece of life was important in some way. I was not going to allow life to be wasted. I would study life and death and discover the true purpose of existence."

Dr. Price nodded his head slightly.

"I took the corpse home with me, an act which puzzled my cousin a great deal.

"There was an old shed in our backyard that had not been used in years. I had cleaned out all the junk and set it up as my own work area.

"In my quest to understand death I had watched several shows on animal biology. Having observed many dissections I felt ready to perform my own.

"It was a messy procedure; after all I was only six. I cut out every organ from that prairie dog and examined them closely. I made hundreds of notes about the feel, smell, color—even the taste in some cases—of every piece of tissue that made that creature whole. I was going to learn just what made something alive.

"I was disappointed.

"The next few years I continued in my quest. I found other rodents to kill and dissect, but I still felt unfulfilled. There was something missing.

"I would ask questions at church and school, but no one could give me a good answer. For some reason the subject of death being talked about to a child was considered a joke. Most adults fed me lies. They would dance around the answers, making it obvious that they did not know a thing about life and death.

"I read the Bible when I was eight years old.

"Yes, I know this is another hard to believe piece of my story, but it is true.

"I understood every word of it. When I started reading it, I thought it would have all the answers I was looking for. Yet, when I was done, I was left with nothing. It had hollowed me out. I saw every contradiction written there, every lie that our society had created. I could not believe that anyone could find answers there.

"I was once more disappointed.

"A new neighbor moved in next door when I was ten. They had a little dog, the kind that could not be quiet. It would yap away in its idiotic tone for hours as I watched it. I grew to love the pointlessness of the stupid animal's actions. For I found it to be below that of anything I had killed. The flies, the bees, the mice, the prairie dogs, the birds, the squirrels, they all seemed to have a purpose. They were truly alive. Yet, in this one domesticated animal I could find no purpose for its existence. It was too pampered by its owners to be able to live without them. It had lost something.

"By this time I was familiar with many ways to trap and kill living creatures. I knew that the dog would be no challenge. I captured it, but I did not kill it. I strapped its mouth close and tied it to my operating table.

"This was the first time I had a living creature to dissect. I watched it struggle for a few minutes although I do not believe that it understood what was about to happen.

"I slowly made the first incision in its chest. Then I stood back and watched as it reacted."

Dr. Price gasped.

"The blood slowly ran out of the animal. It fought and tried to bite me as I moved in for another cut. It ended up tightening its jaws so hard that the teeth pierced through its mouth.

"I took my time opening the dog up. At one point it ripped its lower left leg from its body by struggling too hard.

"Once I had opened up the chest cavity I pinned the skin down and watched as the internal organs did their work.

"It was the most fascinating sight I had ever seen; the heart pumping, the lungs inflating and deflating. It urinated on me and I was able to watch the muscles move that controlled its bladder.

"This worthless creature gave me what I needed. I took notes of course, but they seemed incomplete. I knew I was closer to figuring out the secret of life.

"I was saddened when the dog finally died. It had lived a pointless life with no ambition or purpose. Then in its final hours it made up for all the wasted years by giving me a greater knowledge. Although it had not been willing, it had made a great sacrifice."

Dr. Price swallowed slowly.

"The neighbors of course came looking for the dog. They found it several days later; it appeared to have been run over by a good number of cars at a busy intersection.

"After that I would search the neighborhood looking for new subjects to learn from. The rate of household pets getting loose and playing in traffic increased dramatically in the area.

"That is when I started taking note of the owners of the pets.

"They would burst into tears over their dead pets. These would be the same people who I would watch kill a harmless fly just because they found it annoying. The same people that coldly murdered gophers in their gardens, and all the gopher was trying to do was eat and feed its family.

"I took note of this contradiction. I then decided to pick my subjects by what their owner purchased while shopping.

"Have you ever looked at the amount of deadly weapons that are easily available at grocery stores and such? During the summer some places designate a whole wall to ways to murder 'backyard pests'. Bug spray, mouse traps, rat poisons and fly strips. All are instruments of death on a massive scale.

"When I would see a neighbor buying such weapons, their pet would be the next one found in the street. I felt it was a fair retribution."

Clay paused.

Dr. Price shifted as though just waking up.

"That pattern lasted for many years. I found little else in life that challenged me. I graduated high-school at fifteen, although I knew I could have finished it earlier I did not want to bring that much attention to myself. I then started looking into a career in medicine. I already knew so much about biology that it just seemed the natural course to follow.

"Then one day I found my father in my shed.

"I have not told you much about my father yet, have I?"

Dr. Price had a puzzled look on his face.

"My mother died when I was a baby. My father raised me. He was an idiot. I must have gotten my intelligence from my mother's side. He was an abusive alcoholic. He played a very small and insignificant role in my life. I kept him distanced from me as much as possible. I don't even think he was aware that I was looking into collage at such a young age."

The expression of confusion was obvious on Dr. Price's face.

"But you knew most of that from my files of course. It has been part of your questioning every session after all.

"My father was looking through my notes. After ten years of using the shed as my personal work area, he finally decided to take some interest in what I had been doing out there all those nights. He called me sick and inhuman, denouncing me as his son. He threatened to call the police and get me put into a hospital. Then he hit me.

"He had struck me many times before. I took the beatings and never fought back. This time was different.

"I stood my ground. I did not flinch as his fist struck my face. I made no sound. I was not going to acknowledge the pain. As his hand left my face I grabbed his arm. Pressing inwards at the wrist I soon had my father on his knees. He looked into my eyes and fell silent.

"I looked down at this man that had raised me. I saw something less than the dog. Before me was an animal that had done nothing with the life he had been given. He barely tried to survive. Starving himself in order to buy his most precious beer. Spending most of his days and nights in front of the television, not caring what he was watching. He knew nothing of the world outside the few blocks that he existed in.

"I knew then that I had my greatest subject.

"He fought me when I tied his wrists together. He yelled obscenities and insults. He wanted me to believe that I was more inhuman than he was. I gave him a dose of Valium, one of the many useful drugs I had acquired over the years. He tried to spit it out, but I held his mouth close. I waited for the drug to take effect.

"I strapped my father to an old table. I made sure that the straps were strong and tied properly. I then took out the fly swatter he had given me all those years ago and tied it into his mouth as a gag. I felt it to be the most fitting of gestures.

"As I dissected my first human being I felt the excitement grow within me. I knew that this would have to be the event that gave me the secrets I was looking for. I watched as my father's organs went about their business. I had set up extra lights to kill off any shadows. I wanted to see every detail clearly.

"My father awoke fairly early in the operation. I studied the look of fear on his face. I could see the pain in his eyes. He said nothing as I peeled back more and more skin. Somewhere along the way he had lost the will to struggle. I do not know if it was because he had realized that it was no use or if he had wanted to die.

"I took out the circular saw; I had bought the strongest blade I could find for it. I knew that the human skull would be tough to cut through. As I sliced into my father's forehead he tried to give his last scream. It was a muffled yelp.

"After he died I spent several hours playing with his muscles and such. I used a broken extension cord to give electric jolts to areas of his brain. I had a few interesting reactions, but I could not find what I was looking for.

"Over the next few days I took my father apart, piece by piece. I studied every piece. This time I was not worried about the owner coming looking for the pet. I took my time exploring the human body.

"I thought I had made sure no one would miss my father. I called his work and told them he was deadly sick and that the doctors had told him to stay in bed with no visitors. Whenever someone called for him I took a message and said he would get back to them. I was still working on a long term plan when the police arrived. They had come to arrest him for not showing up to trial on a DUI. It was an irony that did not escape me. I was at a lost as to what to do. They had probable cause to search for him. I tried to keep them in the house. When one of them journeyed into the backyard, I knew they would find my experiment. I pulled out a chair and sat on the back porch as they discovered all I had done. I watched as they vomited and called for backup. They approached me slowly with guns drawn. I did not fight them. I knew it would be pointless."

Dr. Price's eyes were open as wide as possible.

"And that is how I ended up here."

"At first I was very upset with having been sent here. It seemed that the universe was being very unfair to me. I had to play the victim in order to keep those who could not understand my gifts from giving me any real punishments for what they considered crimes.

"It turns out however, that this was just the place I needed to be. Most do not understand what you have here; a collection of people who have been deemed unfit to walk free in the world? Society has decided that there is something wrong with us and unless you kind people 'fix' us, we need to stay locked up here.

"Not a very accurate description. There is so much potential in this place. A smart person can learn a lot from the skills of the youth here. I have learned slight of hand, voice impersonation and forgery just to name a few. All of which can be very useful when used together in the right way.

"Now, please do not think I am saying the young men and women you have here are by any means sane. Most need to be kept away from decent people for their own good. Like Randy, who always has his sessions right after mine. He will become very destructive just to get a quarter.

"I see my time is up for the day."

Clay stood up from his chair.

"I will miss these sessions, doctor. Now I must return to the real world. Two years of this therapy. Makes you feel good that our legal system goes easy on those of us who are too young to be able to be held responsible for our actions. Now I can pursue that medical career I had started planning.

"But first there are a few loose ends here."

Clay took the folder that was in front of Dr. Price.

"My paperwork is awaiting your signature so they will let me leave here today; but you seem to be in no condition to sign them right now."

Dr. Price opened his mouth slightly to protest, but nothing came out.

"Do you know the big trick to forging signatures?" Clay asked as he started to sign Dr. Price's name to the papers. "You need to make sure that each one is not identical. No one signs their name exactly the same each time. You need to know just the basic feel of the signature and then make sure to be casual when signing. It can be tricky, but once you've seen someone's signature enough times and you know what to look for then you can sign their name to anything."

Clay smiled at Dr. Price.

"There, all done. I am a free man once I turn these papers in for you.

"But there is the small problem of you. Even though the Rohypnol seems to be working just fine, and I went through a great deal of trouble to get a hold of that one dose to slip in your water, once it wears off you most likely will remember none of this. The thing is, I see that as a possible problem as well. So here is my solution to that.

"My skill at impersonating another's voice is not that good. It really is more of a talent one is born with. But when using electronic equipment the voice is normally altered as it is. In such cases you just need to make sure you are speaking as the other person would and keeping to a close enough voice."

Clay reached over the desk and touched the button on the intercom system, "Ms. Fines, please send Mr. Carson in. I'm going to let Mr. Phillips wish his friend good-bye before he leaves." It was a not exactly Dr. Prices voice, but Clay knew it was close enough to work.

A moment later a large young man with a muscular build slowly entered the room.

"Hello, Randy," Clay said in a pleasant voice. "I must get going, but first let me show you that secret about Dr. Price that I told you about last night."

Clay leaned over to Dr. Price and whispered in his ear, "Here is the one lie I said I would tell today. Since lies often hurt, I think this one will hurt you greatly. And I feel very sorry for Randy here, who will also be greatly hurt due to my lie. There are times when the innocent must be used to help the greater good. If only Randy had the will to talk, then he might be able to explain why he ended up doing what he is about to do."

Clay moved his hand just behind Dr. Price's ear. With one fluid motion he pulled his hand away from the ear and presented a shinny quarter for all to see.

Randy stood in awe looking at the quarter.

"Now, Randy, there are many more where this came from. Dr. Price's head is filled with them," Clay explained as he walked over and handed the quarter to Randy.

Randy snatched the quarter and turned away from Clay to examine his new treasure.

"I must go now, Randy. And I am truly sorry."

Clay picked up the papers that he had signed and quickly looked through them. He smiled once he was satisfied that all needed papers were there.

Randy had just put the quarter in his pocket and started to move towards Dr. Price as Clay left the office.

Clay smiled at Ms. Fines and handed her the papers.

"I guess you need these," Clay said with a smile. "I hope all is in order then."

Less than fifteen minute later Clay was heading out the gates of the Glendale Juvenile Rehabilitation Center to a waiting taxicab. He heard the alarm go off and the announcement for security to Dr. Price's office.

Clay made no attempt to hide his satisfied smile as the taxi pulled away to take him back into the real world. He was more than ready to get back to work on solving that great mystery called life.

Red Badge

By: John Lemut

Clement sat at the bar facing rows of liquor bottles lining glass shelves down lit and up lit by small, delicate, hot-burning bulbs. The woman bartender who was sometimes allowed to get on stage and sing a song or two she wrote for her now-defunct indie rock band in what she thought of as her signature, slightly growly yet breathy voice served Clement another Jack and Coke.

She added the drink to the tab she was running for him in her head. Clement didn't look at her, but he did notice her. In the month that he had been coming to the club he caught her brief act a few times and one song in particular—he assumed it was called "Me Not You" because those were the words she most frequently repeated—he enjoyed. He didn't like it for the music or the lyrics. She kept her mouth close to the microphone when taking sharp, quick inhalations such that, even with the collective ruckus of the ambient noise in the bar that featured a less than adequate sound system, her inhalations were audible, seeping from the speakers. They made him think about what she would sound like while having sex.

The bartender would not be singing tonight. She only sang on weeknights when the crowd was thin and respectful. Tonight there was a DJ.

She liked the way his glass went untouched until he was ready to take a drink from it. He never ordered a bottle of beer, but if he had, she knew he wouldn't fiddle with it. He wouldn't peel the label off with his fingernails. The glass she set down before him minutes ago still went untouched. The condensation accumulated naturally; perfect little semi-spheres sometimes broke away as demanded by gravity and rolled down the outside of the glass to be absorbed into the cocktail napkin. He drank at his own pace. The word in her mind for it was "deliberate."

Clement didn't know her name. They never introduced her before her performances. She just jumped on stage and started strumming a guitar and singing. He never asked her and she wouldn't volunteer it.

Clement saw Manny's approach through glycol smoke and strobe lights reflected in the mirrors behind the rows of liquor bottles lining glass shelves. Because Clement saw him in advance, he allowed Manny to clasp him on his shoulder without reacting.

Manny slid onto the stool beside him. "Jack!" a clearly excited Manny nearly yelled at Clement. "Babe!" Manny did yell at the bartender. "I'll take a Lite!"

She angrily twisted the cap off a bottle. "Five-fifty," she told Manny.

Clement pointed at himself almost apologetically and her expression softened. She re-totaled his tab while walking to serve the next customer.

Manny was in his early twenties, although he unsuccessfully tried to act a couple years older. Clement's age was difficult for both Manny and the bartender to guess. Clement slept well and that helped his youthful appearance.

"Jack, remember that guy I told you about?"

Clement's eyeballs rolled to look up and to the left to feign the appearance of attempting to recall previous conversations with Manny about the Sandman.

"Remember I was telling you about *the Sandman?"* Manny prodded further, his voice dropped softer for the last two words. "Do you want to meet him?"

"Yeah," Clement replied, now looking at Manny for the first time.

"He's here. He's over in the lounge." Manny motioned to a corner of the club where a man sat alone on a low, black couch secured behind a perimeter of velvet rope. The Sandman was poking at a smart phone.

Clement couldn't quite tell looking through the dance floor crowded with illegally admitted girls and club-dressed men-boys, haze, and the headache-inducing mélange of strobes and barely-on bar lighting; but even seated, the Sandman looked tall (his knees were elevated above his hips), lean but muscular (his thin, form-fitting shirt gave that much away), and possibly part black or Latino (the lighting and dancers obscuring the clear view made racial profiling difficult).

"You know why they call him the Sandman, right?" Manny told Clement this every time he spoke of his "good friend" the Sandman. "…Because he puts people to sleep."

They drank for a couple minutes, ordered another round from the bartender (Clement placed a hundred on the bar to settle his tab and leave more than a one hundred percent tip) and made their way across the dance floor—Manny a pinball in a machine and Clement a stream of water flowing between and around small crowds of girls dancing and boys barely swaying while attempting to look uninterested in general. The Sandman looked up as they approached and waved Manny into his one-man party.

Manny lightly took hold of Clement's elbow to escort him inside the ropes. Clement glanced down at Manny's hand and mentally counted a fast ten. The bass-intense music was no less punishing in the lounge but Manny attempted an introduction of aliases. "Alex, this is that guy I told you about: Jack," Manny said to the Sandman from a respectful distance.

"Jack," Manny leaned in too close to Clement's ear, "just call him 'Alex.'" He then added unnecessarily: "It's not his real name."

The Sandman inclined his head slightly while eyeing Clement and then motioned for the two of them to join him. The Sandman was almost certainly half black, his forearms were a vascular roadmap, and his face was furrowed in an intimidating expression honed in a mirror. Manny sat in the not-quite-middle of the couch and Clement sat crowded against the armrest to Manny's left.

Conversation was impossible so they drank with little talk. Clement could feel the Sandman's frequent glances. Although Clement had finished looking the Sandman over before he sat down, Jack wouldn't have been; so Clement occasionally mocked a surreptitious gaze in the Sandman's direction, timing a few of them with the Sandman's own looks at him so Clement could nervously look away and pretend to be more interested in watching a gyrating dancer's ass than in sizing up the infamous Sandman.

They drank. Clement matched the Sandman's pace, as did Manny. The bartender spied the note Clement wrote on the hundred—JUST COKE—and complied. After several rounds, the Sandman informed Manny and Clement that they were coming back to his house.

* * *

The Sandman told Manny to chauffer Jack, and to follow him. The Sandman appeared to be trying to lose them on the way to his house, but even an over-the-limit Manny could tail the white Monte Carlo with twenty-two inch rims.

Eventually, the Sandman pulled into a driveway and Manny parked on the street in front of a ranch house. The Sandman was a resident of a well-kempt, fifty-year-old neighborhood. A tricycle would sit abandoned until the next morning in a neighbor's lawn near the front step. Porch lights were on but lamps inside homes were not. A couple second-story windows on the block emitted a flickering blue hue.

The Sandman unlocked a dead bolt and then the knob lock and waved his visitors inside. Clement forced himself to lightly stumble over the threshold and then he wiped his feet on the mat inside the front hallway. The Sandman stepped through the door and something started beeping. Manny didn't react, but Clement swiveled his head in all directions, looking everywhere except from where he heard the sound emanating. The Sandman smiled as he entered a code on the alarm keypad attached to the wall above the light switches for the front porch and hallway.

"Relax," the Sandman said. "I had a guy who owed me for a job install a metal detector in the front door." The door jamb was obviously too deep and the metal detector was poorly hidden. The Sandman pulled a Glock 17 from his waistband to prove metal had been detected.

"Let's go in the kitchen," he said stuffing the Glock back in his pants.

The Sandman grabbed three beers from a beer-, Gatorade- and condiment-filled refrigerator. The Sandman sat at the kitchen table with his back to a peninsula counter, Manny's back was to a window, and Clement, across from the Sandman, had the rest of the house behind him.

The inside of the Sandman's home was fairly run-down. The linoleum floor in the kitchen was worn and faded: once vibrant oranges and yellows had become an incestuously related dingy tan. The walls had scuff marks, dings, and nails with nothing hanging on them. The Sandman was not the ideal neighbor.

After another couple minutes of silence, during which Clement looked anywhere except at the Sandman and picked at his bottle's label, the Sandman said, "Ask away, man. I know you want to."

Manny was enjoying Jack's uncharacteristic timidity. Clement had portrayed a bored, confidant, even mysterious figure to hook Manny's desire to impress.

"Manny said…uh, he said that you put people to sleep?"

The Sandman laughed too boisterously. "The name and the, you know, the catchphrase: they get me noticed by people who require my services. People talk, Jack, you know what I'm sayin'? They spread my name around like the clap."

"Where did you learn to…you know?"

"The military. 'Nuff said."

The Sandman was too stupid for SF. Clement deduced that the Army, possibly the Army Reserve, was where the Sandman learned just enough to make a little career out of murdering for money.

"What do you charge?"

"Why, you got somebody you want offed?"

Clement's eyes darted to Manny. The Sandman saw it, took it for an unconscious reflex, and laughed again. "Shit! I'll kill Manny for free." The Sandman smacked Manny on the shoulder, upended his bottle and then braced his palms on the table as a precursor to pushing himself to his feet. Clement innocently put a hand up and went to grab three more beers from the refrigerator.

"Look people in the eye," the Sandman advised. "The eyes tell you everything. When I take a job, I look my client in the eye. When I kill someone, I look that mu'fucker in the eye first. When I meet someone like yourself, someone who wants to know about what I do because he ain't never got closer to nothing like it before, I look you in the eye.

"I already know everything I need to know about you."

"Like what?" Clement asked. He had not expected a statement like that.

"I can see you're scared. You're not scared of my Glock I showed you…you're scared of me. Manny told me you were cold. But you're not. You're trying to hide that you're scared of the things I can do.

"And you know what? You should be. It's okay. It's normal to be. Because I do bad things. I kill people I've never met, people I've never heard about, people I don't care about one way or the other. That's not what my momma had in mind for me when she raised me. That's not what my teachers thought I'd do when they taught me. That's not even what the Army had in mind when they trained me to fuckin' kill!

"…But I kill people and I do it good. And I get paid good for it. Fifteen g's."

Manny had certainly heard the speech in one form or another before, but his reactions were telegraphed to look shocked or possibly aroused to placate the Sandman's ego. Clement maintained a look of blank awe, which he found was surprisingly close to his actual reaction of unmoved neutrality. The Sandman's insight about Jack merely turned out to be an excuse to talk about *himself*—and Clement was mildly disappointed. The Sandman was worked up, though. His breathing was heavy, but he was enjoying talking shop and impressing and scaring some random dude.

"You got anymore questions?" This statement had thin layers of threat running through a genuine desire to field more queries and dazzle his guests.

Clement sipped at his beer. While doing so, he tensed his arm muscles, forcing his hand to shake. A heavy minute passed before Clement asked, "Were you afraid when you killed for the first time?"

The Sandman picked at some crust that accumulated near his left eye's inner tear duct. "I remember my first fuck real good. I don't remember much about my first kill though. I don't remember how many times I shot her and I don't even remember what kind of gun I used, but I do remember how I felt, and it wasn't scared. It was more like…I was controlling myself from outside my body. Now, I'm right there when I do it. I get excited about it. That's closer to feeling scared than I was when I killed that first time."

Clement interlaced his fingers and rested his hands on the table in front of him like an attentive grade school student. "Did you ever read *The Red Badge of Courage*?" he asked.

"I'm not really much of a reader," the Sandman admitted with relish.

Clement smiled, no longer touching the bottle or its label. The Sandman did not take notice of any change, but Manny felt uneasy. "What about *Saving Private Ryan*? Have you seen that?"

"Oh, shit yeah. That's a bad-ass movie. No brothers though, but *Miracle at St. Anna* wasn't really action-packed, you know what I'm sayin'?"

"Remember the character of Upham?"

"The radio guy?"

"No, he was the translator."

After a couple seconds of recall the Sandman slapped the table. "Oh! Shit, yeah. That little chicken shit mu'fucker!"

"Yes, that's the one."

"I would have shot him."

"There's a natural human reaction to war a fairly large percentage of soldiers experience. The first time a man is faced with a battle situation, he often freezes or runs. The military spends a lot of time and money trying to bypass those kinds of reactions to make a soldier's reaction to his first battle one of aggression.

"Upham froze in the stairwell when his Jewish friend and that German were in that vicious hand-to-hand fight. Upham could hear his friend yelling for help, but he was frozen with fear, even though we all saw he could have walked in there and hit the German on the back of the head with his rifle's stock. Instead he cowered and cried in the hallway as the German slowly sunk his bayonet into the Jew's chest. Then the German came out into the hallway. Upham put his hands up from his cowering position and the German walked right past him; he didn't even gauge Upham as a threat."

"Pussy," the Sandman interjected.

"Don't interrupt," Clement said coldly. The Sandman reflexively slumped down a little in his seat. Manny's brain told him that something was different, like a wind shift forewarning the arrival of a swift-moving cold front.

"Later, when the Germans are being beaten and are surrendering, Upham finally stops cowering and a few Germans surrender to him. Upham stopped one of those surrendering Germans from being executed earlier in the film. Upham shot him. A lot of people saw *that* as another cowardly act, but I never did. I took it as Upham finally getting into the spirit of war, you understand? First he froze, as people tend to do. Once he got accustomed to the chaos and insanity of war, he became a true soldier.

"I know I was so scared I was frozen in fear for a minute when I killed for the first time."

The kitchen table didn't have legs. It only had a single metal column that attached to the table top and the x-shaped feet. Clement's foot rested next to it. After what he told them sunk into the Sandman's head, as betrayed by his eyes, Clement forcefully pushed the table with his foot and arms to the right, cracking two of Manny's ribs and painfully pinning him, still seated in his chair, between the windowed wall and table. This burst of action also removed the obstacle between Clement and the Sandman.

Clement stepped forward with his left foot so he stood in the space the table had occupied less than a moment before. He continued applying pressure to the edge of the table with his hip so Manny could not escape. Clement pulled a ceramic diver's knife from a thin sheath nestled in the small of his back and sliced through the Sandman's left jugular with a single swipe of the blade. The Sandman, slow to react due to alcohol, shock, and a sincere lack of skill, did not try to defend against the knife and only put his hand up after his pumping blood coated the wall, the curtains, the window and Manny.

Clement watched for a few spurts. He easily pushed the Sandman back into his seat when he futilely tried to stand. "That metal detector in the door is a pretty good idea. I might have to get one of those at my house," Clement said to the fading Sandman. He stabbed the Sandman in the other side of his neck and turned the blade like a key.

Sandman, real name Edward Jones, died gurgling, in fading pain, moments later.

Manny whimpered and continued trying to dislodge himself.

"Now in *The Red Badge of Courage* the main character, Henry, runs away from his first real battle," Clement told Manny, turning his attention from the Sandman. "He feels ashamed and hides from his regiment. However, he goes on to fight in the next battle and does quite well.

"...You were going to run just now."

"No! No, I swear to God. Please don't kill me." Manny's pleas broke down into sobs which broke down into pain-laced coughing.

"I suppose I was only paid to kill the Sandman. Nobody cared enough to pay me to kill you."

A sliver of hope flickered in Manny's eyes. "How do I know if I let you go you won't come back ready for the chaos and insanity of war?"

"I swear you'll never see me again. Please, just let me go."

Clement considered his options out loud: "On the one hand, I could use a ride back to my car. I'm not real familiar with this town and I noticed you don't have GPS in your car. But on the other hand…I just don't like you. Everything about you makes me want to kill you more."

"Please, *God!"*

"And your begging is starting to get to me."

"I'll do anything!"

Clement set the knife on the table and placed his palms on either side of it. As he thought through what to do with Manny, he dug the balls of his feet into the floor and pushed against the table's edge. Another rib snapped. "Okay! I've decided. I am going to kill you, but I'll do it quickly. Then I'll play in your blood for a little while and then I'll drive your car back to the bar to get my car and then I'll go home."

The ceramic blade was very sharp so Manny didn't feel very much and then Manny didn't feel anything at all.

* * *

Clement found the club again after a few wrong turns and pulled Manny's Neon into the parking lot. He killed the lights and engine and got out of the cabin. As he walked away from the car he tossed the keys over his shoulder; they hit the hood, slid down its length and bounced off the bumper to the crumbling asphalt lot.

The bartender left the club by the service entrance at the back as Clement neared his rental. In her right fist she clenched her key ring with two keys sticking out between her fingers. Clement liked this.

He changed his course to intercept her. She was simultaneously excited and frightened to finally see him alone in the dark. One of the bouncers banged the service door open. "Everything okay?"

Clement didn't look at the bouncer; he knew even his sidelong glance could compel violence. The bartender looked back at the bouncer and said with more than a touch of bitchiness, "I'm fine, *'night.*"

The bouncer threw his large hands up in the air and slammed the door shut.

She considered thanking him for the large tip, but decided against it. She neither wanted to bring up money nor find out what his note meant—if it even was his note. She recalled hearing that some obscene percentage of the hundred dollar bills in circulation had traces of cocaine on them. That note could have been written years ago, states away.

He considered asking her if she could see any blood on his hands in the low light. He washed up before he left Edward Jones' house, but tonight he saw red everywhere. Because she most certainly would ask, his internal conversation expanded, and he decided he would tell her that he had been dropped off by a friend who hit a deer with his car.

Instead neither spoke for some time. They stood closer than strangers would stand, farther apart than lovers would.

Finally Clement broke the silence: "I won't be able to listen to you sing anymore."

"Why is that?"

"I've been in town on business and tonight, or rather today, was my last day."

"That's too bad. You were a—I liked seeing you out there." She sighed. "So, you're leaving, when, tomorrow?"

"I'm not really on a clock. I simply leave town when my job is done."

"What about coffee?"

"Coffee?"

"Yeah, buy me a cup of coffee."

Clement considered something. "I know a place. Follow me?"

She nodded and walked to her car smiling sheepishly. Clement got in his rental. The rearview mirror was tilted so he couldn't see himself. He adjusted the knife resting against the small of his back.

Feeding the Hunger

By: Suzanne Robb

Greg Morrison enjoyed the rhythmic back and forth motion of the saw in his hand. He took comfort in the easy strokes, until it stuttered for a moment, he had hit the femur. Greg laid the handsaw to the side and picked up an electrical one. He started it up and watched the sharp teeth go back and forth in a frenzied blur of motion.

The thing on the table made him angry; she didn't last nearly as long as he had hoped she would. Greg had picked her specifically for her endurance. Every day she ran five miles before work, then did another five when she got home. On weekends he had followed as she went climbing and mountain biking.

Her name had been Sabrina Rogers, and Greg planned to enjoy her for at least two weeks, maybe more. He hoped she would be the one. Imagine his annoyance when after a mere four days of torture she gave in, offering him whatever he wanted. Greg hadn't even brought out the big guns when she folded like a pathetic creature, begging for him to spare her life.

He had been so disgusted at her lack of dignity and fortitude that he grabbed the nearest item and stabbed her in the eye. Greg had smiled grimly when he pulled the pliers out, her eye popped and, leaking clear fluid, blood poured freely out of the socket.

Now he had to clean up after it, chopping the body up into small pieces and then feeding them to the pigs he kept out back. At times like this, he loved country living. People rarely wanted to drive all the way out to see you, no one just dropped in for a visit. Then again, Greg had given up the guise of friend years ago, fully embracing his misanthropic ways.

He started up the electrical saw and began cutting through the femur. A few more cuts and he would be able to toss this waste of a human into the wheel barrel and feed the piggy bank. He laughed at his joke, then shook his head as he remembered no one ever got his sense of humour.

***

Greg watched his prey walk to her car. He looked around the underground garage, no cameras, no security guards, and one exit on the other side. He smiled at the lack of security, people were lazy, and easily lulled into thinking they were safe because they had a clicker to open the garage gates. Their ineptitude made his hunger so much easier to feed.

His prey was lithe and moved with a serene grace. Greg knew she would be a challenge to break, but they were no fun if they gave in right away. He had to choose carefully, study them, and make sure they were up to the task as it were.

The last one surprised him in the most spectacular of ways, making up for the disappointment of Sabrina. Caroline Rogers had endured almost two weeks of torture before giving in. Of course, after he got what he wanted, he no longer needed nor wanted her. Disposal of the body always a messy affair, but oh how he loved to work with his hands.

He closed his eyes for a moment as he remembered the screams of Caroline. They replayed in his mind like a demented opera from Hell. Greg felt his stomach muscles tighten as the look on her face flashed in his mind when he had brought out the nail gun. A look of pure terror which still excited him.

***

Lara Nichols walked to her car, the entire time, the hairs on the back of her neck rising. She didn't so much feel as if she was being watched, as she knew it. For the last few months Lara had felt something, a presence watching her. She tried to chalk it up to nerves, but as she fumbled with her keys and saw a shadow reflected behind her in the driver's side window, the nerves scenario went out the window.

After several tries Lara got the key into the lock and opened the door. She sat inside and locked the door as fast as she could, as if her life depended on it. She saw a figure in her rearview mirror, tall and dark.

Lara forced the keys into the ignition and started the engine, she looked down for mere seconds to put the car into gear. When she looked up again, nothing stood behind her car. She sighed in relief and was about to pull out when a knock to her left caused her heard to leap into her throat.

She didn't look, just pressed on the gas and got the hell out of the garage. Lara hated parking down here, tomorrow she would start parking on the street. The lack of security, and the fact someone was following her, made her want to be out in the open as much as possible.

The traffic flowed smoothly on the ride home, and more than ever all Lara wanted was to go inside her house, lock the doors, and drink until she passed out. Her gaze alternated between her side and rearview mirror multiple times. What if he had followed her?

Lara pulled into her driveway, hit the button for the garage door and pulled in. She kept her eyes on the entrance as she hit the button to close the door. Only then did she get out of the car and use the side door which entered into the kitchen.

The alarm beeped and she entered the code to turn off the 'away' setting, then hit the button for 'at home.' She felt marginally safer, but knew something had to be done, or she would go insane by the end of the week.

Lara went through the house checking all the windows and doors, drawing the curtains, and then allowed herself to grab a bottle of wine from the fridge. She poured herself a liberal glass and went into the bathroom.

She took the time to draw the bath, adding salts and lavender scented oil. She brought out anything with calming, soothing, or relaxing on the label. When she finished, the bath water had a purple pink color and smelled like a florist shop. She sadly noted she did not feel any more relaxed.

Lara tried to talk to her friends about her feelings, but with no proof and the duration of the complaints, they wrote her off as being paranoid. She couldn't blame them after months of talking about it, she annoyed herself with her crazy talk. Gut instincts and hunches didn't carry much weight with the police either.

They told her they would look into it as soon as she brought forth solid evidence. She smiled as she stripped out of her clothes, would her dead body be evidence enough? She stood there naked, and looked at herself in the mirror.

Lara had always been athletic and a bit of a health nut, so when she saw the ribs showing and the dark circles under her eyes she was a bit thrown off, ;he situation getting to her more than she realized.

Slipping into the water she enjoyed a bath and her wine. Once the water became tepid to the touch she reluctantly got out. She had relaxed for a bit, though suspected the wine had something to do with it and not the *'calming aura salts'*. Lara threw a robe on over her pyjamas and went back into the kitchen. She grabbed the bottle of wine and began to pour herself another glass.

Strong arms grabbed her from behind. Instinctually Lara kicked out, using the counter to push back. Her attacker, knocked off balance, fell to the floor. She untangled her legs from his and scrambled out of the kitchen. A hand shot out and grabbed her ankle.

Lara tripped and hit her head on a bookshelf in the hallway. The corner leaving a two inch gash on her forehead, warm blood started to seep down, blurring her vision. She pulled herself up to her feet and felt something grab her from behind.

The attacker grabbed her hair and yanked, her head forced back with such force she thought her neck might break. Then Lara found herself on the floor again, her face lifted then smashed into the tile floor. Everything went black.

***

Greg took a deep breath to calm the anger in him. He had not expected her to fight back, but he had to admit it turned him on. Usually he entered the home and took his prey while they slept. Lara changed her routine tonight; he inhaled deeply and knew she took a bath. She smelled of lotions and soap, her scent aroused him.

He went into the garage and loaded her limp body into the trunk of her car. Returning inside the house, he wore latex gloves while he packed a bag, grabbed her purse, made a few online charges for airline tickets on her laptop, and made sure to grab her passport.

Greg turned off all the lights, set the alarm code, and got into the driver's seat of Lara's car. Putting it into gear, he started to imagine the fun he would have with her. She was definitely a live one with more energy than he suspected.

Lara had to be special, she would be number thirteen. Most people saw it as a bad sign, an omen, but not Greg. Thirteen would be spectacular, it would feed his hunger. Greg weaved into traffic with ease, returning to his own car at the airport.

He made sure never to drive to his prey's home; the less chance of discovery the better. How else could he have been successful with twelve prior victims? Within moments he would be on the highway heading out of the city, past the suburbs, and finally into farm country.

Greg heard thumping from the back of the car and realized his lucky gal had woken up. He turned on the radio and sang along to the oldies song, a smile on his face.

***

Lara opened her eyes and saw nothing. Her head pounded, and she knew she was in a car trunk. A dip in the road caused the back of the car to bounce and her head hit the side. Pain blossomed and she cried out.

This couldn't be happening; this wasn't how she was going to die. She had things to do, place she still needed to see.

She began hitting the lid of the trunk, then kicking with her feet. After several moments, she forced herself to reign in her emotions.

If she intended to make it out of this alive, she needed to be smart, calm, cool, collected, and strong. Lara needed a plan; the only one at the moment was trying to surprise the kidnapper when he opened the trunk. Being in the lower position put her at a disadvantage, but the umbrella her hands had just come across might be enough of a distraction.

She laid there for what felt like an eternity. Then the car stopped, the engine turned off and she heard footsteps approach the trunk. Lara heard the jangle of keys and gripped the umbrella in her hand.

The keys were inserted into the lock and the click of the mechanism echoed in the small space. As the lid lifted she screamed and jabbed with the umbrella, causing it to open. Lara felt no resistance, then, her pseudo-weapon was yanked out of her hand.

In front of her stood a man masked by shadows. Unable to make out any of his features, she simply stared—attempting to come up with an alternate plan of escape. Screaming might be a good idea, the neighbours would hear something.

Lara opened her mouth and let out the most gut-wrenching howl anyone within hearing distance would have ever heard. As she did so, the faintest hint of a smile could be seen on the shadowed face.

Lara stopped screaming, but kept her mouth open. Seconds later, the kidnapper—obviously a man—pulled out a knife. The glint of moonlight on it made it seem far more threatening than it really was. He didn't need to ask, the hand motioning got her out of the car quickly and unscathed.

He held the knife up and motioned once again, this time to a building off to the left of a well maintained, but dark house. She took a few steps, and wondered if she could make a run for it.

What the hell, why not?

Lara took off, pumping her legs as fast as possible. She didn't dare look behind her, her focus on moving forward. As soon as she had crossed the yard she stopped due to the excruciating pain her feet were in. She fell to her knees, feeling the pain once again.

On the ground, broken glass had been strewn about as a way to stop people who had ideas like hers. Though, if she had shoes she could have made it; she guessed the man didn't allow for mistakes and shoes were removed when he knocked his victims out.

The sound of crunching glass behind her set her heart beating. Would he kill her? Would he be mad and torture her? What was he going to do with her?

Rough hands grabbed her and she felt her arms yanked behind her back, rough rope tying her wrists together. Then she was lifted into the air and tossed over a shoulder. The flow of blood to her head caused her head wound to bleed once more, and the pounding to start again.

Lara lost consciousness after a few minutes, hoping she would awaken and all this would just be a nightmare.

***

Greg could not be happier with his thirteenth victim. Lara, in his possession for only an hour, had already proven herself more worthy than the prior twelve. He watched her cross the ground littered with glass, impressed with how far she got.

As he carried her to what would be her accommodations for what he hoped would be a long time, he could feel the snakes in his stomach slithering with excitement. Greg opened the door to the old barn and the hinges protested loudly. Walking down an unlit hallway, he stopped at a rusty door with no window. He inserted a key and opened the door.

The small room held a mattress, a hole in the ground for when his guests had to relieve themselves, and a ragged blanket. Laying Lara down, he smoothed the hair out of her face. The cut on her forehead was caked with hair and blood.

Greg took a rag out of his back pocket and spit on it. With gentle hands, he cleared away the dried blood and brushed a lock of hair behind her ear. Then he laid the body down on the mouldy smelling mattress and stood up. He looked at her bleeding feet and knees; he didn't tend to those because they were her own doing.

"Lara…see you bright and early tomorrow morning."

Greg left the room and closed the creaky door as quietly as possible. He knew lucky thirteen would need her rest to keep up with him tomorrow. As he walked back to his house the pigs snorted in animalistic delight.

He entered the house and started a fire in the huge stone hearth centered in his living room. Greg took out Lara's bag, passport, and everything else. He then tossed it into the fireplace, watching sparks and smoke rise.

No need to worry about a fire alarm, the house too old to have any. The last thing on his to do list, get rid of her car. Getting into it he drove to the airport and took the exit for long term parking. Choosing a spot on one of the higher levels with no cameras, he parked it and got out, knowing there would be none of his DNA or hair to link him to it.

Afterwards he took a short walk to his own car in the short term parking lot. The drive back to his house over an hour, but he filled the time with ideas of all the wonderful things he planned to do to Lara. She would be so much fun.

The snakes in his stomach rattled in agreement.

***

The smell of mould and rust woke Lara up. Her instincts told her to stand and find a way out of the dingy room. As soon as she put her feet on the ground, she whimpered in pain, falling back onto the damp mattress. She held her left foot close as she rocked back and forth.

Splinters of glass stuck out of her bare feet and knees. Lara took her time pulling out the ones large enough to grab, then braced herself when she had to apply pressure and squeeze the smaller pieces out.

Tears ran down her face, and droplets of blood and water littered the floor in front of her. Lara focused on the task at hand, afterwards, she would deal with an escape plan.

Lara tore the cuffs off of her pyjama bottoms, and used them to wrap her feet. She knew it wouldn't provide much relief, but at the least it might help protect her from infection.

A brief glance around the room let her know finding a way out would be difficult at best. She looked at the walls surrounding her and saw fingernails with bits of flesh still stuck to them hanging off the walls. Messages for others were written in blood—

"Just die, the first chance you get."

"Give up, you'll never escape"

"Beg for death."

Lara got a sick feeling in her stomach as she looked around more, a camera up in the corner confirmed her suspicions. She was about to send a message via her middle finger when a noise outside made her freeze in place.

She knew better than to look for a weapon, this person far too smart to make an error like that. The only way she would survive this would be by using her wits.

***

Greg watched as his new acquisition woke up. He smiled when she fell back on the bed after trying to stand. As she began to clean up her feet he debated what the plan would be for today. Too soon for the chair, perhaps starting with something simple like the table was best.

He nodded as he walked towards the old building. The doors groaned in protest, which he intended. A little bit of oil and the problem would be solved; however, he found when his guests knew he was nearby, or possibly coming for them, it helped build up the fear and tension.

Greg walked past the room heading into the center area. He set up the table, a simple gurney with a thin plastic sheet over it. A small tray off to the side had several menacing looking tools. On the walls, ceiling, and floor blood could be seen spattered in various patterns. The stale smell of copper hung heavily in the air.

With the room ready, Greg casually walked towards Lara's accommodations. He wanted to savour his time with her. He took out the key and inserted it into the lock. This part always the same, they thought they could escape when he opened the door.

He waited, and a second later heard a thud as Lara tried to force the door open and knock him over. The door however opened inwards, a special modification he had made after victim number two. As soon as he heard a small moan of pain he kicked the door open, knife in hand.

Lara stood there and stared at him. She held her shoulder in one hand and favoured her right foot. He motioned her forward with the knife, and smiled when she raised her chin at him in a defiant manner.

"Move or I'll cut a toe off."

"Whatever, you don't scare me, you creep. You get off on scaring women? Can't get it up?" Lara moved closer to the wall.

Greg smiled. "Is this your attempt at baiting me? I'm afraid it won't work; others far better than you have tried and failed. Now move."

"Go to hell, you psycho!" Lara let go of her shoulder and started to run towards him.

"Oh, Lara, you have no idea how happy you're making me."

Greg backhanded her as soon as she came within reach. He hit her with such force her body got knocked into the wall and bounced off. She fell to her knees and held her head. Greg leaned down and lifted her onto the bed.

He put his hand underneath her chin and lifted it up. Greg smiled at her, and with his other hand he made a quick motion. The scream she made causing the snakes in his stomach to hiss.

The toe, tiny and painted a nice shade of pink, let loose one large drop of blood as he held it on front of Lara's face. Greg took out a handkerchief and wrapped it up, putting it in his shirt pocket.

"Now, as I was saying, move."

Lara stood up and did as told. Though the look on her face, the pure hatred meant solely for him, excited him more than she could imagine. He walked behind her watching her limp slightly.

***

Lara squared her shoulders, refusing to let this bastard get to her. She wanted to get out of this alive, which meant she had to be smarter than him. The tip of the knife prodded her forward then to the left.

As she entered the room, she almost cried out in fear. The gurney, the tray of tools she knew served one purpose only, and the plastic tarp were enough to make her waiver for a second in her determination.

Once more, the tip of the knife in her back pushed her forward. Lara thought of the hell of living with an alcoholic father who beat her; the agony of a mother who acted indifferent towards her only child; the loneliness of being teased and isolated for being fat and ugly as a child.

She took all the pain of her past and channelled it into this moment. Lara would use it to fuel her strength and resolve. She would live, she would survive, and she would get out of this alive.

"Take off your robe and get on the table."

The voice behind her was icy cold and in control. Lara hoped he would be the typical unbalanced psycho. Someone she could talk into making a mistake somehow. She took off her robe and let it drop to the floor. Lara looked at the table and purposely avoided the tray of red-stained pain-causing implements next to it.

She turned around to sit on the table and saw the man staring at her. His face still managed to hide in shadows, no features struck her. He moved around her, motioning her legs up onto the table and for her to lie down. No matter where he stood, shadows engulfed him. She imagined he attracted the darkness around him and a shiver crawled up and down her spine.

Lara closed her eyes as he tied her ankles to the table then did the same with her wrists. She tried to be strong, but it proved too hard and a few tears escaped her eyes. She felt his gloved hands wipe them away.

"No need to cry, you're going to be my lucky thirteen. All the others were such disappointments, but already you've proven to be better than them."

Lara watched as the shadow-man put down the knife and walked over to the tray. His back was to her so she couldn't see what he picked up until he turned around, when he did she closed her eyes and focused on not screaming.

***

Greg chose a pair of pliers bent at the tip. Pulling out teeth was one of the easiest things to do, but on the plus side extremely painful and the risk of death miniscule. He started out this way with all of his victims; some passed out from the pain, others simply cried.

He jammed a rubber guard in Lara's mouth so she couldn't clamp down and take a few fingers off in the process. Then, with a smile capable of freezing boiling water, Greg grabbed her lower jaw with his left hand and used his right hand to reach in and remove four of her molars.

The first one caused several tears and a few moans of pain. Greg started to get aroused by her struggles against the restraints. The snakes in his belly needed to be fed. The second tooth caused more tears, and groans.

The last two teeth Greg noticed only caused a few tears. He knew she would make him proud. She channelled the pain, he didn't know where or how, but because of it she would provide him with weeks of entertainment.

***

Lara couldn't control the pain when it first began. After the second tooth got yanked out she forced herself to think of worse things he could be doing. She imagined him repeatedly beating her like her father had. She imagined a mother staring at her with vacant eyes not lifting a hand to help her defenseless daughter. She became so enveloped in her thoughts, she successfully blocked out what her body was currently suffering through.

At some point she must have passed out because she woke in her room, the robe thrown across her. Her foot ached where he had cut off the toe. Lara sat up and wondered how she was going to get out of this hell. Her feet were scratched up and still had glass in them, her face was swollen and sore, and one toe missing.

She felt a drop of water on her hand and mentally chastised herself. *'If you plan on living, better buck up and get with the program!'* The only way to escape as far as she could tell was during the time he opened the door to her room and the walk towards the entryway to the torture room.

The facts as Lara knew them were: the guy had a knife and strength on his side. She couldn't overpower him; and with her feet, she wouldn't be able to outrun him either. She knew she was going to have to get the knife he loved to wave around and kill him with it.

She loathed the idea of taking another life, but from what she had seen, this man wasn't human. Lara would be doing the world a favour. She just had to figure out how to get the knife away from him, then kill him without getting herself killed in the process.

A thought occurred to her. It might work, but would be painful. She sighed knowing it was her only option and lay down on the musty mattress to try to get some rest, knowing she would need it all the strength she could gather soon enough.

***

Four teeth with root intact stood out in stark contrast to the black table they rested on. Next to them a small toe, painted a nice shade of pink. Greg stared at the items, a satisfied smile on his face.

Lara had been extraordinary. Not once did she call out for help, or scream at the top of her lungs. She simply went inward, channelled the pain into something else. He knew how special she was. The little trophies spread out in front of him reminded him how much more fun he would be having in the near future.

In a glass case next to him there were twelve toes, twelve sets of four molars, several nipples floating a brownish fluid, and four fingers. Greg had collected them all in hopes they would be the one, the one to feed his hunger.

Greg took a sip from the glass of wine in front of him. He closed his eyes as the sound of opera in the background washed over him. Tomorrow would be a great day, he would test Lara's psychological limits.

***

Lara heard him enter and waited. The door opened after several minutes ticked by. He stood there, made of nightmares and ghostly spectres. He motioned to her with the knife, but she remained on the mattress.

"Come now, Lara." He tilted his head, but once again any of his features eluded Lara.

"Go to hell, you impotent sicko!"

"Every time you do this it brings a smile to my face." Lara watched as he entered the room, the first part of her plan worked.

She watched with a defiant face as he walked over to her and stopped when he stood three feet away. He spoke in a deep calm voice.

"One last chance to move."

"One more time, go to hell!"

With a motion so swift Lara didn't see it, a booted foot hit her in the lower jaw so hard she felt several teeth rattle. When her head hit the wall behind her she felt herself go limp, then everything went dark.

***

Greg carried the body to a different room. Today Lara would experience *The Chair*. He placed the body in the contraption of his own design and took his time to set it up just right.

Each foot went into a bucket which could be sealed. Each arm was placed along the rest with large metal braces, pins jutting out of them. As he locked her arms into position, little droplets of blood could be seen where the pins stabbed her. The last thing he did was to tie her head into place using a strip of leather with little barbs at the end.

Greg stood back to admire his work when he finished. He sat in the corner on a stool and waited for her to wake.

An hour later Lara moaned and went to move her hand, she became instantly alert at the pain in her arms. Greg watched from the corner as she took in her predicament. Fear, worry, concern, and terror all crossed her face. The snakes in his tummy became so excited that they tried to escape.

"Well, now that you're awake, we can have some fun. What do you say?" Greg stood up and walked over to her, a smile on his face.

***

Lara looked up and saw his face for the first time. He looked like any other guy, average on all counts. Brown hair neatly cut, brown eyes, a tan complexion, and an even white smile. He was the type of guy you passed on the street hundreds of times and never noticed.

"Now today we're going to do something different. What scares you, Lara?"

She snorted. "Like I'd tell you."

"That's the beauty of *The Chair*, you don't have to tell me anything."

Lara watched as the psycho went into a corner and switched on a light. The back wall illuminated, full of aquariums. She looked closer and saw they were full of spiders, snakes, and other things she didn't want to think about. Lara forced herself to look forward, then tried to focus on something else to get through the next round of torture.

Seconds later, he stood in front of her, smile in place. He held three tarantulas in one hand, and a few snakes she couldn't identify in the other. Her heart started to beat rapidly in her chest. Breathing became difficult. Snakes terrified her.

He knelt down and she felt the tickle of the spiders on one of her feet and then a lid snapping shit. A second later she felt snakes slithering over her other foot and heard another lid snapping shut.

"Now Lara, all you have to do for this to stop is pull your arms out of the braces, undo the strap holding your head in place, then reach down and pull your feet out of the buckets. I'll be waiting in the corner." He leaned over and gave her a kiss on the forehead; under other circumstances it would have seemed affectionate.

Lara watched him disappear into the shadows. She tried to ignore the twenty-four hairy legs crawling over one foot, and the slithering occurring around her other one. She moved her eyes enough to see her arms were in some sort of medieval torture device.

She pulled her right arm a bit and felt several jabs of pain. The design worked similar to a shark's mouth; the more you tried to pull out, the more the teeth sank into you. Her heart still beat wildly, and she wondered if the snakes were poisonous, or if the spiders would bite her.

Lara tried to force herself to take a deep breath. She tried to focus on all the crap she had been through in her life, but it was becoming obvious nothing would compare to now.

A snake bit her and she instinctually moved her arms, both of them bleeding now. She knew the monster in the corner was getting off on her pain. Using her rage she pulled her right arm out quarter inch by quarter inch.

The pain was excruciating, but she refused to let it show. Only the slightest of grimaces crossed her face. As soon as her arm was free, she reached over to undo the latch on her left arm, only to realize a lock kept it in place. She started the process again, her flesh ripping slowly as the sharp points dug in deeper with each move.

***

Greg watched her, the snakes in his stomach turning into a den of excited rattlers. Lara's right arm looked like ground beef, and soon her left arm would, too. Thirty minutes later, sweat poured down her face as her arm finally came out.

She sighed in relief, but Greg knew it would be short lived. Those arms, with patches of flesh torn off would have to reach up and undo a knot covered in barbs and broken bits of razor. He sat back and smiled as he watched, his excitement growing.

Lara took a breath and reached up with her right hand, she let out the smallest whimper of pain when her fingers came into contact with the straps. Greg stared at her face closely, the small twinges of pain showing through no matter how hard she tried to hide them.

Lara tried several times to undo the knot, putting her hands in her lap each time she needed a break. Her finger tips ripped up and bleeding. Finally, she undid the knot and let out an audible sigh of relief.

Greg grew more and more impressed with her by the second, already she had gone further than most of his prior victims. Lara reached down with trepidation as she undid the tops of the buckets. She tried not to show her pain, but Greg saw it in her slight hesitation to open the lids. He saw it in the tears that fell against her will, and he saw it clear as day in her eyes.

As she fumbled with the tops Greg approached her. Lara stopped what she was doing and looked up at him. Greg merely smiled and motioned with his hand for her to continue.

"Don't let me stop you, you're doing extraordinarily well."

"You getting off on this? You like to make people suffer?" Her words were raspy and broken; Greg could hear the pain now.

"I like to see people in pain, but what I enjoy most is how much pain people will inflict on themselves to survive."

Lara didn't respond, she reached into the buckets with both hands and whipped two spiders and one snake at Greg. He took a step back, not expecting her to do that. He quickly regained his composure, stood up and gathered the spiders and snake.

As he walked towards the aquariums he felt the other ones hit him on the back. Greg smiled, though Lara couldn't see it. Damn, she was exceptional. Most of his victims didn't get to *The Chair* until the fourth or fifth day, and weren't willing to dislodge their arms until they had been locked in it with various things crawling around their feet for up to a day.

Greg wondered if Lara would be the one…the one to stop him, to feed his hunger for doing these things. He could only hope.

***

Lara sat back in the chair, her chest heaved with the effort she'd just exerted. Glancing down at her hands, then forearms, she cringed. There were shreds of flesh attached by sinew and tendon now. If she made it out of here, the damage would be severe, and the scars would be visible for the rest of her life.

She also knew if she stayed in the musty room any longer her chance of catching an infection rose exponentially. She didn't want to die slowly of some infection, watching pus pockets rise and pop on various injuries. She looked at the back of the creep who put her in here. Lara wanted to stand up and kick his ass, bring her wrath down on him. Unfortunately she had no strength left in her.

He turned around and walked towards her, the knife back in hand.

"Lara, you have exceeded my expectations. In a few days I have something special planned for you. I think you'll like it. For now you rest up, let those nasty cuts heal a bit."

"Really? You're going to let me go?" The laugh which followed her comment let her know she would die here.

Lara decided if she was going to die, and she had no doubt that's what this psycho had in mind for her, it would be on her terms. She would not beg for it, nor ask him to put her out of her misery. When she went down, she would try and take him with her.

"Can you walk?" he asked in such a natural way, as if they were old friends.

What would happen if she said no? Earlier she had refused to walk because she wanted him to come in and remove another toe. She didn't want to lose another one, but the day prior he had put the knife down when he wrapped up the newly severed appendage. Lara had hoped to grab the knife today. Too bad he decided to kick her in the head instead.

Would he carry her, or knock her out again? She stared at him as she internally debated her answer.

"I think I can."

She knew it would be a longshot, but worth it. She lifted her feet out of the buckets and began to stand. She wobbled a bit, and as she hoped he instinctually stuck out a hand to balance her.

Lara made her move; she reached for the knife, grabbing hold of it. The shredded skin on her arms protested the movement, but she bit down on the pain. Then she looked up at him… staring into eyes with no shine or sparkle, eyes which were not the doorway to the soul because he couldn't possibly have one.

He yanked the knife back and slit her hand in the process. She watched as three of her fingers fell to the ground. Lara screamed and pulled her hand in close, blood spurting out everywhere.

She used her other hand to hit him, reaching for the knife again, this time he pulled it away and pushed her away from him. Lara tripped over the buckets and fell back onto the chair, her neck grazing one of the sharp points on the arm braces a deep gash began to spit out frothy blood instantly.

Lara reached up to try and stop the bleeding from her neck, and then looked up at the man in front of her. She would not give him the pleasure of killing her; she would die on her own terms. She let her hand fall away, enjoying the feel of warm blood as it dribbled down her neck and onto her chest.

He must have realized what she planned to do, because he rushed towards her, hand out to stem the flow of blood, or so she thought. His hand began to squeeze tighter and tighter. Blackness seeped in the sides of her vision, and sparks started appearing.

Lara saw him lean in close and smile. "You die when I say you die."

Then she felt the knife stick deep into her stomach, and the hand tighten one last time before everything went black.

***

Greg watched his prey, irritated at the fact they were so sloppy with security codes and alarm codes. Didn't they read the papers? Never use birthdays or anniversaries. He sighed; at least this one might be more of a challenge than unlucky number thirteen.

What a disappointment she had been, he had hoped she was the one. The usual joy he got out of using the saw didn't even cheer him up. The greedy snorts of the pigs as they devoured her did nothing to improve his mood, what a waste of time she had been.

Greg looked back up to his new victim, he would take her soon. Just a few more weeks of following her to get the nerves and tension nice and taught; then he would have his lucky fourteen, maybe she would be the one.

The snakes in his stomach hissed, Greg needed to feed the hunger.

Dear Susan

By: Holly Day

DEAR SUSAN

Susan can't wait to get home from work so she can fondle herself. Sometimes, she can't even wait that long—she takes her lunch break in the restroom at work and spends her entire lunch break just touching herself. "Some people might say I have a problem," she says, spreading wide for the photographer. "I don't think it's a problem at all."

May

Tom first saw the real Susan in the grocery store about a half-mile from his house, purely by accident. He followed her through the store, pushing his shopping cart, trying to get a good look at her face to make sure she really was "his" Susan. He continued following her outside the store, following her in his car until she finally parked outside a small white house with a friendly but uncomplicated garden. The next morning, he followed her to work, keeping a good two or three car lengths between them like they always did in the detective shows.

The casual observer might not suspect that Susan was one of those insatiable types. Tom wouldn't have dreamed it himself if he hadn't seen her picture in the one smutty magazine he allowed himself to get once a month. It came to his mailbox in a brown paper wrapper. Not even the name of the magazine was printed on it…just the return address. Of course, everyone who saw the plain brown envelope knew what it was. Once or twice a year, a small, unlabeled box containing a DVD would appear along with the magazine. Everyone knew what that was, too. Tom didn't even have a VCR in his apartment, however, so the boxes just piled up in the corner of the living room.

Tom hardly recognized Susan from the picture in the magazine. She dressed simply and conservatively for work, wearing either the same dark blue suit jacket with a long skirt, or solid-colored slacks and a blouse. She always wore her straight brown hair up in a tight bun on top of her head, pulled back so severely that the scalp looked taut. She wore no conspicuous jewelry and very little makeup.

In the magazine, however, she wore elbow-length white gloves and a white garter belt with no underwear. Her stockings had dime-sized white lace flowers going up one side, and the material was all sparkly as if it had little pieces of silver wove into the fabric. Her hair hung down her back, the tips caressing the points of her shoulder blades, long and straight and thick like a dark brown curtain. Her green eyes were thickly outlined in black, her lips richly pulsing red back at Tom, who lay quivering and cowering in bed. He could easily imagine Susan alone in the tiny bathroom stall at work, long red fingernails gently scratching the ends of her nipples erect, eyes closed in ecstasy as she leaned back against the wall, legs spread wide over the dark bowl of the toilet, stifling her moans of pleasure with clenched teeth and pursed lips as her fellow employees passed by in the hallway outside the lavatory, oblivious to her orgasm.

June

Susan's office only had a tiny window set in the middle of the wall. It was nearly impossible to see into Susan's office from where Tom sat in his car. She almost never went out for lunch. Every so often, Tom would see her walking briskly from the building to the parking lot, eyes sweeping the lot for her car as if she had forgotten where she had parked, even though she parked in exactly the same place every day. Her flat, sensible shoes made no noise against the black asphalt, quite unlike the slow, sensual echo he imagined the stiletto heels she wore in the magazine would make. She would pull out of the lot carefully, looking both ways before turning out onto the road, returning exactly one-half hour later, often still clutching a partially-eaten hamburger as she dashed back from her car to her office.

Could she actually find time to masturbate every day during her lunch break? Tom wondered, dismissing the hamburger. If so, her appetite for orgasm must be truly tremendous—in fact, it must be virtually impossible to satiate her and her voracious sex drive. For some reason, the thought was comforting to him. He would never have to worry about completely satisfying her in bed, because no human being, man or woman, ever really could.

It wasn't long before he was thinking about the two of them sleeping together. He could feel the silk of her soft flesh beneath his callused fingertips, the way the nylon of her sheer pantyhose snagged on the rough bits of skin that outlined his palms. Her thick, red lips smiled back at him in his dreams, eyes half-closed as she watched him move in and out of her. She was the kind of girl who would insist on seeing him put it in her, would watch intently as his swollen penis disappeared inside of her, only to reappear, again and again, wet.

"Dear Editors," he began. It was the first such letter he had penned to the magazine, even though he had been a faithful subscriber for nearly ten years. *"I truly enjoyed this month's spread on "Susan" (pgs. 25-28), and would like to see more of her in the future. Please pass my admiration on to her. Sincerely, Tom Dunn."* It was not much of a first move, but Tom was a shy man.

The Monday after he posted the letter to the magazine, he made up his mind to meet her. He waited until her car turned the corner into the lot before slowly walking toward his office. He timed it so that as she stepped out of her car, he would be walking right past her. It would all appear to be perfectly accidental.

Susan's matte-blue compact sedan pulled into the lot. Tom suddenly felt butterflies tumbling in his gut as he rehearsed how he would say "hello" and smile at her in the most natural and friendliest of ways. Susan parked her car in the same spot she always did and fussed with her seat belt. Tom veered a little from his straightforward path to avoid walking into the fiberglass bumper of her car. Susan opened her door and stepped out of the car, stretching her long legs way out to avoid stepping into a small puddle of rainwater.

"Good morning," she said, smiling at Tom pleasantly.

Tom grinned back, feeling his mouth stretch wide and his head bob idiotically. "Good morning," he said, several seconds too late. She had already walked past him and into her office.

Tom got and his car and drove straight home, heart beating wildly in his chest. "Good morning," she said again and again in his head, from her picture in the magazine.

July

Tom got a different kind of package in the mail. Inside it was an eight-by-ten glossy of Susan wearing the same outfit she had been wearing in the magazine. She smiled invitingly at Tom from the photograph, legs spread wide and hanging over the arms of the chair she was sitting on, allowing for a full and close-up view of her private parts peeking out of a pair of white crotchless panties. A smeary lipstick kiss puckered in the bottom right corner of the picture, with "XXXOOO Love, Susan" scrawled next to it in red magic marker. A small handwritten note accompanied the photograph:

Dear Tom,

it said.

Thank you for the kind words. It is always nice to hear from my fans. Write me any time. I promise to write back.

Love, Susan

it ended.

Tom framed the photograph in the one nice picture frame he had, and hung it up in his bedroom. He tried hanging it up in various places about the room, trying to find the one truly right place to display a picture of a naked woman, and finally settled on the wall directly in front of his bed. It was autographed to him, and was therefore special enough to be on display and not hidden from prying eyes like the rest of his pornography. He lay back on the bed and stared at Susan through half-closed eyes.

"Good morning," he said aloud, imagining Susan in her simple brown skirt and matching jacket.

Dear Susan,

Thank you for the lovely photograph. I was afraid that you would be like all of the other women in the magazines—aloof, unapproachable—but your quick and personal response to my forwarded letter has proved you to be otherwise. I think you look beautiful both in and out of your underwear.

Love, Tom

August

Susan had been out with a cold or a vacation or *something* for almost a week, and Tom found himself standing like an idiot in the empty space where she parked her car time and again. Finally, one day, he saw her pull into the lot, get out of her car and walked briskly towards her own office, radiant in a simple tan blazer and matching pants. Her hair was pulled back in its customary tight brown bun. She dabbed at her slightly-red nose with a white cloth handkerchief as she walked, as if recovering from some sort of sinus problem.

Her hair wasn't really brown, Tom thought to himself as he watched her cross the parking lot. It was actually a sort of reddish-chestnutty color, rich and thick like oxblood or velvet. Her skin darkened to a subtle olive in parts, especially in the crease of her armpits and the dent of her navel. The lips of her vagina were also faintly outlined in gray, almost as if she had applied makeup to the area. Tom knew every nuance of her body, or at least the front of it. He only had a small magazine glossy of her bending over and grabbing her ankles, so he knew just a few faint details about her backside.

Sometimes, when he saw Susan across the street coming to and from her car, he didn't see her in her standard conservative office attire at all. He saw her pacing, like a giant caged cat, slowly across the parking lot, naked in six-inch high heels, hair down about her shoulders, thick red lips pouting at him from across the street. And sometimes, staring at Susan's photograph from the comfort of his antique canopied bed, he didn't see her high heels and white gloves at all—instead, he saw her deep, serious eyes studying him over a dull navy suit, lips tucked in a tight, bleary I-don't-want-to-be-at-work-right-now smile, long hair pulled back into a demure and asexual bun.

Dear Tom,

You sound like a nice man. I have received quite a few thoughtful letters regarding the spread I did in last month's issue of S--. I am contemplating doing another series of photographs for the magazine—am thinking of you as I consider and practice poses for future issues.

Love, Susan

Tom had never been much for forward women. However, he could forgive as well as expect indiscretion from a woman who claimed to spend her lunch hour masturbating in the company washroom. He was actually surprised that Susan's letters were more like the lines blurted out by the 1-900 girls in the back of the magazines—like "Cum All Over My Melons," and "Watch Me Fuck My Sister," and "I Dare You to Pull My Finger." Susan's correspondences were extremely polite by comparison.

September

The weather grew colder. Susan switched from skirts to dun-colored wool slacks; from thin leather flats to lace-up granny boots. She wore her hair down at the office now, obviously more an attempt to keep her neck warm than to look sexy. Tom liked the change in her. The fact that she grew cold in the fall, just like everyone else did, made her even more human. He managed to walk by her in the morning almost every day now, managed to catch her eye long enough to smile and say "hello" or "good morning." Inside, he was bursting. He wanted desperately to say, "I'm the Tom that's been writing you all the letters," but somehow, the moment never seemed quite right.

October

Susan answered every single letter he sent her. She enclosed autographed photos of herself in various stages of undress, in provocative poses, close-ups of her snatch. The letters were somewhat reserved, however, with only the occasional references to sex or self-gratification. She mentioned the men in her life a couple of times, although she flat-out stated that all her previous relationships were transitional things, something to occupy her time while she figured out what to do with the rest of her life. Her interests included modeling, going to movies, and snuggling up with a good book. She especially liked to read pornography, and she encouraged Tom to write her nasty letters.

Tom tried to comply with her request, but always felt his letters falling short of what he really wanted to say. Finally, after many tries, he came up with:

Dear Susan,

I wish we could get together in person. There is nothing I would rather do than follow you into the lav at work and watch you play with your cunt. I want to help. I want to help you get yourself off. I want to hear you say how good it feels, how goodI feel.

Love, Tom

His hands actually broke into a sweat as he wrote. This was what he had meant to say all along. It felt good to say the truth for once instead of beating around the bush with, "Gee, you're so pretty," and, "I'll bet your hair smells nice." He felt strangely empowered by getting this simple truth off his chest and onto paper. He read his letter over and over to himself before finally signing it and stuffing it into an envelope with a photograph of himself. He had to get this thing out with the mail today, now, before he lost his nerve.

Susan's letter came back faster than he could have expected. Inside the large, flat package was a glossy photograph of Susan sitting with the legs spread wide open over the arms of a chair, wearing only a white garter belt with lace hose and elbow-length gloves. The corner was signed: *"XXXOOO Love, Susan."* It was exactly the same photograph and autograph she had sent him with her very first letter. There was no other correspondence enclosed.

Tom drew the bedroom drapes tightly shut and turned off all the lights. She must have made a mistake. The second eight-by-ten glossy must have been intended for another of Susan's admirers, and the letter that was supposed to go to Tom had been sent to that person by mistake. Surely, if Susan had sent another photograph of herself to Tom, she would have signed it with more than all those "X's" and "O's". Not after all the letters they had already exchanged.

Susan smiled at Tom from across the room, the slick surface of the photo catching and reflecting the barest stream of light coming in through the cracks where the drapes met. Her smile seemed sad today, almost apologetic. Of course it had been a mistake. Tom gathered up with little nerve he had left and picked out some casual clothes to wear. He was going to speak to Susan about this, now, in person, like he should have done in the first place.

It was about noon when he pulled into the parking lot. Susan's car was parked in its usual spot. Tom walked quickly to the door of her building and let himself in. The hallways leading to the private offices were dimly lit and cool. The building was quiet, save for the sound of someone typing in one of the rooms, and the voice of a telephone going faintly unanswered in another.

Tom stood in the lobby and held his breath. He had only a general idea where Susan's office lay. He tiptoed past the nearest office and peeked in. A man's suit jacket hung from the coat rack in the corner. The next office was also empty, but a familiar brown leather purse was slung around the desk chair. Tom closed his eyes and breathed in the faint perfume that still permeated the room, a scent that suited Susan perfectly. He thought he could smell her hair if he breathed in deep enough.

The soft pad of high heels on carpet startled him out of his reverie. He quickly ducked into Susan's office and pressed back against the wall. An older woman in a charcoal business suit walked past the open door, glancing quickly at her watch as she did so. Tom looked at his own watch and realized that this was Susan's customary lunch time. Since she wasn't in her office and her car was still here, there was only one place she could be.

Tom waited until the woman disappeared outside before braving the outside corridor. Halfway down the hall, he found the women's restroom and let himself in. He closed the door quietly behind him, careful not to let the latch click as the lock slid into place. There was only one pair of shoes in the restroom, peeking out from under the far stall. They were flat, black, and sensible. They were Susan's.

"Hello?" he said, walking toward the stall. "Hello, Susan?"

"What the hell?" called back a voice with a pronounced East Coast accent "This is the woman's restroom, *idjit*. Is that Jack? This isn't funny."

"Susan, it's Tom!" The words fairly burst out from between Tom's lips, having been held back for so long. He reached the fall wall and tugged at the door. The cheap latch holding the door close came off of the frame and clattered loudly to the ground. The door swung wide open, revealing an angry Susan pulling her stockings up and her shirt down.

"Who the hell are you?" she snarled, trying to stay in control of the situation.

"I'm Tom!' Tom said again, smiling. "I wrote you the letters, remember? To the magazine. You sent me your picture. You sent me a bunch of pictures." He grinned wickedly at her. "I see you've been masturbating in the lavatory again. Naughty, naughty."

"You're the guy from the parking lot," said Susan, recognition slowly dawning on her face. "I'm sorry, but I have no idea what you're talking about. My name's not Susan, it's Jennifer." She had managed to get her hose up around her waist. "And I never wrote you any letters or sent any pictures."

"You're lying," Tom spat the words out at her, and then said it again in a much softer voice. "You're lying. I've been watching you for months now, watching you from across the street in my car, reading your letters in bed at night, trying to write back to you and let you know exactly how I feel. I wrote to you from my fucking *heart*, do you understand? I wrote to *you*." He felt it all then, all the passion and terror and love and pain that had been building up inside of him since he first saw Susan's picture in his magazine, ever since he recognized her as the woman in the grocery store. She was so close now he could smell her, could smell the last traces of urine in the toilet water, the fresh scent of her sweat overpowering the sweeter scent of her signature perfume. She was so close.

"I'm not Susan," Susan said again in a small voice, trying to stand up. She tried to push her way past Tom, out of the little stall. "I'm Jennifer. Jennifer."

"No." Tom took hold of her arm and pulled her back to the toilet, gently at first, then harder. "No."

"Let go of me." Susan opened her mouth and closed her eyes as if preparing to scream; scream, as loud as she could, as loud as they had taught her in those self-defense classes her employer had paid for…the self-defense classes that had never mentioned what you were supposed to do when confronted by a stranger in a cubical too small to move properly in. Tom slammed his open hand across her face to cover her mouth, hard. Susan fell back against the side of the stall and slid to the ground, staring up at him, terrified.

"Oh, shit," whimpered Tom, stepping back. "I didn't mean…please don't scream. I just wanted to keep you from screaming. I don't want t o hurt you. Please don't scream."

Susan pushed herself up with one hand on the toilet and shouted, "Help! Somebody, help!"

Tom caught her across the face with his palm again, stopping the scream again, pushing Susan hard against the side of the stall again. She fell against the flimsy metal frame and slid down to the ground. Her head lolled and smacked the lip of the toilet seat, hard.

"Now look what you've...damn it." Tom held his breath, listening for footsteps, someone coming to investigate the noise. Susan lay on the ground with her face in the toilet. Blood pinked the white porcelain and turned the blue toilet water purple. "It's okay. I won't hit you again. Please don't scream anymore, okay?" He pulled her up into a sitting position. Her eyes stared dully at him, stared straight at him, just like they did from the picture in his bedroom. "See? Nothing happened. It's okay. Right?"

Her body seemed much heavier than the 110 pounds she claimed to weigh in the magazine interview. He grunted as he lifted her up and set her down on the toilet. He leaned her far back against the wall, legs spread out wide to brace her from slipping off the seat. "It's going to be okay," he assured her. Her hose came off easily, over her slim ankles and tiny feet. Her skirt was a little more difficult, but he was able to manage it with her body slung and balanced over his right shoulder. He unbuttoned her white silk blouse and pulled it off, one arm at a time. He left on her slim, white cotton bra, although it wasn't as sexy as the bra she wore in the photographs.

"Everything's going to be all right," he kept saying, over and over, not sure if he was reassuring her or himself. Everything seemed bright and shiny, as if extra lights had been turned on in the room. His breath sounded ragged and incredibly loud in the quiet of the empty restroom. He crawled backwards on his knees from the woman and gave her a little smile. "See? It's just how you like it. It's just how you said you liked it."

Susan was stripped down to just her bra and cotton underwear, head leaning back against the wall, eyes closed, as if she was asleep or overcome with ecstasy. Her right hand was buried deep inside her underwear; her left was just inside the bra, cupping her breast. He had pulled her hair down over the part of her face that still dripped blood.

Tom looked at his watch. It was almost twelve thirty. People would be coming in from their lunch breaks soon. He stood up and patted Susan on the head, awkwardly. "I'll be seeing you around, all right?" he said, smiling again. He had to get out of here before he passed out. The stall had grown so hot and thick he could barely draw a breath without gagging. The hallway was still empty when he crept out of the bathroom.

He drove straight home. Nobody followed him to his apartment; no one stopped him on the stairs. He slammed the door behind him and stood in his living room, heart pounding, head pounding. It was just a bad dream. It didn't really happen. It couldn't have happened.

The day's mail was piled up on the floor next to his feet. Hidden between Victoria Secrets catalogues and books of money-saving coupons he found another letter from Susan. He opened it with trembling hands, expecting to see a picture of her as he left her, propped up in the bathroom stall, blood running down her face, eyes wide and blank. But no—it was a small one of her wearing a short white skirt and a tiny halter top. He could tell from the photograph that she was wearing no underwear.

Dear Tom,

her letter began,

It is always lovely to hear from you. Last night I had a dream that I was lying out on the beach with my eyes closed and I felt firm, strong hands all over my body. I didn't open my eyes, but I knew it was you from the way you took control of me so quickly, from the way you said my name over and over as I pretended to still be asleep. Your strong, callused hands gently slipped my bathing-suit top off, and I felt soft lips and a wet tongue sliding up between the cleft of my breasts...

Rat Man

By: Nichloas Conley

The Rat Man bit into the dog carcass. He ripped out a handful of tender flesh with his sharp fingernails and gulped it down. The colony of rodents that made up his makeshift family followed his lead, sinking their tiny incisors into the meal with relish.

Several rats scurried up the Rat Man's naked back and jumped into the dog flesh. Dinner would be finished soon. His rodent family would be full from the meal, but his yearning stomach made it clear that he still needed more. For him the night was young.

Suddenly, the Rat Man was stunned by the sound of a human voice calling out from the darkness.

"Hey, is someone out there?"

A man stumbled into the alley, wearing a fancy business suit and carrying a briefcase. The Rat Man hissed at the intruder menacingly. The man walked closer, and then recoiled in horror at the sight of the Rat Man's heavily-scarred naked body, caked in a disgusting mixture of blood and slime that smelled like rotten eggs.

As the human's eyes met his vermin gaze, the Rat Man felt a bizarre sense of familiarity; it'd been a long time since he'd seen another human face to face. This was quickly replaced with animalistic rage. The Rat Man shrieked into the sky, calling out the attention of his rat followers.

The intruder tried to run. He wouldn't escape. The Rat Man shot down the alleyway on all fours to catch up. He jumped onto the man's back. His rage was white hot; his fury had taken on a breathing, heart-pounding life of its own.

The Rat Man thrust his claw-like fingernails into the man's back. The man screamed in pain as he toppled to the ground. This opened the door for the family to join in. The rats swarmed around the man, taking their own little bites out of him. Victoriously, the Rat Man ripped the man's throat out with his teeth.

But then, he spat the piece of flesh out. For some reason he couldn't bring himself to swallow it. Why? It was just another piece of meat, wasn't it? Why couldn't he bring himself eat human meat?

The Rat Man's fragile psyche was suddenly overcome with unfamiliar feelings of guilt and uncertainty. He fell backwards. The taste of the man's fresh, salty blood was still on his tongue. The Rat Man licked his lips and hissed, putting aside this unexpected attack of conscience. If the intruder stood up again, he'd make his next attack.

The human pulled away from all the rats. He choked on the blood drizzling from his throat, and searched through his pocket. He pulled something out: a pistol.

The Rat Man studied the weapon. It seemed so familiar; why were all of these things suddenly so familiar? By the time he remembered how dangerous it was, it was too late.

The pistol went off. The Rat Man shrieked at a sudden sharp, throbbing pain in his thigh. He tried to scramble up from the ground. Blood poured out of the wound.

The rats jumped onto the intruder again, knocking him back to the ground. He shot the pistol again but hit nothing. The Rat Man didn't wait around for him to shoot a third time. He dashed out of the alleyway.

The bullet wound burned intensely. Normally, he'd run for miles without tiring, but tonight he was already worn out. His arms and legs dragged him down like massive bags of sand.

As he ran down the sidewalk, a silver-haired old woman walked directly into his path. The Rat Man tried to hiss a warning at her, but the sound that came through his teeth was little more than a whisper. He collapsed in front of her.

"Oh my God," the old woman gasped.

The Rat Man struggled to pull himself from the ground, but it was too late. His wound became fixed to the sidewalk by dried blood. His eyes closed. He fought unconsciousness away as long as he could but in the end, it overcame him. He passed out at the old woman's feet.

He woke up several hours later in a painfully bright room. He closed his eyes again in horror. Then, slowly, he pried open one eyelid. Once the one eye had adjusted to the light, he opened the other.

The first thing he noticed was that the wound in his thigh was bandaged up. The second thing he noticed was the room itself; it was small, square and white. There was a simple bed in the corner, which he examined with a bit of uncertainty. The walls were padded. Finally, there was a heavy metal door. The Rat Man tried to reach forward and crawl over to it.

Instead, he collapsed face first onto the cold floor.

His arms wouldn't move. They were strapped to him by some kind of strange white garment. He hopelessly tried to claw his way out of it.

As he cried out in misery, a window slid open on the door. The face of a bearded man became visible. This "bearded man" stared at the Rat Man with contempt, then turned around and looked over his shoulder.

"Hey, you're in luck, the guy is actually awake now. Why the hell do you wanna go in there, though?"

There was mumbling in the background. The bearded man listened to it. He eyed his prisoner, and then spoke again.

"Wow, you sure? I dunno what's wrong with him. Guy is a freak."

More mumbling.

"Fine, but talk to him through the window first, would'ya? We can't cover any kinda injuries you get from this guy."

The bearded man stepped away. His face was replaced by that of the same old woman that the Rat Man had stumbled upon earlier. He awkwardly scrambled up to the door.

"Remember me?" she asked in a delicate voice.

The Rat Man's throat produced an embarrassing whining noise. He crumpled up into a ball on the ground. As he lay there whimpering, he dug his fingernails into the cloth of the straitjacket and scratched against it.

"I brought you here to make things okay. You're going to be okay now, you hear? The doctors will fix whatever is wrong with you."

The long, sharp nail of his index finger hit a snag in the fabric. Carefully, he clawed back and forth at the snag.

"They're trying to find out who you are right now. I'm going to be visiting you. Don't ask me why, I mean, I know you don't talk but…I don't know why, I feel like you falling in front of me was some kind of sign that I have to help you. I…well, goodbye. Goodbye for now."

The old woman disappeared. The Rat Man listened to her footsteps clomp away slowly. As his nail finally cut through the fabric and emerged on the other side of it, the face of the bearded man returned.

"Good night, freak."

The window slid shut. He was alone now. He rolled to the corner of the room and curled up behind the bed. With his one exposed claw, he began scratching a small hole in the padded wall.

This was the beginning of his escape plan; he would work on this hole every day, until it was big enough for his entire family of rats to crawl inside. They'd come. He knew they'd come. Eventually, when his family freed him, they would all feast every human in this torturous place.

The Rat Man squealed out in delight. He clawed at the corner of the wall for hours. Finally, he fell asleep.

He was awoken the next morning by the sound of the window sliding open again. The bearded man's face reappeared. He had a sick grin on his yellow teeth.

"Rise and shine! Dr. Brundle would like to speak to you."

The metal door opened. The Rat Man bared his teeth. Normally, he would've readied himself for attack but unfortunately, he was still limited by the straitjacket.

No, he would have to bide his time. For now.

Dr. Brundle stepped into the room. He was a man with broad shoulders, a box-shaped body and beady little eyes. He had a disturbingly blank, unsympathetic expression. What little hair he had left was jet black. A fake grin decorated his face.

"Well hi there, Gregory," he said in a southern accent.

The Rat Man shuddered. That word…Gregory. It seemed so familiar. So scarily familiar. A coldness ran down his hunched over spine.

"Yes, Greg. We found a fingerprint match. We know who you are. You've been gone a long time, haven't you?"

Dr. Brundle grinned.

"We'll just have to run some psychiatric tests to see what made you develop this…this little psychological condition you have, because it's quite strange. In the meantime, I have some shots to administer to you, so things are easier on us and well, easier on you. Don't worry, Gregory, we'll make you better."

The doctor pulled out a long needle and took hold of the Rat Man's bare leg. He screeched. Brundle held him to the ground and injected it.

His body became stiff and heavy. His eyelids sagged. As Dr. Brundle left the room, the Rat Man took advantage of what little consciousness he had left and inched over to the corner of the room. He continued his methodical scratching against the wall.

In his head, he already heard the family's vermin cries. As the drugs knocked him out again, he imagined Dr. Brundle, or the bearded man, or any of those awful humans screaming as they met their deaths. Soon it would come, soon, soon, soon…

The Rat Man woke up much later. As he opened his eyes, Dr. Brundle and several other doctors were in the room. His eyes caught the glimmer of a needle and he growled a warning at them. Brundle plunged the fresh needle into his skin.

This time, he wasn't going to go down without a fight. The Rat Man reeled forward and bit into Brundle's arm. The doctor cried out in pain as blood splashed from the open teeth wounds; a vein had burst. He and the other doctors stepped back fearfully. The bearded man ran into the room and kicked the Rat

Man on the side of head. Again, the Rat Man slipped into unconsciousness, his mouth filled with the surprisingly delicious taste of warm human blood.

Another day passed. This time, as he awoke, the Rat Man held his eyes closed fearfully. First, he sniffed the room around him and listened for sounds. Someone else was in there, watching him. Was it Dr. Brundle? The bearded man?

The Rat Man didn't waste time thinking about it. He snarled, ready to take another bite. However, as soon as he opened his eyes, the rage died down. He sank to the floor, unsure of his next move.

Sitting on the bed was the old woman. She was knitting something with red and green yarn. Slowly, she raised her spectacles and looked at him. She smiled nervously.

"Hello, Gregory."

The Rat Man whimpered. That word again. Why was that word so powerful to him?

"That's your name, isn't it?" she spoke softly. "Gregory. It's a very nice name, I think. But if you don't like that, I can call you something else. Would you prefer that?"

The Rat Man crouched silently. He stared at the elderly woman and tried to piece her words together. It all made sense as much as it didn't make sense.

"Here, if you like a name, nod your head up and down like this," she said, demonstrating, "If you don't like it, shake it back and forth like this. You ready? Nod if you are."

With some trepidation, the Rat Man imitated both gestures she had shown him. He then curled up and began to claw at his little hole on the wall.

"Yes or no?"

The Rat Man resisted. Somewhere in the back of his mind he knew both gestures very well, but using them again would open a floodgate, some kind of barrier that he wanted to keep shut at all costs.

He looked into the old woman's gentle eyes. Her expression convinced him. He nervously nodded his head yes.

"All right. Do you like the name Robert?"

The Rat Man hesitated. He shook his head no.

"John?"

No.

"Well, is it Gregory then?"

Despite all his reservations about "Gregory," the Rat Man found that his automatic reaction was to nod yes.

"Well, Gregory it is, then! Here, Gregory, I brought you some food."

The old woman took out a muffin. Cautiously, Gregory crawled forward. The thing had a sweet scent to it. Again, it seemed familiar. Too familiar. Nevertheless, Gregory reached his head forward and grabbed the muffin in his teeth. He dropped it to the floor and ate it. As he did so, the old woman smiled and continued to knit.

She left shortly afterward but Gregory knew she would come back soon. He licked the muffin crumbs from the ground and glanced over at his hole on the wall. He gave it a single scratch and was content for the day.

Just as he was about to make himself comfortable, the window slid open again.

"It's that time again," the bearded man called out, "Ready, ready, ready!"

Gregory braced himself.

Two guards stepped in. Gregory stayed calm as they took his shoulders and held him down. He could get through this. Dr. Brundle stepped in next, dragging a small wooden chair behind him. The doctor took his seat on it. His lips settled into that disgustingly fake grin. Gregory snickered a little bit at the bandage that was now wrapped around Brundle's arm.

"We're going to try doing this the easy way, Greg."

Gregory didn't reply.

"Right here," Dr. Brundle said, taking out a bottle of pills, "I have some medicine that could help you. It might change the improper chemical balance going on in your brain. If you don't want it, though, we could just continue to inject you every day. So do you want to do this the easy way or the hard way?"

Gregory remained silent. With a head gesture, Dr. Brundle signaled the guards to come to him and then whispered something in one of their ears. The guard seemed uncomfortable with whatever the doctor had said but went ahead and signaled to his partner. Both guards left the room, leaving Brundle and Gregory to themselves.

"Listen, Greg," Brundle whispered, "I know there's more going on inside that dense skull of yours than you like to let on. Let me fix you. You have no idea how much I stand to benefit from this if I fix you. The media will be all over this story. The infamous Rat Man, not only a real person but cured at last! Just play along with the game. We'll be famous."

Gregory snarled, baring his teeth.

"You little…" Brundle started, slanting his eyes, "Oh shut up, you piece of shit. You do what I tell you to, okay? You'll take these fucking pills. You'll play the game I tell you to play."

Gregory clawed at the inside of his straitjacket. Dr. Brundle threw the pills to the ground, expecting Gregory to go for them. He didn't. In response, Dr. Brundle took out another needle, then swooped forward and injected Gregory with it. He then fled from the room.

The next several weeks passed by in the same way. Every day, Dr. Brundle would try to talk to him. It always resulted in new drugs and new injections. Gregory learned not to fight, to simply sit through the torture and let it pass. Occasionally, the bearded man would come in during the middle of the night and slam his head against the wall, for no explainable reason. It was the bearded man that Gregory hated most of all.

But he put up with it. He accepted all of it and lived through it. This was because of one reason. One person. One person and one alone.

"Here, Gregory, I have some more cookies for you," the old woman said.

Gregory brushed his long, ragged hair behind his ears and smiled. He leaned forward to take the cookie in his mouth.

As usual, he dropped it on the floor and ended up licking up the crumbs.

The old woman was still knitting something out of green and red yarn. It had grown bigger and bigger as the weeks went by. Gregory looked up at her from the ground, eyes wide, ready for another cookie.

"No," she said, "This time, we need to learn something new. You need to ask for it."

Gregory fell back. He smiled. When his smile didn't work, he whimpered.

"Say 'please,' Gregory. Then you'll get the next cookie."

"Pl…Pl…" Gregory stopped. He was surprised as she was at how fast the first two letters had come from his mouth. He hadn't even thought his throat was capable of it. How could a rat like him speak in human tongue?

"Yes, that's it," she said.

"Pl…Pl…Plea…" Gregory paused, "P-Please."

She gave him the cookie. He gobbled it up, watching her knitting fingers with fascination. Carefully, Gregory laid his head down on her leg. She was warm. The way she cared about him filled him not with bloodlust, not with craving…but with something else.

Something different.

A few days later, Gregory was reminiscing about the warmth of the old woman's leg as he lay alone on the ground of the cell, clawing again at his little hole in the wall. It had gotten much deeper as time went on, to the point where it was surprising no one had discovered it yet. He didn't know why he still clawed at it anymore, though. He'd forgotten his prior motivation.

The sound of footsteps in the hallway made him shiver. The bearded man was coming, which meant either Dr. Brundle was going to inject him or he was about to be beat up again. He couldn't decide which would be worse.

Then he heard something else. Soft squeals coming from the hole in the wall. He could've sworn he'd heard a shuffling of tiny little feet. Was he imagining things?

The door of the cell was thrown open. Two guards entered, as usual. This time, they threw Gregory onto his bed. A bed he'd never slept on. They strapped him on top of it as tightly as they could until he was unable to move.

Dr. Brundle walked up to him. He looked down on Gregory and smiled. He pulled out a small needle filled with an unfamiliar blue fluid.

"It's time for a change of pace, Greg. We're going to test your psychological limits. This will freeze your body; put you into an induced coma until we can figure out the proper way to fix you. You ready for that?"

The doctor lowered the needle. Gregory panicked. He desperately struggled to free himself from his bonds. He finally pulled his leg free and kicked the needle out of the doctor's hand.

Dr. Brundle cursed wildly. His hand was scratched but not quite to the point of bleeding. He backhanded Gregory across the face and called for "William," the bearded man, to come do the procedure for him.

Gregory again heard squealing inside the walls. His ears perked up. They were close now, closer than ever before…

The bearded man elbowed Gregory in the nose. Snot and blood dribbled down his face. The bearded man then took out a fresh needle.

"Where do I stick it, doctor?"

"Right here," Brundle said, pointing at the vein.

There was a quiet tiny hissing sound, somewhere under the bed. The guards, doctor and the bearded man looked around with some confusion, and then returned to the procedure. Dirty rodent feet dashed up the side of the bed and climbed down Gregory's leg. The smell of rotten food, corpses and leftovers greeted his nostrils. He shuddered.

He started remembering who he was. Who he had always been. And that person had never been named Gregory, now had he? No, he had a different name…

Several more rats clawed their way up the side of the bed and quickly nibbled through the straps holding Gregory down. Other rats gnawed through the straitjacket that had kept him imprisoned all this time.

The needle was inches away from Gregory's skin. If his rat family couldn't chew through his bonds fast enough, it was all over.

"Wait," Dr. Brundle said, stopping the bearded man, "did you hear something?"

"Um…"

A mass of dark, black-eyed rats exploded out of the hole in the wall, scampering across the floor of the cell. There were hundreds of them, one swarm arriving after another. They surrounded the men in the room.

The rats scrambled up Dr. Brundle's leg. He anxiously pulled his pants off and jumped onto Gregory's bed to get away from them. His coworkers were also panicking. Gregory was no longer strapped to his bed.

Dr. Brundle whipped his head around. Gregory was standing behind him. He'd torn his straitjacket off. His long, lanky, naked body was hunched over. His eyes appeared red with anger.

The Rat Man spread his claws and screeched.

Dr. Brundle fell off the bed. He plunged to the floor. The swarm of rats took advantage of this by jumping on top of him.

The Rat Man hissed and stepped on top of Dr. Brundle. He sunk his claws into Brundle's torso and punctured his stomach. The Rat Man took a vicious bite out of the doctor's flesh, followed by another. His rat family joined in, all taking their own sharp little nibbles. Dr. Brundle screamed out in horror and the Rat Man walked away.

He surveyed the scene before him. The two guards were struggling with rats; they'd already been defeated. The bearded man had escaped. That didn't matter. His scent could be followed.

The Rat Man grabbed both guards by the ankles and pulled them to the ground. He scratched their faces and left them to his rat family. He followed the trail of the bearded man.

As it turned out, it wasn't a long trail to follow.

"Hold it right there, freak!" the bearded man yelled angrily, "If you think I'm gonna hold back on gunning down your fucked up, abused little ass for even a second, you got another thing coming!"

The bearded man was holding a pistol; it reminded him of the man in the alleyway. The Rat Man had learned from his mistakes.

He swooped down and slid across the floor, grabbing the bearded man by the knees and knocking him down. The pistol went off several times but the bullets hit nothing but ceiling. The Rat Man scrambled on top of "William" and ripped the majority of the man's hair and beard out with his teeth.

The formerly-bearded man urgently tried to get a better grip on his pistol. The Rat Man grabbed the barrel and threw the pistol away like a piece of trash. He dug his fingernails into William's hand until he screamed and begged for him to let go.

There was a pause, as the two men looked into each other's eyes with pure hatred. William spat in the Rat Man's face.

"Fuck you."

The Rat Man sank his sharp nails into the bearded man's eyes, popping them like soft grapes and tearing into the man's brain. His rat family squealed in amusement and began to feast. One rat scuttled into his left eye socket.

The Rat Man screeched out victoriously and jumped away from the body. Then, he heard another person walking up behind him. Grinning madly and covered in a thick layer of blood, he tackled his new victim to the floor.

The Rat Man raised his claws, fully prepared to slash the victim's face into ribbons. She quickly blocked his attack with a large sweater. He stopped; the sweater was composed of yarn;

green and red yarn, to be exact. Horrified, the Rat Man fell backwards.

The sweater had the name “Gregory” emblazoned on the front of it.

The Rat Man curled up into a fetal position as the old woman pulled herself to her feet. He moaned in misery. The blood slathered across his body now smelled sickening.

He was brought out of his gloom by the sound of the elderly woman screaming again. His rat family was climbing onto her, taking little bites from her flesh. They had betrayed him. The Rat Man hissed.

He grabbed one of them by the tail and threw it down the hallway like a baseball where its guts splattered across the wall. He tore all of rats from the old woman’s body with several thrashing gestures. She was still breathing. Good.

More rats climbed onto her; like the others, they were swatted away. The Rat Man went on a killing rampage, stamping out his old rat family. After a few minutes of this, they fled. Soon, they were all gone. The Rat Man whimpered quietly. All that remained was him, the old woman, four human corpses and hundreds of dead rats.

The old woman, still shaking, tapped him on the shoulder. The Rat Man was startled by the gesture. She handed him the red and green sweater. If he were not still horrified, the Rat Man would have smiled.

He turned down the kind gesture. He reached over to the bearded man’s corpse and took his pistol off the ground. He handed it to her and pointed it at himself.

“No,” she whispered. “No, Gregory. Put the sweater on, please. I made it for you.”

She took the pistol from him and dropped it on the ground. She handed him the sweater again. Finally, he accepted it and she helped him put it on. He looked down at himself in the sweater. Again, he almost smiled.

“I-I…” the Rat Man whispered, “I’m sorry.”

“I know.”

The Rat Man lowered his head and crept away from her. He picked up the bearded man's pistol again. His hand was shaking. His throat closed up in fear. He stuck the pistol inside his mouth and put his finger on the trigger.

Gregory shot himself.

Eighteen

By: Joseph Schwartz

The sun broke the horizon, its golden focus ready to light and heat the cold, wet grass until dry to the touch. I've begun to notice these things now that it is too late to appreciate them. I guess that's how it always is. People think they got all the time in the world.

A key was unnecessary to open my trunk, but I still fumbled for it. All that pointless frustration when there wasn't a lock even if I had found a key. The Cadillac's emblem shone magnificent against the pearl white paint. When the sunshine hits it, I won't be able to look at it directly without sunglasses. Now, in the pre-dawn, it is a great whale's ghost that lies in wait to be discovered.

I used to not believe in ghosts when I was a younger man. Then, inevitably as all things in life do, something changed. The dead cling to you. Stick to you with Super-Glue strength and linger. I'm not talking about death in terms such as the family dog or your Great Aunt Edna. You'll get another dog or whatnot, and after a proper period, Auntie Edna will be nothing more than a dust-covered memory. No, pal, I'm talking about the ones I've killed.

I took the golf club bag by the built in handle. It seemed to get heavier every time I picked it up. The truth was that the thing in my stomach was growing with a splendid efficiency. *It is akin to what women must feel,* I thought. The anticipation of birth, a countdown to something millions of others had done, but an experience theirs alone to possess for a little while. This thing in my stomach was not a bringer of life…but death. The medicines for pain worked well and were exquisite with alcohol. I couldn't have picked a better way to check out.

I held up a five and a Latino boy about sixteen jogged over. With my money in his hand he smiled as he carried my bag. He had flawless white teeth that were beautiful against his cream colored brown skin. He reminded me of my first.

Your first is either by accident or by order. I had flatfeet so it wasn't Uncle Sam who popped my cherry.

My buddy Jonah was an amicable guy with a real bitch of a wife. She nagged him every minute and chastised his every action despite his obvious devotion to her. He worshipped the ground she walked on, and she deliberately shit in his face. Didn't matter much to me; I wasn't married to her. If Jonah could stand her abuse, then he could have his precious Nancy.

It was a cool Sunday afternoon when I went over to Jonah's place. Nancy was alone. Jonah had gone to help his brother move and wouldn't be back for hours. I was about to leave when she told me next time I felt so inclined to drop by, I'd better call. Not an unreasonable request. It was how she talked to me that flipped my switch. I looked at her in disbelief. With that snide, contemptuous grin she saved for her dog Jonah, she dispelled any doubts I had toward her.

"You fucking heard me," Nancy said. Almost funny in hindsight that they were the last words she ever spoke. I lunged for her throat with both hands. Instantly, I brought Nancy to her knees. My grasp was an adrenaline charged vice-grip.

After I was sure she was quite dead, I opened the fridge and drank two beers, moreso to calm down than to quench my thirst. After I pulled my car into the garage attached to the house, I dumped Nancy's dead ass into the trunk. Later that night, I dropped her into an infinite void called the Meramec River. Nobody ever found her.

I realized I had begun to squint and put on my sunglasses. The dark black lenses allowed me to see as clearly as if I were inside. Sancho or Pedro or whatever-the-hell-his name-was said he knew how to caddy for another ten. Fine by me. I gave him a twenty and told him if he did a *bueno* job, he could keep the over as his tip.

The kid drove me to the first tee in an electric golf cart. As I slowly stretched my back, hips, and calves, Juanito teed up my ball dead center between the markers. In his hand he held my

3-wood ready. It was a measly three hundred-yard par four. My new best friend's choice was excellent. A good scratch golfer could probably score a birdie. If I shot par or a bogey that would be a nice start.

As I took the club and swung away, the ball quickly sliced to the right. I was so pissed I could have bitten through nails. Of all the goddamned terrible breaks. I would be lucky to make double bogey from such a horrendous mistake.

I tossed my club back toward Jose. He had a good eye and drove me within a stones throw of my wayward ball. The Elm tree had stopped its forward progress but that did little to soothe my self-loathing. Last time I had been this angry was closing time at a little podunk-shit bar called 'The Tinker's Dam.'

A giant redneck by the name of Johnny Ray with a melon shaped beer gut and sweat stained cowboy hat made for me the second he came through the door. Jesus, it was like being back in high school. The asshole had a comment on everything from the presumed size of my dick to my 'faggot' drink. I tried to be cool and roll with the punches. It's when that overgrown moron poured the beer I bought him over my head that I quietly walked outside.

It took three hours for the ignorant son-of-a-bitch to come stumbling out. I watched as he staggered to his oversized four-by-four import truck (fucking hypocrite!) and pulled out of the gravel parking lot. When he parked under the lean-to that connected to his single-wide trailer, Johnny Ray never saw me get out of my car with the tire iron. Before the jack-off could say 'boo' I caved his fucking skull in. I didn't stop until he lay motionless in a puddle of his own piss, blood, and brains.

I swung my pitching wedge hard as I had swung that tire iron so long ago. The ball popped high up into the air. As it landed an impressive fifty feet safely on to the fairway, I remembered how Johnny Ray's eyeball had burst with my first strike. Not many things in life are simultaneously that pleasant and violent.

My good mood enhanced my swing. With a relaxed follow through, I put the ball twelve feet from the flag with my five iron.

The kid was next to me in an instant. "Nice one, Señor," he said as he took my club and drove me up to the green.

I misjudged my speed on the putt and came up short. Another par shot to hell. If bogey was the name of the game I could have went pro twenty years ago.

The business of killing is quite different than the passion of murder. No different than a duffer like me who whacks balls versus a pro like the Golden Bear. In my hands these bent hammers could do as much harm as good. For all the polish and chrome, they're nothing more than primitive caveman tools. Give Fat Jack my bag and he would destroy this course. As a hobby though, I like the game. That's why I always play alone. Competition, be it friendly or not, would spoil the joy it brings me.

The kid teed my ball up for me again. Done he came back to the cart and again pulled my three wood. I had to give him credit, he knew his clubs. The second hole was a par four with a wicked dogleg in the middle meant to grind down your confidence. I swung for the fences and connected with that perfect 'ping' sound every golfer yearns to hear as titanium and rubber explode. The ball lofted straight and high. It was by far one of my best tee shots ever.

Not unlike many small businessmen, my first professional job came from a family member. My father-in-law was at his wits end with his second wife's daughter. She was a junkie who had cost him a heap on bail, lawyers, and most especially the raising, clothing, and shelter of her five-year-old son. The boy was smart and handsome and scared shitless of his mother. I could personally recall a broken arm, a broken ankle, a black eye, and a broken rib the boy had already suffered. The idea that any kid got hurt that much seemed abnormal to me, but nobody was asking for my opinion, so I left it alone.

That is until one night my father-in-law and I were watching the game and drinking too many beers. He was edgy. When he didn't so much as budge when the Blues scored a last second goal that forced the Blackhawks into OT, is when I knew he had troubles.

Jenny, his stepdaughter had threatened him. Told him she would do as she pleased, when and with whom she wanted. If he so much as lifted a finger to stop her she would take her kid, split, and it would be a cold day in hell before he ever saw the boy again. The old man said if there was a way that he could get away with it, he'd kill the rotten little bitch.

My father-in-law was a good man. A stern and grumpy asshole if there ever was one, real old-school, but fair. When my wife and I needed a down for our house, he gave us two grand in cash with nothing more than a handshake. The day our first son was born he co-signed the loan on a new mini-van for us, then insisted he pay the tax, title, and license fees. "A gift for the baby," he said.

I told him if he was serious, there was a way. He didn't say a word. I thought he was trying to forget what I had said the way you try to ignore a pungent fart in an elevator. When the Blues lost, he turned to me and said, "Okay." He further explained to do whatever I had to do, but if it went bad, if the cops tapped me, I had to promise to keep his name out of it. I promised.

Jenny had a real scumbag of a boyfriend that was about an inch shorter than me. In two months I deliberately gained thirty-five pounds to match his fat, cheeseburger-engorged pouch. I grew my beard in the exact same style he wore his, that long Vandyke style popular among potheads. By the time Halloween rolled around, you couldn't tell us apart at fifty paces if we stood side by side.

It was around two in the morning. I had followed them home from a bar and parked down the block. My father-in-law had taken his wife and Jenny's boy on a spontaneous trip to Branson. I figured this shit could take all week, but when that greasy mongrel came out fifteen minutes later and fired up his shit-mobile, I couldn't believe my good luck.

I kept to the shadows until I was at the door. Underneath the porchlight when I could have been seen it would have been but for the briefest of moments. The second I stepped inside through the unlocked front door the strong odor of marijuana hit me. And sex.

I found Jenny in my father-in-law's bed smoking a joint. There wasn't shit for light except candles. The sight of her alone pissed me off. Her deliberate pollution to my father-in-law's inner sanctum gave me all the fuel I needed to complete my work. I was damn near standing next to the bed and she still didn't recognize me. "Where's the fucking tequila?" she asked in an exhale of pot smoke.

"You stupid bitch," I said as I raised the knife high above her. She screamed for less than a second before I jammed the eight-inch double-sided blade downward through the crown of her skull. The look on her face was priceless as her blood ran hot over my gloved hand. I left the knife in her wide-eyed, silent corpse and used her discarded jeans to wipe my hands.

Under the driver seat I had stashed an industrial trash bag that I shoved my gloves, black rain slicker, and shoes inside. After I tied it off in bunny-ears fashion, I threw the sack on to the passenger seat, got behind the wheel, and waited.

When the dufus came back an hour later, I pulled away with my lights off until I came out to the main road. Unfortunately for him, his story about going to the store didn't wash with the DA. He got fifty-to-life less than a year later, right about the time my father-in-law was awarded full custody of his step-grandson.

The sudden stop of the golf cart brought me back to the task at hand. I had to have driven the ball at least two hundred yards. Not bad for a guy with a stomach cancer. I refused chemo and radiation without much thought. My doctor considered it stupid, and unless I reconsidered his recommendation for treatment, he would no longer see me. I shook his hand and wished him well. With as much death as I've seen in my time, I felt it pointless to fight that which was inevitable.

A burning pain like I swallowed a hot piece of coal seared in the pit of my stomach. The suddenness caught me off guard, but the pain was becoming a bit more familiar with each attack. It would pass in a minute or two. Until then, I would have to grit my teeth.

The kid rushed to me, his mouth ablaze with words like 'emergencia' and 'medico.' I told him to cut it out. He was my caddy not my nurse. I must have yelled by the way he suddenly shut up and began to examine his feet.

"Why don't you hit this one?" I asked him. He already had my four iron in his hand, but seemed intimidated by my offer. "Seriously, go ahead, kid. I need a break."

He approached the ball slowly, looking back once over his shoulder at me. I assured the kid with the old thumbs up that all was well. His address over the ball was nothing write home to mom about, but his swing was wonderful. Jesus, to be able to hit with that much power was enough to make me forget the pain. It was a goddamn shame to see it pull left and drop in the sand. Still, it was an easy punch out. With any luck, between the two of us, we could make par.

"Nice shot, Zorro."

"Diego," he said as he put the club back in my bag.

"Come again?" I asked knowing full well that the kid had put the kabosh on my ass. It was easy enough to correct me behind my back, it was another to look me in the eye and do it.

"*Me llamo, Diego*," he told me as he sat behind the steering wheel. He paused and turned to me. In a voice low with determination he asked, "*Si*?"

The pain in my gut had passed and I couldn't help but smile. "Okay, Diego," I said, "Let's play some fuckin' golf."

Diego was a good kid. There was no reason to bust his balls. Besides, if the situation was reversed, I don't think I would have been so polite. The whole 'no habla Englas' song-and-dance was a smokescreen. As we gently rocked and bounced in the golf cart to the sand trap I couldn't have gave a damn. He was an excellent caddy and handy with a club. I had gotten much less help over the years from close friends.

I once did a job on a golf course. A real hotheaded jackass who could drown more balls in an afternoon than most guys did in a season. Manly Stanley wore lots of jewelry and smoked a huge cigar. I could hear him swear and laugh a mile away. It was no wonder to me how this guy could have pissed somebody off bad enough to want him dead.

He was playing in a foursome with three carbon-copy minions. If he downed a beer, they did. When he made a joke they laughed as if the re-animated corpse of Richard Pryor told it. The guy's swing had a hook that surgery couldn't correct. Every time he swung, his pals congratulated him with 'good shot.' After watching them play the front nine, I was certain the others were much better than Manly Stanley, but were holding back. Why these assholes worshipped an even bigger asshole wasn't a mystery to me. Birds of a feather and all. Besides, even assholes needed friends.

After a pitiful eleven shots, Manly Stanley finally cupped his ball. Not bad…a mere seven above par. Why loaded pricks like him had such an indifference for a sport handed down by kings was a mystery to me? From what I heard, this Jew treated everything like this. The world was his playground and all of us his inconvenient playmates. I had meet and known guys like his faux-majesty before. They were nothing but spoiled, delusional children wearing the clothes of men.

At the turn, they drunkenly drove their carts in serpentine designs to the brickhouse. Public courses, if you were lucky, had a couple porta-johns dispersed randomly over eighteen holes. Private clubs like this one had real bathrooms that were bigger than a two-bedroom apartment. You had to love a place that didn't discriminate against anyone due to race, color, or religious organization. The sole color considered here was green, and if you didn't already have a heap to burn, you were never going to see the inside of this place except as an employee.

I went inside a few seconds ahead of Manly Stanley's group and sat down in the first of four shitters. I could easily see the urinals through a slit where the jamb of the door didn't quite meet the frame. My guy was half-shitfaced already as he pissed everywhere but inside the wide open porcelain mouth. The other guys were laughing as they shook and flushed. Manly Stanley rocked like a sailor riding a dinghy. I saw it coming before his friends. In a sloppy one hundred eighty-degree turn, Manly Stanley thrust himself toward the handicapped stall with all the strength he could muster. A trail of beer and beef jerky vomit hit the floor and drenched his polo shirt before he made it.

I don't know if he heard his buddies leave, one saying they would wait for him outside, but I couldn't have been happier. Certain Moe, Larry, and Curly were outside again, I slid back the sliver handled lock and quickly went to where Manly Stanley was doubled over and blowing considerable chunks.

There was about a dozen ways I could off this idiot; everything from poison to an old fashioned bullet between the eyes. This, however, was as good as it got. Manly Stanley was in between heaves. As soon as he started his next upchuck I grabbed him by his sweaty, curly hair, and slammed his head as hard as I could against the rim. Manly Stanley went limp at once. I held his head face down in the bile-polluted water. After he kicked once or twice, it was over. By my watch it had been about two minutes. A quick check with my fingers against his carotid artery confirmed it. Manly Stanley was done. A coroner would later hypothesize that Mr. Siegel had probably tried to stand, slipped, knocked himself out, and inadvertently drowned due to the accident.

It occurred to his buddies while I was casually walking out that maybe they should check on their beloved leader. As they went in I took the keys from their carts and peacefully drove mine back to the parking lot. By the time any of the three jerks were able to make it back to the clubhouse on foot I was gone.

I drove the speed limit back home without a care in the world. Middle-class suburbia no more suspected that I wasn't the independent corporate consultant I pretended to be than the honest-to-God hitman I was.

My neighbor Bob was washing his custom '69 Chevelle when I pulled into my driveway. In his friendly, jovial manner he came over as I stepped out of my car. I shook his soapy, wet hand and realized mine was still slightly pruned. "How was work?" he asked with a grin.

With the same knowing smile, I answered, "You know how it is. Another boring day at the office." We casually laughed at our pathetic banter, said we should have a beer together later, then I went inside and took a nap. Christ, I was tired.

A courier delivered a check two days later. It was made out to 'American Consultants' the phony name I had given my business. As long as my taxes were paid regular, there was nothing suspicious about how I made my money. To this day I don't know what the fuck a consultant actually does, but it's assumed they make embarrassing amount of money to do it.

I chopped the ball free from the white sand bunker and landed it about six feet from the flag. The lie was all uphill and had an invisible slant that could leave the clubhouse pro dangling on the lip. This time I faked a stomach cramp and let my new golf buddy Diego putt. Son-of-a-bitch if he didn't make it look easy. I envied his natural ability. A kid like him could go pro with a little help.

I finished the front nine with considerable help from Diego. It was on the tenth hole that I let him tee off. The hole was vicious par five that was rife with thorny brush to left and a dense mongrel forest to the right. Both sides were automatic out-of-bounds. There was no way in hell, that if you could find your ball in the deciduous mess, you could hit out of it. It was by far cheaper to take the penalty stroke than try. If you were able to avoid that, there was the lake. It cut the middle in half. Most times, I would try to lay up and hit it short. If I knew one thing in life it was when to play it safe. I didn't have to be a mind reader to see Diego had no such ambition. The kid had already proven to me that he had the touch when it came to my other clubs and irons, now I was curious if he had it with Big Bertha, my illegal USGA driver, and most expensive stick in my bag.

The kid was nervous, but excited, too. Even though this was a public course, it had regulars. A kid like him could probably make more in a week hustling hacks than his buddies did in a month busting their asses mowing grass.

Most of the cheap knuckleheads here though would have only used Diego to carry clubs and a porta-cooler with iced-down beers. The kid was built for it. Diego's shoulders were wide and strong with thick knotty triceps that bumped out below. His chest was square with a torso that came to a perfect V shape into his hips. His thighs were oversized with muscle and his hairless calves bloomed out from his cargo shorts thick with veins. The kid must have spent every day he could here carrying bags for chump change. It was a weird form of strength training but it worked. Any port in a storm I guess.

The air surrendered in a torturous whine as Diego took the business end of my driver down from high noon to six o'clock. The ball launched like a guided missile. I watched in awe as the white dot sailed straight. Diego's eyes never left the tee. There was no doubt he hit it perfectly straight, but too god-damned hard.

When the kid did look up, the damndest thing happened. The ball gracefully curved thirty degrees to the left. It felt so surreal. I had a moment of doubt that I had possibly become delusional. Then I saw the kid's cocky smile. The ball landed with a soft bounce and in the safety of the left quarter. Christ, any competent player from that point could make par. The kid—regardless of his age—knew every bump and turn this place held.

If I played here six times a year, that was a lot. I suspected Diego was here everyday open or closed. Probably had a set of clubs scrounged from garage sales, thrift stores, and occasionally, outright theft. Sweet Jesus, what this kid could do if he had a real manager and a little money was limitless.

I walked over to Diego and held out my hand. The kid immediately handed over my driver and started that 'looking at his shoes shit' again. I wasn't mad at him, but I'm sure that's what he expected. No man, in light of age, intelligence, or station accepts it when another makes him look like an asshole with his own gear. Even at Diego's tender age—and me at the end of my life—he intuitively knew this rule, as did every man since the dawn of time. When I put my hand on Diego's shoulder he looked up. Maybe he expected a smack to the head or to be fired. Either was what I would have done ten years ago.

I said, "Nice draw, kid."

We walked back to the cart, my hand still on his shoulder and him with a smile like he was about to get laid by the head cheerleader. From a distance we could've been a father and son silently bonding over the game that surpassed all the money, speeches, and bad advice each generation coveted. I let Diego play the entire hole. He had earned it.

There was a job that haunted me. Diego had reminded me of it. His youthful exuberance and natural skill for the game were precarious things. Fate, destiny, chance, God's divine will, whatever the hell you called it, had a funny way of fucking with a person's best laid plans.

I used to be a drinker. Not a Joe-six-pack, but more like a drink-twenty-beers-throw-up-and-repeat kind of guy. My main drink near the end (not that I wouldn't drink anything with alcohol to excess except Listerine) was Canadian whiskey. I drank rivers of the shit. The only thing that I would dare to give myself credit for is that I never did a job under the influence. Work always came first. My old man, a guy who never met a drink he didn't like, was the same way. As long as the bills were paid, my Mom never would've said shit if she had a mouthful.

He was always a faithful provider. My sister and I had what we needed and more. If he wanted six or seven cold ones after work everyday and thirty or forty on the weekend, so what. He worked his ass off, didn't fuck around on the old lady, and never laid a hand on us kids. It wasn't until he retired that he became what could only be classified as a pathetic drunk.

One night, smashed on boilermakers, he crashed his precious Buick headfirst into a concrete light pole three blocks from the house. The cops said he was doing at least eighty and, of course, wasn't wearing his seat belt. What was left of him we buried in a closed casket funeral.

How most men viewed mountains, I saw the biggest bottles on the shelf. A challenge to be conquered not savored or enjoyed. So many mornings I would take a moral and actual inventory to my misspent evening. A sense of pride and shame would greet me as there wouldn't be two-fingers of the brown liquor left to be had. Did it stop me? Hell no. Did it slow me down? Sometimes. More often than not, I would trade whiskey for pot. Similar in potency, but void the nasty hangover. The best was when I mixed the two drugs. Jesus, if there was a more stupid thing to do to myself I haven't found it.

It was the week of a big job. My wife had taken the kids to Florida to visit her mother. We agreed that after I had finished my business, I would follow them down to shoot the works. The beach, Disneyworld, sailing, whatever. Nothing but fun in the sun.

I parked a mile away in a still coming-of-age subdivision. Dressed in black from head to toe, I walked to the guy's house and waited. The place was a McMansion in a neighborhood of look-a-likes. He was the brain trust of some red-hot Internet thing that would eventually make him rich. His biggest mistake was not keeping his intellect to himself.

His partner in this thing was about done. Sales to the website were practically automatic now. There was no more need to court big companies to invest. They had paid everything back, and given a couple more years, theirs would be one of those super-user sites like Google or Yahoo that people simply could not live without. That's when the genius predicted upwards of an eight-figure buy-out. He had, in advance, generously offered an eighty-twenty split to the man who had hired me.

At around nine on the third night he showed. I watched as he pulled into his garage and the door automatically descended. After ten minutes, I heard the TV go on. The guy was getting comfortable, settling down, maybe about to crack open a beer. I rang the bell. It didn't surprise me that a guy so smart would just open the fucking door without a second thought. Before he had it half swung to himself, I bum rushed it full strength with my shoulder. The solid wood door knocked him flat on his back. Before he had a chance to think about it, I kicked the dumb bastard in the balls. Satisfied he wasn't about to jump up to call the cops or go hide in some part of the house, I gently closed the door.

His face was a shade of purple as he gasped for air. I was sure he wouldn't die from it, but goddamned did it had to have hurt. I sat across his chest and pulled out a syringe from the inside pocket of my leather bomber jacket. The salesman said it had to look natural, no funny business. Any suspicion of foul play would tie the company assets into a receivership and that would fuck everything up. My challenge was how to kill the goose and preserve the golden egg. I lifted the genius' arm and injected a 10cc needle filled with pure liquid potassium into his armpit. Ten minutes later he was dead.

I left the TV on and took the keys to his car. If a neighbor saw his Volvo pulling out at this time of night with the lights still on, they would presume he had gone out to run some bullshit errand. Nothing to worry about, or fuck me, and call the police. For these rich cocksuckers they would be here at the speed of light. When I used the clicker tucked above the visor to close the garage, not so much as a stray dog saw me leave.

I parked his car about twenty feet from mine. In the darkness, it was impossible to see clearly ten feet away much less from a hundred yards. I removed the genius from his own trunk, put him behind the steering wheel, cranked the heater to full blast, and laughed as I drove away. An autopsy would only be a formality. Cause of death would be ruled a major heart attack. Stress at the office, the salesman would insist to coworkers, as the board of directors assigned him full control of the company.

I was so pleased with myself. My wife called the next morning and was excited to hear my job had gone well. I promised I would be down south the next day and could already taste the Gulf of Mexico's salty waters. By noon I was shitfaced. That's about the last thing I remember.

When I woke up, I had casts on both legs, my chest hurt like a bitch, and there was no doubt that I was in a hospital. A cop came by later and told me I was definitely going to be charged with DUI. *Big fucking deal*, I thought. That's why God invented attorneys. Then the cop got this weird look on his face like he had eaten a bad egg. That's when he let me know the DA would contact me soon enough.

Unlike my old man I hadn't driven into city property. In

my drunken stupor I had crossed the median and killed a mother blithely driving home from school with her two kids in the family mini-van.

In my life I've dealt a lot of death; men who deserved it, and women who should have known better than to fuck with dangerous people. But I never hurt anybody without a damn good reason, be it revenge or a paycheck. This miserable feeling of regret made me want to vomit. I couldn't work anymore. Two years later I was divorced. We sighted irreconcilable differences as the cause, but we knew better.

I went to Florida a dozen times to visit the kids, but eventually stopped going, then calling, then everything. Somehow, I didn't feel right about still having my family after what I had done.

When the cancer came, unique to most patients receiving a death warrant from their physician, I felt relief. In my mind, I was finally going to get as good as I had gave; a slow, painful, terrible death that would eat me from the inside out.

The memory made me feel like shit and it showed. After Diego birdied the eleventh, I told him I wasn't feeling well. He drove the cart back to the clubhouse, shouldered my bag, and waited for me as I settled my green fees.

Once outside, we walked back to my car. The sun had risen fully in the sky and in another hour would begin its slow descent into the west. I reached for my wallet and held out a fifty for Diego. The kid sternly refused the tip.

"No, *Señor*," he said, "you owe me nada."

"You're a good caddy, kid. I'm not blind. You need this money."

"*Sí, sí.*" He took the money. "Gracías, Senor. You are very kind."

"Kid, I'm the worst kind of asshole there ever was. You just caught me on a good day."

Diego and I both laughed. He unholstered the bag of heavy clubs from his shoulder as I got into my car. When he saw the reverse lights come on, he moved out of the way, maniacally waving his arms for me to stop. I did but not until my open driver's side window was even with his waist.

Before he could start, I held my hand out the window. He took my palm in his and we both squeezed hard.

I drove away feeling better than I had in some time. Diego, if he didn't go pro, could sell those clubs for a small fortune. I know he didn't understand and how could he?

Sometimes, life was nothing but chance, being in the right place at the right time. Mostly though, it was about doing the right thing, no matter what it cost or how much it was going to hurt.

The unthinkable has hap-
pened. The dead are
walking!
Humanity's fragile thread
may be reaching its bitter
end.
Individuals and groups
struggle to survive…some
at any cost. Will there be
anybody left?
Or, is this just…

The Ugly Beginning?

Book 1 of the *Dead* Series

DEAD: REVELATIONS

THE SECOND BOOK
IN THE 12 PART
ZOMBIE EPIC
Steve…the Geeks…and
all the rest continue to
learn on the run.

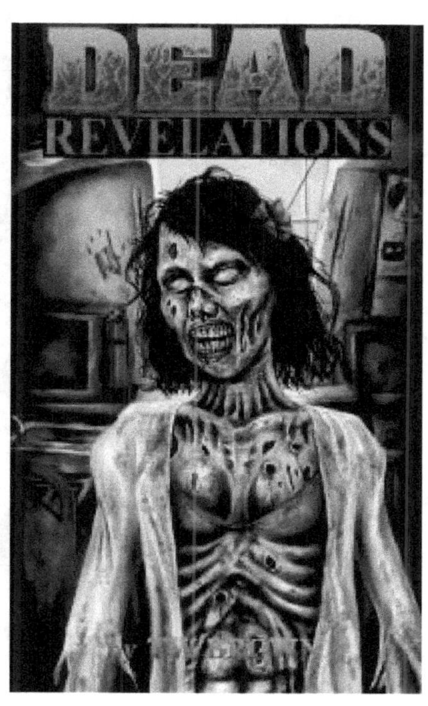

(Book 3 available in December)

THE DEAD WALK!

Samuel Todd is a regular guy:
...Failed husband...
...Loving father...
...Dutiful worker...
...Aspiring rock star.

He had no idea if anyone would care, or take the time, to read his daily blog entries about his late night observations. But what started as an open monologue of his day-to-day life became a running journal of the first-hand account detailing the rising of the dead and the downfall and degradation of mankind...

Meredith Gainey is a survivor…and determined to retain that status as the zombie apocalypse wipes out most of humanity. Unable to accept an existence behind walls and fences, she finds herself in constant danger…and she wouldn't have it any other way.

Look for Zomblog: The Final Chapter coming August 2011

The legions of the undead continue to grow. First Time Dead proudly presents a host of brand new names to the genre pantheon. Each writer contained herein might be the next "it" writer on the rise…the one to watch for. You never know where the next Romero, Kirkman, Brooks, Keene, or Wellington may emerge to scare and entertain the masses.

Our matched set anthologies
Available Mother's Day and Father's Day 2011

It has been said that women are the "gentle" sex. Apparently, not all of them got the message. Within the pages of this anthology are a dozen zombie tales by women who will help you discover why they say something else about the ladies: **Hell Hath No Fury…**

"Ladies first" So say the gentlemen.
This is the companion anthology to Hell Hath No Fury…Inside, you will find an undead bakers dozen that will remind you of how dark and desolate the minds of men can truly be. Vowing not to be upstaged by the dark musings of their female cohorts, the men offer up a usceral, gore-drenched collection that strives to prove… **Chivalry is Dead**

Slip into the skin of common men and women and experience the horror through their eyes. Follow the Zombie Apocalypse from its initial stages to the brink of the abyss, and over…into the pits of an unthinkable Hell on Earth. Tune into your local radio stations for the latest updates or stay here and follow the story as it unfolds on…

Eye Witness: Zombie

Gruesomely Grimm Zombie Tales Vol 1

For the Not So Young!

Follow the Grimms Fairy Tales #1-25… but with Zombies added to the mix.

GOT HORROR?
ATOMIC
DEAD GUY
THE ART OF SHAWN CONN
ATOMICDEADGUY-COM

The growing voice in horror and speculative fiction.

Find us at www.maydecemberpublications.com

Or

Email us at contact@maydecemberpublications.com

The growing voice in horror and speculative fiction.

Find us at www.maydecemberpublications.com

Or

Email us at contact@maydecemberpublications.com